Getaway With Murder

Diane Kelly

St. Martin's Paperbacks

First published in the United States by St. Martin's Paperbacks, an imprint of St. Martin's Publishing Group.

GETAWAY WITH MURDER

Copyright © 2021 by Diane Kelly.

For information, address St. Martin's Publishing Group, 120 Broadway, New York, NY 10271.

www.stmartins.com

ISBN: 978-1-250-81597-2

Our books may be purchased in bulk for promotional, educational, or business use. Please contact your local bookseller or the Macmillan Corporate and Premium Sales Department at 1-800-221-7945, ext. 5442, or by email at MacmillanSpecialMarkets@macmillan.com.

Printed in the United States of America

St. Martin's Paperbacks edition / November 2021

10 9 8 7 6 5 4 3 2 1

ACKNOWLEDGMENTS

I'm so grateful to have such an extensive and talented team working with me to bring my stories to life.

Many heartfelt thanks to the fantastic people at St. Martin's Press. Nettie Finn, you are a skilled editor and a pleasure to work with. Thanks as well to Allison Ziegler, Kayla Janas, Sara Beth Haring, Sarah Haeckel, Talia Sherer and all the other St. Martin's staff for everything you do to get books into the hands of readers, reviewers, and librarians. I appreciate all of you!

Thanks to Danielle Christopher and Mary Ann Lasher for creating the perfect cover for this book. Your image is the perfect invitation for readers to visit the Mountaintop Lodge.

Thanks to my agent, Helen Breitwieser, for all you do to advance my career.

A shout out to all my friends who have encouraged me along the way, as well as to my fellow authors who have helped to further my career and made it so much fun. I'd like to specially acknowledge author Melissa Bourbon (also known as Winnie Archer) who has become a critical part of my support system, a valued business ally, and, most of all, a good friend.

Thanks to Heike Goerres for the help with the German. One can never know how to say "Hello, kitty" in too many languages.

And finally, thanks to you readers who chose this book. Enjoy your time at the Mountaintop Lodge!

CHAPTER 1

I went to the woods because I wished to live deliberately, to front only the essential facts of life, and see if I could not learn what it had to teach, and not, when I came to die, discover that I had not lived.
—Henry David Thoreau (1854: *Walden*)

Misty

I'd just finished signing the divorce papers when my trim, tanned husband walked into the conference room, carrying a paper cup. He sat the steaming chai tea latte in front of me. The barista had written "Miss T" rather than "Misty" on the cup, but I supposed that name wasn't heard often anymore. It belonged to ladies of a certain age—ladies like me, who'd turned fifty years old this very morning. As I sipped the delicious brew, both my stomach and heart warmed. I gave Jack a grateful smile. "Maybe we should rethink this divorce."

We shared a chuckle. It was no secret I wasn't a morning person. If not for my snowy-white cat standing on my chest and demanding her breakfast each day, I'd sleep until noon. Jack, on the other hand, liked to rise with the sun. Our biorhythms weren't our only difference. Jack couldn't get enough of the Outer Banks but, while I enjoyed the sandy beaches, North Carolina's notorious riptides terrified me. I preferred the mountains in the western part of the state.

I loved altitude and everything that went with it. Hiking in dappled woods. Long-range views from a mountaintop. Snowflakes falling in a peaceful hush. Unfortunately, Jack felt carsick on the winding roads up the mountain, cursing every hairpin turn. He never got the hang of skiing, despite several lessons. He feared frostbite if the thermometer dipped below fifty degrees, even if dressed in a parka and fleece-lined boots.

Opposites attract, but sometimes the attraction doesn't hold forever. Still, while Jack and I had agreed to go our separate ways, we had no regrets. We'd enjoyed two decades together and raised two wonderful, well-adjusted sons, but our relationship had run its course. So, here we were, "consciously uncoupling." We'd easily agreed on the division of our property. Jack would keep the house in Raleigh. I'd get the anniversary clock we'd bought to celebrate our first year of marriage, plus the investment accounts. I'd reinvest the funds in a new venture this very afternoon.

Mitchell, our younger son, sat at the table with us, playing games on his phone while Jack signed the paperwork. Both boys had my pale freckled skin, dark brown hair, and hazel eyes, but their physique was all Jack, tall and lean. My body was rounder and softer, more so each year despite brisk daily walks. But if the price of aging was a few extra pounds, I'd gladly pay it. Growing old had its downsides, but it sure beat the alternative.

I turned to Mitch. "Good thing you're grown so we don't have to fight over you."

"I'd let you have him," Jack teased, "and all his laundry, too."

Mitch rolled his eyes. He knew Jack and I couldn't be

prouder of him and his brother. Both had been honor students in high school, and members of the marching band. They'd landed in occasional trouble that could be chalked up to kids being kids, but who'd want a perfect kid anyway? I was glad they had minds of their own. While our older son Jack, Jr., or J.J., was a sophomore at Duke, Mitch would start his first year at the University of North Carolina in Chapel Hill very soon. In fact, once we finished here, Jack and I would move Mitch into his dorm. It was mid-August, and classes would begin in just a few days.

Fortunately, our boys had been neither surprised nor upset when we'd told them we were calling it quits. J.J. had put it best when he'd said, "You two seem more like roommates than a couple." He wasn't wrong. I couldn't even remember the last time Jack and I had engaged in marital relations. *Maybe after his office holiday party last December?* But even though our marriage didn't last, we'd always hold a special place in each other's hearts.

Jack finished signing and set the pen down. Our mission here complete, we thanked the attorneys and stood to go.

An hour later, the three of us were in Mitchell's dorm room. I made my son's bed for what I both hoped and feared was the last time. While tears filled my eyes, Mitch champed at the bit, wanting his parents to leave so he could stroll the halls and meet the other new Tar Heels. I wiped a tear from my cheek, plumped his pillow, and glanced around to determine if we'd forgotten anything. "Where's your phone charger?"

"Right here." Mitch pulled the cord from the front pocket of his jeans.

I took it from him and plugged it in at his desk. "Keep your phone charged. I worry when I can't reach you."

My son groaned. "Trust me. I know."

It was Jack's turn to question him now. "Got your electric toothbrush?"

"Yes!" Mitch snapped. "Five tubes of toothpaste, too. Enough for the whole semester."

Jack worked in sales for a dental equipment supplier. "What about floss?"

Rather than answer his dad, Mitch pointed to the door. "Go!"

I stepped toward him. "Not without a goodbye kiss."

He made a gagging sound, but suffered through me giving him a peck on the cheek. Jack ruffled his hair. "Stay out of trouble, dude."

Jack and I stopped at our cars in the parking lot, and he turned to me. "Your birthday gift is waiting for you at the lodge."

"What is it?" Jack was a famously thoughtful gift giver, always finding the perfect thing. Over the years he'd surprised me with a seat warmer for my car for ski trips with the boys, high-powered binoculars to enjoy the birds and views on my hikes, and a pair of spiky metal crampons to attach to my snow boots so I wouldn't slip on the ice.

He grinned. "You'll see." He stepped forward and enveloped me in a tight hug.

I hugged him back, my throat tight with emotion. "There's no one I'd rather be leaving."

Taking my words in the spirit intended, he concurred. "We had a darn good ride." He cleared his throat, overcome with feelings too. After a last squeeze, we released each other.

As Jack headed off on sales calls, I swung by the house to round up Baroness Blizzard. My boys nicknamed her Yeti for her ice blue eyes and bountiful white fur. She'd skitter off if I grabbed at her, so instead I crouched and held out a treat. "Here, girl! It's tuna! Your favorite!" She swished her tail and eyed me suspiciously. I raised the treat to my mouth. "If you don't want it, I'll eat it." Her smug expression said *Go ahead. Eat it. I dare you.* She'd called my bluff. As I reached for her, she leaped off the couch and bolted. Luckily, I'd had the forethought to close all the doors. She found herself trapped at the end of the hall. I snatched her up, squashed the wriggling cat against my chest, and ran for her carrier. I shoved her in, tossed the treat in after her, and fastened the lock. "Off we go!"

CHAPTER 2

All good things are wild and free.
—Henry David Thoreau, "Walking"
(1862: *The Atlantic*)

Yeti

How dare Misty shove me into this box! Normally, being forced into the carrier meant Yeti would be taken to the veterinarian for poking and prodding. But, surely, they'd passed the vet's office by now. Misty had slid a plush mouse through the bars, too. But the cat wouldn't fall for the ploy no matter how strongly the nip called to her. She refused to be kidnapped *and* catnipped.

Yeti put her front paws on the bars and raised up to look out the window. All she could see were trees. If Misty thought she could cart Yeti off to who knows where without getting an earful, the woman was sorely mistaken. Yeti gave Misty a piece of her mind. *Meowww!* When Misty failed to respond, Yeti escalated the conversation. *Hisss!* Still nothing from Misty. *This situation calls for the full-blown growl-hiss combination. Rrrowwwl! Hissssss!*

Misty eyed Yeti in the rearview mirror. "Drama queen."

Though Yeti didn't know precisely what the words meant, she could tell from the tone she'd been summarily dismissed. *The nerve of that woman!*

CHAPTER 3

What a noble gift to man are the Forests! What a debt of gratitude and admiration we owe to their beauty and their utility! How pleasantly the shadows of the wood fall upon our heads when we turn from the glitter and turmoil of the world of man!

—Susan Fenimore Cooper (1850: *Rural Hours*)

Misty

Three hours, 175 miles, 5,000 feet in elevation, and a fifteen-degree drop in temperature later, I was making my way into the Blue Ridge Mountains of northwestern North Carolina. I'd stopped briefly in Boone to sign more legal documents and pick up the keys to the mountain lodge I'd purchased. The Watauga River tumbled alongside the road, the tumultuous water topped with whitecaps, fueled by a recent downpour. After turning onto the winding road that would take us to the mountaintop, I switched into a lower gear to increase power to the engine. My ears popped as we weaved our way up the steep switchbacks. Finally, we reached the pinnacle, flattened out temporarily, and cruised past the business district and the sign declaring Beech Mountain's claim to fame as the highest American town east of the Rockies.

My dashboard clock read 6:03 as I started down the backside of the mountain, approaching my destination. The air vents delivered the delicious aroma of the all-day, all-you-can-eat pancakes offered by the Greasy Griddle Diner across from the lodge. My heart soared like the hawks above as I turned into the parking lot. With wings stretched out on either side of a vaulted foyer, the log-cabin-style lodge appeared to be welcoming me into an embrace. Though the hotel had been built in the 1950s, the traditional style was timeless. My parents brought me and my siblings here dozens of times on family vacations when I was young. I'd stayed here on college ski-club trips, too. Jack and I even spent half of our honeymoon here. We'd spent the other half at the shore, climbing the lighthouse in Hatteras and strolling the beach. Once the boys were born, we'd carried on the tradition and brought them up the mountain for hiking and river rafting in the summers, and sledding, snowboarding, and snowball fights in the winters.

Throughout my childhood and up to my mid-forties, the place had been operated as The Ridgeview Inn by a jovial married couple. When they'd retired five years ago, they turned the place over to their shiftless grandson, who had little interest in the inn and no head for business. *No wonder the lodge ended up in the red.* There were several other hotels for sale in the area, too, some of which had gone out of business and languished on the market. Only a handful of inns still operated successfully. With the rise of internet sites like Airbnb and Vrbo, the vacation lodging market had changed. There were plenty of privately owned rental properties available, cabins and condos with full kitchens and multiple bedrooms where families and friends could spread out. With listings easily searched online, competition for guests was stiff. What's more, weather could severely impact tourist traffic. A bad year for snow meant fewer skiers. Heavy rains, such as those that hit the area over the weekend, deterred even the most ardent outdoor enthusiasts, though they made for great waterfalls afterward.

Buying the place was risky, but I felt certain I could run a successful lodge. I knew the place, the property, and the people well. I knew why vacationers up and down the eastern seaboard chose to come here. I had no doubt I could turn things around. To that end, I'd developed a targeted marketing plan. While cabins and condos offered certain amenities, they didn't offer a central meeting space or the ability for groups to stay together in immediate proximity. Rather than merely hope individual guests would register for rooms on my website, I planned to actively seek out groups who would enjoy having the lodge to themselves, taking it over as their home base for days at a time. I planned to get in touch with regional hiking clubs, ski clubs, bird-watching groups, you name it. The lodge could even host small weddings, family reunions, and similar events.

I swung around to park in the covered drive-through in front of the lobby and squealed in delighted surprise. Standing next to the front door was a piece of chainsaw art nearly as tall as me—an adorable black bear standing on his hind legs as if to get a better look at something that had made him curious. A bright yellow bow sat atop the bear's head. It was a perfect gift. *Jack has done it again.* I climbed out of my car, whipped out my phone, and stepped across the stone walkway to snap a selfie with the bow-topped bear. I sent the pic to Jack with a text that said *I LOVE IT!* The words were redundant. My smile spoke for itself.

After retrieving my suitcase and my cat, I stepped back to the glass door at the entrance, unlocked it, and pushed it open. The place had gathered dust in the two weeks since it was last cleaned, but otherwise looked to be in good shape. The check-in counter took up the front right corner of the lobby and looked out over an expansive great room with wood flooring and a vaulted ceiling. The gathering space served as the heart of the lodge. Comfortable rustic furniture surrounded the stone hearth, ready for guests to enjoy the cozy fireside come winter months. A colorful rug adorned the floor.

The broker who'd listed the inn had touted it as a turnkey operation and offered to have management continue taking reservations for a seamless transition of ownership. But when the few remaining employees jumped ship, I advised the broker I'd prefer to replace the staff myself. I wanted full control over the operations. The Ridgeview Inn had hosted its last guests two weeks ago. I'd reopen the lodge on my own terms with staff I'd personally selected.

I'd purchased the place as is, but only after having it thoroughly inspected. The lodge needed some minor cosmetic repairs, but the inspector noted only one significant structural item, a rainwater runoff issue. Drainage was a common problem with high country properties, especially in Beech Mountain, which averaged forty-five to fifty-five inches of rain annually. I'd get the matter taken care of right away.

I freed Yeti from her carrier. As she strutted out, I scooped her up and carried her to the plate-glass windows at the back of the room. The view of the treetops and distant peaks was awe-inspiring. The ridges appeared in ever-lightening shades of bluish grayscale as they receded into the distance. The sun had begun its daily descent, slipping soundlessly behind the forested peaks as I gazed out. Though I'd seen the view many times, it never ceased to astound me. I ran a hand over my cat's head. "Isn't it beautiful?"

Yeti, too, seemed impressed, putting a paw to the glass as she looked out. She purred in my arms as if sensing the same feeling I always had in the mountains. *This is where I belong.*

The rumble of the cat's purr was interrupted by another rumble, this one coming from my stomach. It was dinnertime for me and my furry companion. An elongated creak met my ears, too. *Creeeeak.* My first thought was that the sound must have come from the woods. The trees often made creaking noises as their limbs rubbed against a neighboring tree or as they swayed in a brisk wind. But there was no breeze at the moment, and the forest seemed still. *Hmm.* Maybe one of the trees was about to shed a rotten limb. One had to be careful when hiking in the area as branches could crash down without warning.

Another creak followed. *CREEEEEAK.* Not only was this sound longer and louder, it was now clear where it was coming from—directly under my feet. I'd just looked down when—*WHUMP!*—the floor dropped several inches. Clutching Yeti, I toppled forward and smacked my forehead against the window frame. At the same time, a crack appeared at the bottom of the glass, shooting up. Yeti clawed her way over my shoulder, her nails scratching first my skin, then the wood floors as she scrambled to hide under the sofa. I put my hand on the window frame and pushed myself back onto more solid flooring. A gap appeared between the bottom of the window and the frame. The back of the great room had collapsed. That *minor* drainage problem was now a *major* drainage problem. *Darn that weekend storm!*

I left Yeti cowering under the sofa and exited the lodge. The shifting foundation had cracked the front window, too. *Ugh!* I circled around to the back of the inn to assess the damage. I issued a sharp exhale and a G-rated curse: "Son of a bleep!"

The recent heavy rains had swept away a chunk of earth behind the lodge, turning the mountainside lot into a precarious precipice. Without dirt to hold it in place, a support beam had collapsed under the great room. The wings of the inn, which had seemed to welcome me only moments before, now looked like the arms of a person desperately clinging to the cliff. Even Yeti seemed to realize the place was in peril. She'd emerged from under the couch and stood in the back window, looking out at me, her tail twitching in agitation.

I closed my eyes and groaned. I'd just broken free from the bonds of a dying marriage, only to shackle myself to a dilapidated lodge. *What had I been thinking?* I'd romanticized the idea of owning the inn, bought it out of nostalgia in an attempt to hold on to the past. But now, the reality of owning the lodge rolled over me like so many rough-hewn logs. *Have I just made a huge mistake?* Maybe hot flashes had fried my brain. I could only hope the lodge wouldn't slide off the cliff tonight and take me and Yeti with it.

I walked the length of the inn, crouching several times to visually examine the foundations under both wings. Fortunately, my closer inspection confirmed the wings were on solid footing. Unlike the great room, they rested on bedrock rather than dirt.

I went back inside and headed to the registration desk. Yeti skittered ahead of me, jumped onto the counter, and sashayed across it to the plastic sign that read No Pets. She paused and eyed it. If I didn't know better, I'd think she was reading the sign. She lifted her tiny pink nose as if in indignation and raised her paw, swiping the sign off the counter and into the waste basket below. I reached out and ruffled her ears. "Thanks, girl. The no-pets policy was the first change I'd planned to make."

I circled around the counter and pushed through the swing gate to access the area behind the desk. There were two workstations, each with a desktop computer and padded stool. Between the stations was a locked drawer divided into numbered compartments for the guest room keys, as well as master keys for the staff to access guest rooms, storage areas, and the housekeeping closet. The lodge had just twenty guest rooms, but that was a plus in my opinion. A modest operation would be easier to manage on my own and make for a boutique experience for guests.

I unlocked the drawer and fingered the keys. As many times as I'd stayed at the property over my lifetime, I'd likely slept in every guest room. The place had been my home away from home. Now it would simply be my home. I planned to live on the premises so I'd be available 24/7 to handle any matters that might arise. The simplicity of living in a smaller space appealed to me. Besides, I had no need for a separate residence. The boys could stay in guest rooms when they came to visit. I was neither a picky eater nor much of a cook, and could make do for meals with the in-room microwave, a toaster oven, and a hot plate.

I retrieved the sets of keys from the compartment marked

#1. Each set included two keys, one for the room and one for the exterior doors so guests could let themselves in after hours. The keys hung from a kitschy keychain crafted from a small pine cone. For security purposes, the keychains didn't note the name of the inn or the room number. As I rolled my suitcase down the west wing, Yeti ran forward to pounce on a shadow of leaves caused by sunlight filtering through the glass door at the end of the hallway. I stopped at the last door on the right.

While most of the rooms had a single wide window at the back, the rooms at the end of each hall had a second window on the side wall. It might have made sense to keep these special end rooms available for guests, but I'd decided Yeti and I would take one of them. She was used to having a domain of 1,800 square feet, but now she'd have a mere 352. The least I could do was provide her with more scenery. She'd enjoy watching the birds flit among the trees and the deer wander by. I unlocked the door and stepped inside. The room was dark. I opened the shutters, letting in the dappled sunlight that streamed through the woods surrounding the lodge. Yeti sauntered into the room and glanced about her new abode.

The space was well designed, with a large bath, a wide closet, and an in-room coffee bar equipped with a mini-fridge and microwave, plus a small sink for filling the coffee pot and rinsing mugs. The ceilings were coffered, a common style in rustic structures, wherein support beams were exposed and the ceiling materials were laid over them rather than attached to the underside. The dark-stained beams complemented the lighter-colored ceiling panels and mirrored the exposed beams in the great room. The wood-paneled walls were decorated with framed watercolors of deer, bears, and birds, species native to the area. The furniture was versatile. Along with a king-sized bed covered in a black-and-red buffalo-plaid spread, the room featured a fold-out sofa upholstered in sturdy leatherette. The square oak table pushed back against the wall came with four chairs, and could be used as a dinette, desk, or card table. Over the broad dresser hung a mirror and a flatscreen television on an adjustable mount. It was a cozy, comfy space. *Yeti and I will enjoy living here.*

As my cat explored the room, I set up her litter box, filled her bowl with water, and unpacked my suitcase. Our new home now ready, I opened a can of Yeti's favorite feline fare and spooned it onto a saucer. She hopped down from the sofa and strolled over to sniff the food. I gave her a quick scratch behind her ears. "Enjoy your meal. I'll be back once I've had some dinner myself."

CHAPTER 4

The goal of life is living in agreement with nature.

—Zeno of Citium

Yeti

Yeti stared at her saucer, disgusted. Misty had left her with a meal of salmon pâté. *How dare she!* Misty had proffered the same cuisine the preceding evening. Sure, the fare tasted fine yesterday, but Yeti could not be expected to eat the same meal two nights in a row. She wasn't an undiscerning dog.

Leaving the food uneaten, she hopped up onto the window ledge and stared out through the glass. A faint shadow swept across the rocky ledge behind the lodge, a mere wisp or suggestion of shape that seemed to be floating in the sky. A skuttling cloud, perhaps? Maybe an errant leaf falling? A moment later, the wisp darkened into a wide, winged shadow as the creature forming it descended as if to see whether the cat in the window might make a suitable snack.

HAWK! Instinct seized control. Yeti sprang from the sill and skittered under the bed. *What is this horrid place Misty has dragged me to?*

CHAPTER 5

I love places that make you realize how tiny your problems are.

—Unknown

Misty

Weighted with worry, I headed across the parking lot to the Greasy Griddle. I needed comfort food, stat. The classic diner sported shiny aluminum siding, black-and-white checkered floors, and red vinyl booths. A sign on a stand inside the door invited me to seat myself. I chose a stool at the far end of the counter. I might be fifty now, but I still found it fun to spin and swivel. I could certainly use a little fun right now. *How much will the damage at the lodge set me back?*

It was a weeknight and schools were back in session, putting an end to the summer tourist traffic. Even so, the diner did a brisk business, bustling with vacationers and locals alike. I was the latter now. A local. One of the few who lived in the mountains year-round.

The same bright-eyed, dark-skinned woman I'd seen before was running the place, as usual. She made her way down and gave me a warm smile. "Welcome back to the Greasy Griddle. What can I get you to drink?"

She'd recognized me, too. Not a surprise, I suppose, given how many times I'd eaten at the place over the years. "Coffee, please."

She eyed me, her smile faltering as she took in the bump on my forehead and my worried face. "Shall I make it a decaf? You look anxious. Caffeine will only make it worse."

I cringed. "Is it that obvious?"

She flipped the dish towel she'd been carrying over her shoulder and rested her hands on the counter, leaning in to speak to me more privately. "What's going on?"

I hiked a thumb over my shoulder to indicate the lodge, which was visible through the window behind me. "I bought the inn today."

"You'll be our new neighbor, then. Wonderful!"

My lips twisted wryly. "I thought so, too. But the lodge is about to fall off the cliff." Okay, maybe that was an exaggeration, but while the inn might not literally go over the precipice, it had definitely suffered substantial damage. I told her how the place collapsed under my feet. "I feel like I've thrown myself off a cliff, too."

She looked from me to the lodge and back again, her gaze locking on mine. "You didn't throw yourself off a cliff. You took a leap of faith. *Believe in yourself.*"

"I'm trying," I said, "but I'm having a hard time. I don't know what I was thinking. How would I know how to run a lodge? I haven't held a full-time job in twenty years."

"You spent those years doing something. What was it?"

She listened intently and asked occasional leading questions as I detailed my volunteer work and part-time jobs. Over the last two decades, I'd managed my family's home and finances, finding ways to cut corners so we could save for the boys' college expenses. I'd spearheaded the most successful fundraiser in the history of the band boosters, organizing a team of parents and students and raising enough cash to send the marching band on a bus trip to Disney World. Every Christmas, I worked part time at the mall to cover the cost of gifts.

The woman straightened, rallying resolve on my behalf. "You might not have held a full-time job with a fancy office or title, but between your volunteer work, seasonal retail gig, and family responsibilities, you've learned to be resourceful, thrifty, and good with people. Those are the skills you'll need to run a successful lodge. The building can be repaired. Buck up, buttercup. Take it from a woman who's been there. You'll be fine."

I straightened, too. She might be blunt, but she was also right. I could do this. I *would* do this. My confidence restored, I thanked her for the pep talk. "I'm Misty, by the way."

"Patty," she replied. "Now that I've talked you off the cliff, let me get you that coffee."

I glanced down at the laminated menu, which doubled as a place mat. Dinner would be pancakes, for sure, but should I go with the blueberry or banana nut? Patty returned with a carafe of fresh coffee and a yellow mug embossed with her diner's logo, the name Greasy Griddle in red letters underneath a cartoon cast-iron skillet in which a square of melting butter had left the letter *G* in its wake. It was a simple yet eye-catching emblem. I'd have to come up with a logo for my lodge, too, once I decided on a new name. Its current moniker would have to go. The Ridgeview Inn had garnered far too many one-star Yelp reviews recently.

Patty set the mug on the counter and filled it with coffee. "What did you decide on?"

"I'm on the fence." I fished a sugar packet from the plastic bin in front of me and flicked it with my middle finger to loosen the crystals. "I'm going with the all-you-can-eat pancakes, but I can't decide between blueberry and banana nut."

"No need to decide," she said. "I'll bring you some of both."

"Thanks! No wonder the Greasy Griddle has five stars on all the review sites."

She cocked her head. "Been checking our customer feedback?"

"I have," I admitted. "I eat here often enough to know your food is consistently scrumptious, but I wanted to see what others had to say. In fact, I've got a proposal for you."

"Yeah?" She slid the pot onto a burner behind her before turning back to me. "Shoot."

"Hotel guests expect an on-site breakfast these days. I can add some tables to the great room, but the lodge doesn't have cooking facilities and it wouldn't be cost effective for me to install a commercial kitchen for only one meal a day. There isn't space for a kitchen, either." I'd have to lose a guest room to do it, not to mention the hassle of health inspections, hiring cooks and dishwashers, et cetera. "I'm wondering whether the Greasy Griddle could cater a breakfast at the lodge each morning. Your usual southern breakfast staples. Some continental items, too. Muffins, maybe a bowl of fresh fruit."

Patty nodded thoughtfully. "That way your guests would have a choice between sitting down for a hot meal, or just doing a grab-and-go before they hit the trails or slopes."

"Exactly. Catering would provide an easy solution for me and more income for you."

She glanced around the diner as she mused aloud. "We do get busy here most mornings, run out of seating and have to keep folks waiting. If I could feed your guests at your place, it would solve a problem for both of us." She tapped the tip of her index finger on her chin as she appeared to mentally calculating. "I can do it for five bucks per person. I'll need a headcount by nine each evening. I'll loan you a warming table to keep at the lodge."

I extended my hand. "We've got ourselves a deal."

Two days later, I was back at the Greasy Griddle. But this time I sat in a booth and I wasn't alone. Patty was bent down behind the counter speaking with a man who was fixing her industrial-sized oven. All I could see were the top of his head and his broad shoulders pulling his plaid flannel shirt taut across his back. His sandy hair bore hints of gray, like the fur of the bobcats that lived among the mountains. I surmised he was the man who drove the blue king-cab pickup parked outside. The truck had a shiny metal toolbox mounted to the bed and a sign on the driver's door that read High Country Handyman Service.

Across from me sat a contractor I'd called for a bid on fixing the drainage problem and repairing the damage to the lodge. He slugged back a gulp of coffee and pushed his proposal across the table, turned to the signature page. He held out a ballpoint pen. "Sign at the bottom, give me half down, and I can get started as soon as I wrap up another job."

Not so fast, buddy. I flipped back to the first page. As my eyes perused the terms, my temper started to sizzle like the hash browns on Patty's grill. It didn't take an expert to know that $157,000 for diverting runoff, shoring up the foundation, and replacing some damaged flooring and a couple of windows was outrageous. "Surely there's a less expensive way to fix the problem than drilling through solid bedrock."

"Not if you want it done right."

"Couldn't you lay pipe above ground to divert the water?"

"That would look terrible."

I pointed out that bushes, ground cover, and decorative latticework were common and inexpensive ways to disguise eyesores. "An aboveground solution wouldn't require repaving the parking lot, either." His bid had included the cost of replacing the asphalt once the digging was complete. When I turned to the next page, my blood ran as hot as the coffee in my cup. "You're proposing to refloor the entire lobby with travertine tile? I only want the current floor repaired."

He scoffed. "You can't compete with the luxury resorts if you go cheap."

"I'm not trying to compete with the luxury resorts," I told him. "If you'd listened to me, you'd know that." My goal was to provide people with a comfortable, affordable getaway. I looked the man in the eye. "When my boys didn't listen to me, I put them in the time-out chair."

Patty turned my way. So did the handyman. My heart

did a *ba-bump*. He sported a light, nicely trimmed beard along his square jaw. Casual yet masculine. His eyes were the same blue-gray as the haze that topped the Blue Ridge Mountains. They twinkled with amusement.

The pompous jerk on the other side of the booth argued with me again. "You've got wood paneling on the walls. You don't need wood floors, too. It's best to mix up the materials."

"It's a mountain lodge. A lot of wood is to be expected." Not to mention that I liked wood. It brought nature inside. Besides, the walkway, the fireplace, and the check-in desk had enough stone to provide visual appeal. "You realize this is *my* lodge, not yours, don't you?"

He had the nerve to snort. "You realize *my* company's sign will be displayed out front?"

"No. It won't." I pushed the contract back across the table. Staring him down, I calmly picked up my coffee mug and took a sip. *Kiss my asphalt.* He stood, snatched up his pen, and jammed it into his breast pocket, leaving the contract behind as he stormed out of the diner.

While the handyman packed his tools into the toolbox on the counter, Patty walked over with a pot of coffee and refilled my mug. "You didn't let him push you around. Good for you."

"That man didn't listen at all."

Patty sighed. "Do they ever?"

"*I* listened," said the handyman. His voice had a deep timbre and a smooth southern drawl, like a deejay on a country radio station. He stepped out from behind the counter. Along with the plaid shirt, he wore a pair of nice-fitting jeans, a tool belt, and work boots. His clothing was clean, not a grease or paint stain to be seen. His neat appearance said he took pride in himself and his work. To my surprise, he was followed by an enormous, furry black beast with tan paws. A white stripe ran down the dog's forehead and between his eyes, encircling his snout. Surely it was a health code violation to have the dog in the diner, but nobody seemed to mind. Mountain folks tended to be laid back.

The handyman walked over to the booth, circled his screwdriver in the air as if to signal he'd rounded up my concerns, and paraphrased me. "You said you want to bring the lodge up to snuff without going bankrupt."

"That's right," I said. "You know someone who could do it?"

He pointed the screwdriver at his chest, giving me an excuse to ogle his pecs. No *dad bod* here. This guy was in great shape for his age, which I guessed to be around mine.

"You licensed?" Handyman work was one thing, but this job might require specialized skills.

"No, unlike Molasses here, I'm not licensed." He reached down and ran a hand over his dog's head. "But there's no licensing required for the things you need done."

Patty gave me her two cents. "He's the first person I call anytime something goes wrong here at the diner. The guy can fix anything, and he doesn't charge you an arm and a leg."

"I worked in construction for years," he added. "Everything from drywall to plumbing."

In light of my new friend's rousing endorsement, as well

as the man's experience, I figured there was no harm in letting him make a bid. "Want to come take a look?"

He picked up his toolbox and gave me a roguish grin. "I thought you'd never ask."

I left some cash on the table to cover my coffee and led the man and his dog over to the lodge. Both had their focus on the ground, the dog snuffling about and the man carefully eyeing the wide, shallow trench the rainwater runoff had created. We walked down the side of the inn and around to the rear. Yeti lay in the window, napping. She lifted her head with a lazy gaze, but when she spotted Molasses, she rose into an arch, lips curled back in an unheard hiss.

Once we'd reached the collapsed spot, I turned to the man and extended my hand. "I'm Misty Murphy. I know your dog is called Molasses, but I didn't catch your name."

He took my smaller, softer hand in his big, calloused one. His rough touch sent a little tingle through me. *Sheesh.* Divorced only two days and already getting the hots for another man.

"Rocky Crowder." He gave my hand a shake. "My given name's Rockford, after Jim Rockford of *The Rockford Files* television show. My mother had a hopeless crush on James Garner back in the day. His sideburns did her in."

"My mother never missed an episode, either."

Rocky bent down to inspect the exposed structural supports before lowering himself to all fours, turning over onto his back, and wriggling under the lodge to take a closer look. He disappeared up to his waist. My heart pitter-pattered in my chest. *What if the lodge comes down and crushes him like the witch from* The Wizard of Oz*?* Thankfully, he soon wriggled back out from under the structure, stood, and brushed the dirt off his shoulders. "You're in luck. The rest of the foundation looks solid. It'll be an easy fix."

Relief brought my shoulders down from my ears. "Thank goodness."

"Epictetus said, 'The greater the difficulty, the more glory in surmounting it.'"

"Ah. You're not just a handyman, you're a philosopher, too?"

He shrugged. "Live in the mountains long enough, you're bound to become a guru."

"It that why you do handyman work?" I asked. "For the glory?"

"Glory, craft beer, and cable television. That's all a man needs." When Molasses looked up and whined, Rocky laughed. "And a dog." He reached down to ruffle the dog's ears. "That goes without saying." Rocky wandered to the edge of the cliff, examining things in detail. He took measurements with a measuring tape and made notes on a notepad. When he finished, he angled his head to indicate the lodge. "Let's take a look inside."

I led the man and his dog back around the lodge and into the lobby. I showed Rocky the cracks in the glass and the damaged floor below the back window. He knelt down to examine the flooring and the window frame. He ran a hand over a floorboard and rapped on it with his knuckle. "This is top-quality wood. Replacing these floors with tile would have been an abomination." Using his tape measure again, he determined the dimensions of the window. "Plate glass this size is gonna cost you. Would you consider going with a set of French doors instead?"

"But where would they lead?" Outside the glass was a four-foot drop to the ground.

"If you put a deck back there, your guests could watch the sunrise and sunset from it. A deck would conceal the pipe, too. I wouldn't have to bury the part that ran under it."

My mind went to work, envisioning a deck. There was enough room for a good-sized one. It could run the width of the lobby and be twenty feet deep, stopping at the tree line. A deck would give my guests more room to spread out, and it would offer another event space for groups. I mused aloud. "I could put some tables out there, maybe chaise lounge chairs and rockers."

"A fire pit, too," he suggested. "People like to gather outside around a fire."

"You've got great ideas, Rocky."

"I like to think so." He took a seat in one of the chairs and I dropped into another. While he added things up, Molasses wandered over to me. He stood at my knees and gazed up at my face, waiting patiently, demanding nothing. *Yeti could take some pointers from this sweet dog.* I took his enormous head in both of my hands and treated him to a behind-the-ears scratch. His mouth fell open slightly and he closed his eyes in canine zen.

Rocky glanced up from his calculations. "The only outstanding question is the landscaping. I'll cover the part of the pipe that's not under the deck with dirt, but you'll need foliage to hold the dirt in place. Ferns do well up here, and the deer don't eat 'em. 'Course you could go with rhodo-dendrons, instead. They're colorful and stay green all year round."

Rhododendrons' cold-hardiness made them a great choice for the mountains. They grew naturally here in abundance, their flowers adorning the mountains in bright pink blooms each spring. "Let's go with rhododendrons."

Rocky finished his calculations and pulled his chair next to mine so we could discuss his bid. When I turned my attention from Molasses to his master, the dog flopped in front of the fireplace, his chin flat on the floor and limbs splayed in a near-perfect impersonation of a bearskin rug. Rocky tore the sheets off his pad and handed them to me. The proposal included the addition of the deck and a raised berm along the edge of the parking lot to keep the water off the asphalt. A channel drain would allow rain-water to flow down through a metal grate and into a pipe that would carry it off the cliff at a point where it would not cause further erosion. A truckload of dirt would be brought in to cover the exposed pipe so that it wouldn't be an eyesore.

The bid was on the bottom line: $18,000. "How can you do all that work for that price?" I asked.

"I've got the efficiency that comes with experience. I've built upwards of two-hundred decks and laid enough pipe to run from here to the coast. I've also built a solid reputa-tion that keeps me busy enough to make a living and gets me discount pricing with my suppliers." He offered his pen. I signed the contract with a flourish and handed the pen and paperwork back to him. He separated the pages and gave me the bottom yellow copy.

I retrieved my checkbook and wrote a check for half down as per the terms of the contract. As I handed him the check, I said, "Thanks, Rocky. You've restored my sanity."

He flashed his roguish grin. "Keep a little of your crazy. It makes things interesting."

CHAPTER 6

Normality is a paved road: It's comfortable to walk, but no flowers grow.

—Vincent van Gogh

Misty

I'd spent Monday and Tuesday nights consumed with worry, but thanks to Rocky coming to my rescue, I slept like a baby Wednesday night. Yeti did, too, curled up on the pillow beside me. A rumbling engine woke me just after eight o'clock Thursday morning. I opened the shutters on the back window to see Rocky maneuvering his pickup along the cliffside. A flatbed trailer bounced along behind the truck, piled high with two-by-fours, PVC pipe, and gallon cans of wood stain and sealant. The brake lights flashed and the truck rolled to a stop. Rocky slid out and let Molasses out of the rear cab. He was the first contractor I'd ever hired who'd showed up on time.

I hurriedly cleaned myself up, dressed, and fed Yeti her breakfast. My anniversary clock chimed the half hour as I scurried out of my room, out the wing exit door, and around to the back of the lodge to greet Rocky. I raised a hand in hello as I approached, then lowered it to run it over the head of Molasses, who'd ambled forward to meet me. "You're here bright and early."

"You don't have much choice when the baby in the room next door goes off like an alarm clock at six a.m." His smile said he'd forgiven the baby for rousing him.

Did Rocky have a younger wife or girlfriend who'd recently given birth? Maybe he lived in an apartment, and the baby belonged to a neighbor. Though I was curious whose baby he'd referred to, I didn't want to seem intrusive by prying. "Coffee?"

"I wouldn't say no to a cup. With sugar. Lots of it."

I hustled back to my room and started a pot of coffee. Yeti finished her breakfast and climbed onto the wide windowsill to supervise Rocky's work. I rounded up a mug and filled it with the hot brew and five packets of sugar. When I went outside to deliver it to Rocky, the strains of Bachman-Turner Overdrive singing "You Ain't Seen Nothin' Yet" came from the phone sitting on his tailgate. Rocky sang along with the tune, not stopping when he spotted me. In fact, he pointed a section of pipe at me as he belted out the chorus. The words seemed prophetic, and I wondered—*If I ain't seen nothin' yet, what might he show me?*

He took the mug of coffee from me and in return offered a grateful nod and more off-key caterwauling. I couldn't help but smile at his carefree confidence. He paused his singing to looked down at his dog. "Mo, fetch my flathead screwdriver."

Molasses sauntered over to Rocky's toolbox. He poked around with his snout for a few seconds before turning around with a screwdriver in his mouth. He carried it over.

"Wow!" I exclaimed. "What a smart dog."

"Not really." Rocky held up the tool. "He brought me the Phillips head."

Even so, it was more than my cat would ever do for me. Before turning to go, I said, "I'll leave the front door unlocked for you to take a break. If you need me, I'll be either in the lobby or Room One." With that, I went back inside to fix myself a chai latte. It wasn't as good as the drinks from the fancy coffee places, but it wasn't bad, either. As I exited my room this time, I left the door open so Yeti could venture into the lodge and explore. I'd be working at the front desk where I could make sure she didn't escape. Not that she was likely to try. She seemed to sense the outdoors was for lower-class cats, street-walking strays and feral felines. A cat of her stature was intended to live in indoor luxury.

Planner in hand, I made my way to the registration desk and plunked my bum on one of the stools behind the counter. Several tasks filled my to-do list for today. The first was to place an ad online for an assistant. The next was to select patio furniture for the deck. Once those jobs were done, I'd tackle a more formidable mission, choosing a new name for the lodge. I knocked out the first two items in short order, scoring durable aluminum deck furniture half off in an end-of-season sale. *Now, to name my lodge* . . .

Two hours later, Yeti was lying languorously on the registration counter and I was still scribbling on a legal pad, mulling over names for the inn, when Rocky came through the door. He scratched Yeti under the cheek. "Gorgeous cat." As if realizing he'd paid her a compliment, the shameless feline launched into a purr and pressed her head into his hand. She seemed to like his rough touch, too. Rocky eyed me. "You look perplexed. What's up?"

"I've been brainstorming names for the lodge, but I

haven't come up with one that feels quite right." I handed him the pad so he could read over the ideas I'd had so far.

He read the list out loud. "Summit Guesthouse. Tranquility Lodge. Serenity Inn." His lip quirked. "Hope you don't mind me saying, but these names sound a little uppity."

While I hadn't liked the other contractor attempting to force his opinions on me earlier, Rocky made a good sounding board. Besides, I agreed with him. I wanted the inn to sound friendly and accessible, not snooty. "Are there any you like?"

He continued down the list. "Treetop Lodge. The Hawk Nest. The Buck and Bear. That's getting closer." He finished the list and frowned, like me not finding any of them suitable.

I raised my palms. "What's a good name for a mountain-top lodge?"

"You just said it."

"I did?"

"Mountaintop Lodge. It's simple, straightforward. That's what you're going for, right?"

"Exactly." I slapped a palm to my forehead. "I was over-thinking it, but you nailed it."

"Didn't need a hammer, neither."

He handed the pad back to me and shot me a wink. Heat rushed through me. I wasn't sure if it was a blush or a hot flash. Either way, I fanned myself with the pad as he strode across the lobby, motioning for me to follow him to the cracked window. I gazed out to see that he'd already laid a length of pipe to divert the water.

"The channel drain's installed, too," he said. "I'll start on the deck after a lunch break."

"How about I treat you to lunch at the Greasy Griddle? I owe you for helping me name the lodge." Though the quiet inn was peaceful, I had to admit I'd felt a little lonely since moving here. I was used to having a husband and son around, and now all I had was Yeti.

To my disappointment, Rocky declined. "That's a nice offer, but I packed a lunch."

My heart fell, but it probably wasn't a good idea to get chummy with the guy, anyway. After all, he was working for me. Better to remain professional and keep him at arm's length.

That afternoon, I contacted the web designer to have the inn's domain and website updated with the new name. With those changes in progress, I turned my attention to signage. Fortunately, I wouldn't incur any expense having old signs removed. The only sign designating the lodge as The Ridgeview Inn was a freestanding wooden one on sawhorse-style legs that stood next to the parking lot. I wrangled it into the storage shed and ordered a new sign online, opting to spell Mountaintop Lodge in a playful rustic font that resembled twigs. The new brand was really coming together.

Now that the place was nearly ready for guests, it was time to find some. As I searched for specific groups online, I hit paydirt. According to a post on the website for the Third Eye Studio & Spa in Charlotte, they were searching for a new retreat venue after an ashram in Asheville had turned to ash, the fire caused by unattended incense. I was on my phone in an instant. After extolling the virtues of my lodge, including its magnificent mountain views, I'd convinced the owner, a woman named Sasha Ducharme-Carlisle, to move the retreat to my inn.

"I can only sleep on a down pillow," she said. "Do you have down pillows?"

"No," I said. "Some people are allergic to down, so we provide hypoallergenic bed linens instead." Besides, geese needed their feathers for their own use, and my own experience with down pillows involved being repeatedly poked with tiny quills that pierced the pillowcase. Not exactly conducive to a good night's sleep.

She sighed dramatically. "I suppose I'll have to bring my own pillow, then."

At least our pillows had not been a deal breaker. "Your group will love it here."

"We'd better," Sasha shot back. "The reputation of my studio relies on it."

While I'd like to think it was my marketing savvy that convinced her to give the Mountaintop Lodge a try, it was more likely her desperation. Where else would she find a place her group could have all to themselves on such short order? "See you soon!" I said before hanging up the phone. They'd arrive in just ten days. *I'd better get ready for them!*

Rocky was banging nails out back Friday morning as I waited at the desk for a woman named Brynn O'Reilly to arrive for her job interview. She'd been the most experienced person to apply for the assistant position, and her references gave her rave reviews. What appeared to be a first-generation Prius pulled up in front of the lodge. Though the vehicle was old, the exterior was spotless. The chrome and glass gleamed, and the hubcaps bore no road dirt or grease. *That's a good sign.* A willowy woman climbed out. Her thick, wavy red hair cascaded over her shoulders and down the back of her loose-fitting bohemian-print dress. She glanced about as if assessing the lodge as she walked to the door.

I met her there, noting the pretty pendant hanging from her neck. It was round and made of silver or pewter with a Celtic symbol on it. I introduced myself and held out my hand. She angled her head as if visually inspecting it for cleanliness before taking it in hers. I led her to a table and pulled out a chair for her. Again, she glanced around, taking everything in. She'd be expected to clean the place. She was wise to determine what she'd be getting herself into.

I'd printed out her online application and referred to it now. "I need help with both housekeeping and administrative matters, so the fact that you've operated your own cleaning business for the past ten years caught my eye. Can you tell me why you'd like to work here?"

"Cleaning rentals comes with a lot of uncertainty. Investment properties turn over frequently, and I'm constantly scrambling for cleaning contracts. I'd prefer a regular paycheck."

The woman doesn't beat around the bush. Would she mind beating a rug?

Before I could ask, she said, "I enjoy cleaning. I find it therapeutic. I'm happy to do whatever you need, inside or out. Windows, walkways, whatever. Same goes for administrative tasks. I'm very organized and good with computers. But if I'm hired, I'd have two conditions."

"What are they?"

"I'll only use nontoxic and organic cleaning products."

"No problem. Send me a list of your preferred products, and I'll order them. What else?"

"I'll need September twenty-second off."

I opened my planner and checked the calendar. September 22 would be a Wednesday. My calendar noted that the day would mark the autumn equinox. "No worries. In fact, how about we make Wednesdays and Thursdays your days off? There are fewer guests midweek. I'll need you from eight to five the other days."

She agreed to the schedule. We negotiated her hourly and overtime rates, and I saw her to the door. "I'm looking forward to working with you, Brynn. See you a week from Sunday."

At half past five, Rocky came into the lodge. "I'm done for the day. How'd things go in here?"

"We'll host a yoga retreat the first week of September. They booked eighteen rooms!"

"Congratulations," he said. "I suppose I ought to put in some hours over the weekend to make sure the deck is done in time. The weather forecast for next week looks iffy."

I'd promised the owner of the yoga studio that the deck would be ready for outdoor practices when the group arrived. I'd feel more at ease once the deck was complete and the landscape installed. Still, while I appreciated Rocky's offer, it wasn't fair for him to work unplanned overtime. "I don't expect you to give up your weekend."

"Don't know what I'd be giving up. Didn't have any plans." He rested an elbow on the counter. "I could put in more hours if I didn't have the drive to and from Boone every day. How about you let me hole up in one of the rooms until the deck's done?"

"Won't your wife miss you?"

"Horribly," he said, "if I had one." He flashed that grin again.

While I hardly knew the man and it felt odd allowing a stranger stay in what was now my home, I realized my feelings were ridiculous. I was going to be running a lodge and having strangers stay in my home every night. That was the whole point. "You're welcome to stay."

"I was hoping you'd say that. I even brought my suitcase along this morning."

I reached over, unlocked the key drawer, and retrieved a set. "Here you go. Room Twenty." The room was at the end of the east wing and on the opposite side of the hall from mine, as far from my room as I could put him. Still, it felt too close for comfort. *Or perhaps too far . . .*

Rocky was hard at work by nine o'clock Saturday morning. Meanwhile, I unpacked boxes of games, puzzles, and paperbacks, and placed them on the shelves in the great room. I arranged a selection of books about the Blue Ridge Mountains on the shelf nearest the check-in desk. Guests would enjoy learning the history and geography of the area, and the books would help them decide which sights to see. The display of brochures for regional tourist traps would help with that, too. The area offered everything from ziplining and gem mining to the annual Scottish Highland Games. The breathtaking valley view from the legendary Blowing Rock was something to behold, and the Tweetsie Railroad was a family favorite. When my boys were young, they'd insisted on riding the steam train every time we came to the mountains.

I gave Rocky some distance over the next few days, remaining in the lobby or the west wing and avoiding the east wing altogether, so as not to make our cohabitation uncomfortable. On Monday, Brynn's organic, nontoxic cleaning supplies arrived. I moved the leftover cleaning products to the bottom shelf in the housekeeping closet and put her products on the rolling carts.

Tuesday afternoon, I was checking emails at the desk when Rocky entered through the new French doors. "All done! Voilà." He swept an arm to invite me to inspect his handiwork.

The French doors were precisely framed, the rhododendrons were planted, the deck was sanded and stained to a shiny smoothness, and the drainage pipe was obscured underneath it. You'd have to get down on all fours and peek through a knothole to know the pipe was there. "Everything looks perfect!"

"Aristotle said 'Pleasure in the job puts perfection in the work.'"

"Did Aristotle build decks, too?"

"I believe he installed a pillared portico at the Acropolis."

I wrote Rocky a check for the remaining balance. "Thanks for your hard work." There was more I wanted to say, but I was afraid of sounding corny. His idea of adding the deck helped make this place my own, and would attract guests seeking an intimate event space. And even though I'd tried to give him space while he'd stayed here, I was sad he'd be leaving now. It had been nice to know there was someone else under the same roof. I'd be totally on my own now.

He folded the check and tucked it into his breast pocket. "I suppose I should pack up."

He stared at me a long moment, as if he, too, were debating whether to say something, when brakes squeaked out front. We turned to see a delivery truck at the door. The driver hopped down and came to the door. "Got some patio furniture for you."

Though he'd been poised to depart only a moment before, Rocky insisted on helping me assemble the tables and chairs. I wasn't about to pass up his assistance. He was far more adept with tools than I, and completed four pieces to each one of mine. Still, when he inspected my workmanship, he agreed it was solid. When we finished, it was half past six.

"If you won't let me pay you for your extra help," I said, "at least let me buy you dinner."

He agreed this time, and an hour later we were sitting across from each other at a booth in the Greasy Griddle, polishing off pieces of Patty's delicious blueberry pie. When he finished, he pushed his plate back and eyed me. "What do you plan to do for maintenance at the lodge?"

"The sellers left me a list of people to call."

"It would be better to have someone on-site in case of an emergency."

He had a point, but I couldn't afford a full-time maintenance worker. Rather than admit this, I said, "There won't be enough work to keep someone busy full-time."

"What if I took care of maintenance?" he asked. "I'd still

do my side-hustle handyman jobs, but I'd make your lodge my top priority. The room could be my pay."

Patty, who'd come over to top off our coffee mugs, liked the idea. "Seems I'm always calling Rocky to fix something here at the diner. It'd be nice to have him just across the parking lot."

I looked from her back to Rocky. "You don't want to go home?"

"It's crowded," Rocky said. "I had my house to myself until six months ago when my son-in-law lost his job. The company closed down. He and my daughter moved in until they can get back on their feet. Their baby girl, too. I love 'em to pieces, but there's no peace or privacy."

"The arrangement would be temporary, then?"

"That's right. When your lodge starts filling up, I'll ske-daddle. What do you say?" He angled his head, waiting for an answer. Patty did the same.

Is this a good idea? From a business perspective, it made perfect sense. According to the financial records I'd reviewed, the previous owners had spent around two grand a month on maintenance. I had little cash left to pay for maintenance, but I did have an empty room that could serve as compensation. It could be difficult to get reliable help up here, too, so it seemed silly to pass up the offer of a hardworking handyman. Unfortunately, I'd developed a little crush on the guy. How could I not? He'd rode in after the lodge collapsed like a knight in shining armor—or at least a knight with shiny tools in his tool belt. I'd been able to mask my feelings so far, but would things get awkward if he stuck around? After a moment's thought, I realized I had to set aside my personal feelings and put my business interests first. After all, I'd moved up here to run a mountain lodge. Besides, it would benefit Patty, too. "I say 'enjoy your stay.'"

Chapter 7

I learned this, at least, by my experiment: that if one advances confidently in the direction of his dreams, and endeavors to live the life which he has imagined, he will meet with a success unexpected in common hours.

—Henry David Thoreau (1854: *Walden*)

Misty

Brynn arrived ten minutes early Sunday morning, ready to work. We went to the housekeeping closet and I handed her a lanyard with three keys—one for the drawer at the registration desk that contained the guest keys, one for the exterior doors, and a master key for the guest rooms, housekeeping closet, and storage spaces. I was always delighted when hotel housekeeping folded towels into cute shapes, and I'd found a YouTube video that showed how to turn a towel into a bear. I taught Brynn what I'd learned. As we rolled the two housekeeping carts out of the closet, the front wheel on Brynn's cart rattled. I made a mental note to ask Rocky to fix the loose wheel.

Brynn and I tidied up the rooms, leaving a towel bear in each bath. She worked the east wing, which included Rocky's room, while I handled the west wing. With the guest rooms freshly dusted and vacuumed and the pillows plumped, we spent the afternoon polishing the paneling and planting colorful goldenrod in whiskey barrels on either side of the front door. When we were done, Brynn went to the housekeeping closet and returned to the registration desk with several items in her arms, including a small bowl, a bundle of plant stems tied together with string, and a large feather from a red-tailed hawk, a common raptor in the area.

"What's all that for?" I asked.

"Smudging," she replied. "It purifies the space and creates positive energy. It's a Wiccan ritual. But don't worry. I grow my own sage so it's sustainable."

The sustainability of her sage was the least of my worries. I'd heard of Wicca, but what, exactly, did Wiccans believe? Would her unconventional ways alarm the guests? Immediately, I chastised myself for my hypocritical thoughts. Spirituality took many forms, and a reverence for nature was one I understood. Coming to the mountains had always been as much a spiritual experience for me as a vacation adventure. Who was I to fault her for her beliefs?

She proceeded to light the bundle on fire and, once it had burned a few seconds, blew it out. She carried the bowl and feather around as the bundle burned, waving the feather to disperse the smoke and tapping the ashes into the bowl. The air filled with a scent similar to incense.

Rocky walked in and eyed Brynn. "Getting high on your own supply?"

Brynn waved the smudge stick as she walked toward us. "It's sage, not marijuana."

"Good," he said. "The last thing we need is the sheriff showing up and arresting you."

She raised the feather higher, sweeping it through the air. "Been there, done that."

Rocky and I exchanged looks. *What had Brynn been arrested for?* Before I could ask, a hiss of air brakes sounded in front of the lodge. The minibus chartered by the owner of the yoga studio had arrived from Charlotte and pulled to a stop outside. I scurried over to open the door to the lodge, pushing the stopper down with my foot to hold it in place so the guests could easily enter with their luggage. Brynn extinguished her smudge stick in the bowl before joining Rocky and me as we stepped outside to greet our first guests and help them with their bags.

The bus door opened with a hydraulic *whoosh*. A trim woman of about thirty appeared in the doorway and descended the steps like royalty, one hand raised and clutching a shiny metal water bottle like a scepter. A designer tote hung from the crook in her elbow, a rolled-up lavender yoga mat sticking out of it. In her other arm she held a pillow in a pink satin pillowcase. The woman had silky black curls, creamy skin that appeared to have never seen the sun, and vivid green eyes trimmed with impossibly thick lashes that were likely glued to her lids. She looked like an old-fashioned porcelain doll who'd grown up, thinned out, and time-traveled from yesteryear, trading her ruffled petticoats for sleek Lycra. She wore a pair of athletic mules with a gold ankle bracelet, hot pink spandex pants, and a fitted black tank top with the studio's logo printed on it, a white triangle with a green eye—just like her own—in the middle. A black strap with a buckle encircled her wrist, and an amethyst glittered from the piercing in her nose.

A curvy blonde slid down from the bus after the human doll. The strap of a cross-body purse cut a swath across the studio logo on her tank top, bisecting her bulging breasts. She held her water bottle aloft, too, mirroring the first woman's mannerisms like an understudy practicing her performance. She also wore a strap around her wrist and a jewel in her nose, though her strap and jewel were both turquoise in color.

Next off the bus was a young man with a NASCAR ballcap on his head, black wraparound sunglasses, and a well-trimmed goatee the color of gingersnap cookies. He was slightly on the short side, around five feet-seven inches or so, and had a fit athletic build. On spotting my birthday bear, he strode over, draped an arm around the bear's shoulders, and curled back his thumb and pinky so that his three fingers formed a letter *M*. He opened his mouth, stuck out his tongue, and snapped a selfie.

"Is that Madman Maddox?" Rocky asked. "I didn't realize we'd be hosting a celebrity."

Although I'd seen the name Dax Maddox among the registrations, I hadn't clued in that the guest was the NASCAR star better known as Madman. I didn't follow racing myself, but you couldn't live in the Carolinas and not have heard of Madman Maddox. Last year's Rookie of the Year had made quite a name for himself, both on and off the track. On the track, he'd beaten more experienced drivers by incredible leads. Off the track, he'd gotten himself into hot water for accusing his rival of executing an unsportsmanlike bump-and-pass maneuver that cost him precious seconds. After the race, Madman had given the other driver a curse-laden dressing down, and performed his own bump and pass by slamming his shoulder into the other driver as he stormed past him. Madman claimed the contact was unintentional but few bought his story, including NAS-

CAR officials who put him on a short suspension. My guess was his attendance at a yoga and meditation retreat was primarily a PR stunt, but so long as he behaved himself that was fine with me. He could bring some attention to the lodge. After he'd snapped his selfie, he glanced around before settling his gaze on me. "What's the name of this place?"

"The Mountaintop Lodge," I said.

"Gotcha." He worked his thumbs over his phone, posting his pic to social media.

Rocky stepped over to offer a hand as people continued to trickle out of the bus. Three Asian American women chatting amiably. Two thirtyish women, one white and one black, with high-end sneakers and muscular calves that identified them as runners. A woman around my age with a virtual clone twenty-five years younger, clearly a mother and daughter. A young Latino with short hair and a horseshoe-style mustache. An elderly woman with snow-white curls who might have wrinkled a bit but hadn't lost the bounce in her step. She led a small, short-haired tan dog on a leash, a chihuahua-pug mix, or chug, if I wasn't mistaken. He, too, had a bounce in his step, his tail curled up tight against his rear like a ballerina's bun. When he spotted Molasses, he launched into a *yap-yap-yap* and pulled his owner over so they could get acquainted. I had to give the tiny dog credit. He was as fearless as he was cute.

I bent down and ran a hand down his back. "He's adorable. What's his name?"

"Chugalug," said the woman. "And I'm Norma Jean, in case you're interested." Her wide grin said she took no offense at my showing more interest in her pup than her.

Last off the bus was a skinny, sixtyish man with impossibly long, lanky limbs. Other than thin gray eyebrows, his head was hairless. Like Sasha, he was remarkably pale. Thanks to a wide forehead, his bald white head resembled a light bulb, oddly appropriate for someone who was enlightened. He wore a pair of earthy sandals and faded jeans along with his Third Eye T-shirt. A colorful open-top bohemian bag hung from his shoulder. Next to me, Brynn softly hummed the notes from *Close Encounters of the Third Kind*—*Re, Mi, Do, Do, So*. The man did indeed resemble an alien, or the subject of the famous Edvard Munch painting known as *The Scream*. Maybe the artist had had a close encounter of his own before painting the iconic oil.

Now that all of the occupants of the bus had disembarked, the dark-haired doll woman stopped in front of me, tossed her hair, and looked at me expectantly, blinking her long lashes.

"Welcome to the Mountaintop Lodge," I said. "Are you Sasha Carlisle?"

"I'm Sasha *Ducharme*-Carlisle." She circled a finger tipped with a long, pink nail, indicating the group milling around her, retrieving their luggage from under the bus. "These are my students and staff." She glanced over her shoulder at the alien-like man. "Glenn! Get my suitcase." As if realizing she'd forgotten her manners, she added a curt, "Please."

"I'd be happy to," Glenn replied with a serene smile, seemingly unfazed. He set down his own vintage avocado-green Samsonite suitcase, then reached under the bus to retrieve an oversized piece of luggage with wheels. He rolled it over to Sasha. She took the handle and flounced inside.

I gave the man a nod. "Nice to meet you, Glenn. I'm Misty."

"Namaste." He bowed his head. I figured I couldn't go wrong by returning the gesture.

While Rocky helped Norma Jean with her baggage, I held out my hand to invite the group into the lodge. "Welcome, everyone. Let's get y'all checked in."

Brynn and the guests followed me to the registration desk, where Sasha stood, drumming her fingers on the countertop. As the host of this retreat, who stood to make a pretty penny from her students, she might be expected to let them check in first. But Sasha seemed used to putting herself ahead of others. Forcing a smile, I pulled up her registration on the computer. Her email address was no surprise: bosslady@thirdeyestudiospa.com. I opened the drawer and retrieved the keys for Room 19, which sat directly across the hall from Rocky. I pointed to my right. "Your room is at the end of the east wing. It has a lovely view of the woods out back."

"Great." She snatched the keys from me and turned to the towering blonde in line behind her. "Meet me for drinks on the deck at eight."

"Fun!" said the blonde, though she said it to Sasha's back. The studio's owner had already grabbed her suitcase and was wheeling it away, not having waited for an answer.

While Brynn checked in one of the other guests at the computer next to me, I gave the blonde a smile. "May I have your name?"

"Kendall McFadden." She presented her identification and credit card. "Can I have the room next to Sasha? We're best friends."

"Of course." I planned to be as accommodating as possible, especially with groups. If they enjoyed their stay, maybe they'd make the trip an annual event. I reached down to retrieve the keys for Room 17, which adjoined Sasha's, and handed them over. Brynn and I registered the other guests, sending them off to the right until the east wing filled up, then sending them to rooms in the west wing.

A sturdy woman around my age stepped up to the counter carrying a portable massage table folded in half. She plunked it down on the floor in front of the desk. *Klunk.* "I'm Heike," she said in a heavy German accent. "The room can fit my massage table, ja?"

She must be the spa's masseuse. I assured her there'd be plenty of room for her table.

"Gud. I need space to do my work." As if to demonstrate, she held up her hands, flexing her fingers. After I gave her the room keys, she pointed them at me, jabbing the air. "You get massage. Fifty dollars only. I put signup sheet on my door."

Her offer sounded more like an order, but either way I'd take her up on it. Getting the lodge ready had been exciting but stressful, and a relaxing massage sounded divine.

She reached out her freshly flexed fingers and plucked a white fur from the sleeve of my shirt. She held it up. "You have cat."

"I do. Her full name is Baroness Blizzard, but we call her Yeti."

She pulled out her wallet, flipped to the section with the clear plastic pockets, and showed me a photo of three tabbies, one in each variety: Brown, gray, orange. "My babies."

"Such cuties." I pointed to another photo, one of four teenaged children, all very close in age, who resembled Heike. "And who might these be?"

"My other babies." She waved a dismissive hand. "They have no time for their mother."

I offered her a sympathetic smile. "Been there. I've got two boys in college. Spending time with me is the last thing on their minds."

Rocky walked past, carrying two pieces of luggage for Norma Jean. Molasses and the puggy pup followed them, the little dog's nails *clickety-clicking* on the hardwood floor.

"Hund!" Heike barked, patting her leg. Either Molasses spoke German or he recognized the universal hand signal for *Come here, doggie!* He waked over to Heike and received a nice scratch courtesy of the masseuse. I wondered if he realized he was in professional hands.

My final guest to check in was Glenn. After carrying his ancient suitcase up to the counter and setting it on the floor, he wheeled something up to the desk that was tall and flat and wrapped in a fringed yoga blanket held fast with rope.

It was probably nosey to ask, but he'd made no attempts to hide the odd contraption and my curiosity got the best of me. "What do you have there?"

He removed the rope and blanket to reveal a large metal gong. "It's for the meditation sessions. I lead transcendental, focused, visualization, mantra, metta. The whole gambit."

"I didn't realize there were so many types of meditation."

"Each has distinct techniques and purposes," he said. "You're welcome to join in our practices, gratis. You were kind to open your lodge to us on such late notice. We'd thought we'd have to cancel the retreat. The fire at the ashram was a tragedy, but the universe must have wanted us to be here instead."

Brynn glanced over, a thoughtful look on her face. It seemed to be dawning on her that she and the meditation leader might share similar worldviews.

When I completed Glenn's registration and handed over his keys, he replied with a soft smile and a light tap of the padded mallet on his gong. *Gongggg.* I could see why he used it in their practices. It was a mellow, melodious sound. "Beautiful."

The final woman to check in with Brynn had "harried mother" written all over her. Her hair was pulled back in a sloppy ponytail and she wore no makeup, though she did wear a smear of grape jelly on the sleeve of her blouse. *I remember those days.* She was just about to hand over her credit card when her phone blasted a ringtone at full volume. She scrambled to pull the device from her purse and eyed the screen. "It's my husband. This can't be good." She jabbed the button to accept the call and put the phone to her ear. "What's up?" She paused to listen. "A fever? How high?" Another pause. "One hundred and three? No!" She put a hand to her forehead in frustration, a subconscious act of empathy, or both. "I'll head home as soon as I can."

As she ended the call and returned the phone to her purse, I asked, "Sick child?"

"Yes. Strep throat." She groaned and closed her eyes for a moment. "This was my first chance to do something for myself in years. Why do kids always get sick at the worst times?"

I was disappointed to lose the income her room would

generate but, even more, my heart went out to the woman. It was hard to see your children suffer. "I'll waive your cancellation fee." Maybe she'd appreciate the gesture and bring her family up for a vacation another time.

"Thank you," she said with a grateful, if wry, smile. "Now I've got to figure out how to get back to Charlotte. The bus already left. Can you get an Uber up here?"

Rocky had returned from bellhop duty and overheard our exchange. He stepped up and stepped in. "I'd be happy to drive you down to Boone. You can rent a car there or catch a bus."

I reached under the counter and retrieved one of the teddy bears I'd ordered as a perk for guests with children. "Take this, too. Maybe it will cheer up your child."

The woman took the bear from me and looked from me to Rocky. "You two are so kind."

As she called her husband back, Rocky waved me aside to speak privately. "If you want to fill the empty room, there's bound to be someone who wants to get off the A.T. for a night or two. When I'm done in Boone, I can swing by the Mountaineer Falls Shelter if you'd like."

"Thanks, Rocky." Though I'd only taken day hikes on stretches of the Appalachian Trail, or A.T. as it was commonly referred to by avid hikers, I'd seen the shelter Rocky had referenced. It was located at Big Pine Mountain in Tennessee, a half-hour drive from the lodge. The shelters were primitive, covered platforms enclosed on three sides with an open front, basically doghouses for humans. Stopping by the shelter to see if anyone wanted to trade the hard, cold platform for a soft bed, hot shower, and laundry facilities was a smart idea.

The time was nearing five o'clock and, with all of the guests checked in, I let Brynn leave a few minutes early. She rounded up her purse from the locker in the housekeeping closet and raised a hand in goodbye as she headed out the doors. As hard as she'd worked today, I felt confident I'd hired a solid worker, though I still wondered about her run-in with the law. Brynn followed Rocky and the worried mother out the door.

With all of my staff going off site, my nerves buzzed with equal parts anxiety and excitement. Here I was, running a lodge all by myself. *Gulp.* On the other hand, here I was, running a lodge all by myself. *Hooray!* I supposed it was normal to feel both apprehensive and proud at the same time. If worse came to worst, I could call on Patty. She'd run her own diner for decades and was just across the parking lot. We were already business partners of sorts. Maybe we'd become friends, too.

CHAPTER 8

Who wouldn't be a mountaineer! Up here all the world's prizes seem nothing.
  —John Muir (1911: *My First Summer in the Sierra*)

Misty

With my guests otherwise occupied, I decided to take a peek at social media and see whether Madman had posted the pic he'd taken with the bear. Maybe the NASCAR driver would drive some traffic to the lodge. I found the photo on his Instagram feed. More than a hundred people had already commented on it. Unfortunately, his post read *Just arrived at the Mountainside Lodge. It's wild up here. HAHAHA!*

Ugh. Too bad he hadn't gotten the name straight. *Speaking of names . . .* I mentally ran through the guests, trying to commit their names to memory so I could greet them personally when we crossed paths in the lodge. Vera was the woman who'd come with her daughter, Vivian. The two names, both starting with *V*, would be easy to remember. The white-haired woman with the pug mix was Norma Jean. The guy with the mustache was Joaquín.

Sasha sailed into the lobby with Kendall in her wake. While Sasha carried a stack of folded shirts, Kendall juggled an assortment of merchandise in her arms. Water bottles. Towels. Yoga mats, bags, lightweight foam blocks, and long colorful yoga straps with metal D rings on one end. All imprinted with the Third Eye Studio & Spa green eye logo, of course.

Sasha looked around the great room, emitting an *"mmm"* as she seemed to be evaluating her options. "There," she said, pointing at a bookcase. "Move that junk to the bottom shelf." The *junk* she referred to was the books, puzzles, and games I'd placed there to entertain my guests.

Kendall placed her load on a table and proceeded to relegate my things to the bottom shelf, cramming them in haphazardly. Once the upper shelves were cleared, the two filled them with Third Eye merchandise. As Sasha swept by my desk on her way back to her room, she said, "Make sure nobody takes anything without paying me first."

I hadn't expected to serve as loss prevention for a pop-up shop and, frankly, I didn't want to be liable if things went missing. "I'll do my best," I told her. "But I'm not always at the desk."

She replied with a *"hmph"* and went on her way.

Rocky returned two hours later with a young man and woman in tow. Their shaggy hair told me they hadn't had haircuts since heading out on the trail. They looked weary but cheery, dirty but undeterred. On their backs they carried enormous packs that started at their hips and extended up over their heads, containing everything they might need on the trail.

Rocky introduced us. "Misty, this is Cole and Sammie. They got married in Maine back in May and started hiking south on the A.T. right after the reception."

Sammie groaned dramatically. "Longest. Honeymoon. Ever."

Cole teased her right back. "It was *your* idea, remember?"

The two obviously adored each other. It was also obvious from the trail funk permeating the lobby that the two could use a shower, stat. I pulled up the screen to input their information. "How many nights will you be staying?"

When Cole looked to Sammie, she said, "Let's do three nights. That'll give us two full days to wash our clothes and buy supplies before we get back on the trail."

"Great." I clicked on the calendar icon. "I've put you down to check out on Wednesday."

They lowered their packs and retrieved their wallets, counting out bills on the counter. A glimpse into their wallets told me they had scant money left, with hundreds of miles to go before reaching the end of the trail in Georgia. My mind went back to when Jack and I spent our honeymoon here. We hadn't had two nickels to rub together, either. Besides, building goodwill was as important as making a buck, right? "Your stay is on the house. Honeymooners' special."

Cole gaped. "For real?"

When I nodded, tears welled up in Sammie's eyes. "Thank you! That's sooo generous!"

I rounded up their keys and handed them over. "If you need anything, just give me a buzz." I'd programmed the front desk phone to forward calls to my cell if it wasn't picked up in three rings. "The breakfast buffet will be open from six thirty to nine thirty."

As they headed down the hall, members of the yoga retreat group began to emerge from their rooms, their unpacking complete. Some wandered across the parking lot to have dinner at the Greasy Griddle. The two women with the shapely calves went for a jog. Others decided to take a hike on one of the many trails accessible nearby. But as the evening wore on, nearly all of them ended up outside on the deck, enjoying the cool evening air and the stunning sunset view. Rocky had been right. A deck was just the thing this lodge needed to give it some zhuzh.

Kendall headed past the registration desk, a bottle of white wine in hand. The label identified it as one of the Biltmore's offerings, from their high-end Antler Hill line, which meant she'd paid around forty dollars for the bottle. The Biltmore Estate was a North Carolina tourist staple. I'd visited a dozen times and sampled many of their wines. She carried the bottle onto the deck along with two water glasses from her room, and took a seat at a table. Sasha soon sashayed by the desk, too. At the French doors, she turned back to me and circled her finger in the air like she'd done earlier. "I'll need all the deck furniture moved by seven a.m. for sun salutations."

Having issued her orders to me, Sasha joined Kendall on the deck, taking a seat opposite her friend and snatching the bottle from the table. While Kendall had only filled her glass halfway, Sasha poured until the wine reached the brim of hers. The two threw their heads back and laughed at her indecorous act.

Madman Maddox ventured out on the deck with a bottle of beer in one hand, his ever-present phone in the other. He walked over to the rail, set his beer down, and held up his phone for another selfie. He formed the *M* with his three fingers and stuck out his tongue again before snapping the photo. *Click.*

As he lowered his phone and began typing, I scurried

out to the deck and gave him a smile. "Thanks for mentioning the lodge in your earlier post. Just a minor correction, though. The name is the Mountain*top* Lodge, not Mountainside." *My new sign can't arrive soon enough.*

Madman gave me a thumbs-up. "Got it."

When he finished posting, Sasha patted the empty seat next to her. "Sit here, Madman!"

He hesitated, but then walked over to her table and sat down. Sasha leaned over from her chair, her hair brushing against his shoulder as she draped an arm over it and gave him a naughty grin. "Tell me how it feels to go fast."

Sheesh. Sasha could use some lessons in the subtle art of seduction. Didn't she know the guy was already attached? He dated a "Honey Bee," a cheerleader for the Charlotte Hornets basketball team. His girlfriend stood three inches taller than him, more in heels, towering over him in photos. The two made an attractive couple and were a constant subject of celebrity gossip.

Sasha laid her head on Madman's shoulder and batted her eyes. He shrugged her off, scooted his chair back, and glanced around, as if to make sure nobody had snapped a pic that could land him in trouble with his sweetheart. If Sasha had thought her efforts might lead to a second hyphen in her last name—Ducharme-Carlisle-Maddox—Madman made it clear that wasn't going to happen. I felt sorry for her. She was at that age when hormones could make a woman do stupid things in search of love. *Whoa.* A sudden spike in my body temperature and an instant sweat on my upper lip reminded me that my hormones hadn't given up on me yet, either.

I headed back to the desk, where I fanned myself with a

travel brochure for a nearby zip-line park. Once I'd cooled off, I checked Madman's Instagram feed. He'd posted the photo along with: Sunset at the Mountainview Lodge.

Maybe I should write out the name for him on a sticky note, I thought.

An hour later, after finishing his beer and politely rebuffing Sasha's repeated attempts to throw herself at him, Madman excused himself.

Sasha slurred, "See you later," punctuating her words with an exaggerated wink.

Kendall was no longer laughing. In fact, she frowned as Sasha shook the now-empty wine bottle over her glass, making sure she hadn't missed a drop. They were like frenemies in an overwrought soap opera. Sasha had drunk three-quarters of the bottle. Now that both the wine and the NASCAR star were gone, she no longer seemed interested in chatting with Kendall. She stood and called to the crowd, "Be here in the morning at seven sharp!" She staggered inside, leaving her dirty glass behind.

As Sasha passed by the registration desk, I called out "Sleep well!" She looked my way but didn't seem quite able to focus on my face. She weaved her way down the hall to her room.

By a quarter to ten, all guests had returned to their rooms and the lodge was quiet. I returned to mine, as well. I slid into my nightgown and was brushing my teeth when the Westminster Chimes on my anniversary clock began to play, the sound reverberating in the room. Lest the clock annoy Vera and Vivian, who were staying in the room next to mine, I rushed over and slid the battery compartment open, removing the batteries to silence it. At our house in

Raleigh, the sound barely garnered my attention. But with people in close proximity here, I was more aware of just how loud the chimes were. Clearly, I still had a few things to learn about living in a lodge.

My cell phone alarm went off much too early Monday morning. Irritated to be awakened from her beauty sleep, Yeti cast me a look of disgust and rolled over on her pillow. While most folks would be sleeping in on the Labor Day holiday, Rocky and I had to be up before daybreak to make preparations for the yogis. We met on the dimly lit deck at six to move the furniture aside for the group's sun salutations. Though lights shined in some of the guest-room windows, we worked as quietly as possible so as not to disturb guests who might still be sleeping. Chugalug had heard us outside and watched through the window, but at least he didn't yap.

We'd just cleared the deck when I noticed Patty standing outside the front door with one of her kitchen staff. Both held heavy warming trays in their arms. I rushed through the lodge, unlocked the door, and let them in, taking a tray to relieve her load. "Sorry to keep you waiting!"

Patty grunted. "Two more seconds and your welcome mat would be coated in gravy."

Rocky rubbed his tummy and took a tray from her helper. "This food smells delicious."

We set the trays in the electric warmer atop a portable table I'd covered with a whimsical bear-print tablecloth. Before Patty left, I said, "Hold on." I went around the desk and retrieved one of the extra keys for the exterior doors. I attached it to a pine-cone keychain and held it out to Patty.

"You should have a key of your own so you and your staff don't have to wait on me."

"Good idea." She took the key from me. "How's everything going so far? From the headcount you gave me, it sounds like you've got a full house."

"We do," I said. "It's a group from Charlotte on a yoga retreat. It's been smooth sailing so far."

"See?" She smiled. "I told you things would work out fine."

"You did, and you were right. If you have some free time one of these evenings, come over and enjoy the new deck with us."

"I will," she said. "Holler if you run low on anything."

Lured by the enticing smells of a hearty southern breakfast, many of the guests came out to fill their plates. Others opted for just coffee or juice, planning to enjoy a full meal after their sun salutations.

The phone at the front desk rang at six forty-five and I hustled over to grab it. The readout told me the call came from Room 19, Sasha's room. I remembered to use her full last name this morning. "Good morning, Ms. Ducharme-Car—"

"Send a bellhop. I need someone to carry my things to the deck." *Click.* She was gone.

I hung up the phone, scurried down to her room, and rapped lightly. The door opened a few inches and Sasha's manicured hands thrust a yoga mat, yoga strap, water bottle, and what appeared to be a metal mortar and pestle at me. The black wrist strap that seemed to be a constant accessory peeked out from the sleeve of her pink satin pajamas. I glanced into the room, which was still dark. I saw only Sasha's bloodshot right eye, no doubt courtesy of the three glasses of wine the evening before.

She barked more orders. "Set those up at the back of the deck." Once the items were out of her hands and in mine, she shut the door without another word. *Okay, then.*

Rocky had propped open the French doors to allow the students easy access to the deck. I carried Sasha's things outside and spread the mat out on the deck near the back railing. I placed the water bottle next to it. Seeming to recognize the mat and bottle as Sasha's, Kendall unrolled her mat and placed it close, so she'd be in the front row of students. Her behavior triggered a high-school flashback. Kendall reminded me of the wannabes, girls on the fringes who were desperate to belong and swarmed around the queen bees, hoping to gain their favor. *Shouldn't Kendall have outgrown that notion by now?* I supposed some people never did.

I held up the bowl. "What's this for? Burning incense?"

"It's a singing bowl," Kendall said. "Sasha uses it to signal the start and end of practice."

As I went to set the bowl down, Kendall threw up her hands. "Be careful! Sasha paid five grand for that bowl. It's an antique from Tibet. It was hand-forged by monks centuries ago."

What could one say to that but "Wow." It was the most valuable thing I'd ever held in my hands. My engagement and wedding rings together hadn't even cost that much. I gently placed the bowl on Sasha's mat before returning to the front desk.

Other students went outside to set up on the deck. Glenn did, too, though he took a place at the back of the group.

It was probably standard protocol for the studio's staff to let students have the prime spots. He wore another Third Eye Studio & Spa tee today, but he'd traded his jeans for a loose-fitting pair of striped cotton pants that looked like pajama bottoms.

Once she'd kept her class waiting a few minutes, Sasha flounced fashionably late into the lobby, dressed head to toe in bright gold spandex as if she herself was the sun to which her group would pay homage. Her blood-shot eyes had cleared, perhaps with the help of eye drops. She turned to me and said, "Have maintenance replace the bulbs around my bathroom mirror. They're not bright enough. I could barely see to put on my makeup." The copious quantities of foundation, lipstick, and mascara on her face said otherwise, but I didn't argue with her. She sailed gracefully out the doors, tossing her students a flippant "Namaste, yogis!"

Sasha picked up the singing bowl and ran the mallet around the rim. The bowl emitted a resonant yet soothing tone. Having studied piano and listened to my sons practice their trombones for untold hours, I identified the note as an E. It was the same note my anniversary clock played when tolling the hour. My clock played what was known as the Westminster Chimes, the same as those played by Big Ben at Westminster Palace in London. Sasha confirmed my guess when she said, "The E note represents the solar plexus chakra. We'll focus on that chakra today."

As the class proceeded to follow Sasha's lead through various poses, Heike wandered into the lobby and gave me a guttural grunt in greeting.

I gestured to the group outside. "Planning to join them?"

She scoffed. "The sun has risen for thousands of years and it will do the same for thousands more whether I thank it or not." She proceeded to the breakfast buffet, where she piled a plate with home fries, grits, and biscuits and gravy. While Heike refused to worship the sun, her heaping plate paid homage to Patty's skills in the Greasy Griddle's kitchen. Heike poured herself a mug of coffee, too, and carried her meal back to her room to eat alone.

A twentyish busboy with hair the color of maple syrup came over from the Greasy Griddle to collect the tub of dirty dishes. The skillet-shaped nametag on his shirt read Brock. As he lifted the tub, the sleeve of his T-shirt inched up to reveal the tattoo of a mountain range on his bicep. The image was accompanied by the words High Life. His gaze moved to the windows at the back of the room and the dozen derrières raised in the air as the group posed in downward dog. When he realized I'd caught him ogling my guests, he blushed. "I'll get these dishes back to the diner." With that, he scurried off with the bin.

The melodic sound of the singing bowl told me Sasha had concluded her class. Murmurs of "namaste" followed. The group rolled up their mats and came inside. Several, including Kendall, lined up for the buffet. She'd just picked up a plate and was poised to drop a heaping spoonful of grits onto it when Sasha returned from stashing her things in her room and shrieked.

"You can't eat that! Do you know how many carbs are in grits?"

Kendall dropped the serving spoon into the warming tray as if it had burned her. *Clang!* "You're right. I don't know what I was thinking."

She'd been thinking the breakfast smelled and looked delicious, that's what she'd been thinking. I found myself again realizing that growing older had its benefits, a big one being that you no longer worried so much about other people's opinions. It was freeing.

Sasha lifted each lid in turn, emitting a series of sound effects to evince her disgust. *Hash browns?* "Uck." *Biscuits?* "Augghh!" *Gravy?* "Ewww!" *Pancakes and syrup?* "Nuh-uh!" She shook her head at the basket of muffins and even bypassed the oatmeal. By the time she reached the end of the line, the only item she'd put on her plate was a banana. Same for Kendall, who'd followed her along. Kendall glanced back at the food with longing as she trailed Sasha to a table.

Patty had come over to fill the coffee urn with fresh brew, and witnessed her food being summarily rejected. She pursed her lips, as if holding back choice words for the women. Brynn, who'd watched from behind her housekeeping cart, did not hold her tongue. She stopped at the desk and leaned toward me to whisper, "Sasha Doohickey-Carbuncle is a piece of work."

While I'd prefer my staff not gossip about the guests, I agreed with Brynn.

Patty left to return to the Greasy Griddle, and Sammie and Cole came up the hall, looking well rested and smelling shower-fresh. Their response to the buffet was the exact opposite of Sasha's, their eyes going wide with delight. Cole gave a play-by-play as he made his way down the line. "Hash browns! Score! Biscuits and gravy? Yay! Pancakes with maple syrup!" He pumped his fist. "Yesss!" The two loaded their plates with so much food I feared they'd make themselves sick. Weeks in the woods subsisting on trail mix and tree bark had taken its toll.

I was cleaning up behind the guests a few minutes later when Rocky returned. He eyed the newlyweds shoveling food into their faces. "Hiking sure can give people an appetite."

I wiped a smudge of syrup from a table with a rag. "You speaking from experience?"

"I am. I hiked the entire Appalachian Trail after I graduated from high school."

The young honeymooners must have overheard Rocky. Cole's mouth was full, but he jabbed his knife in the air to indicate the seat across from him. Sammie put words to her husband's motions. "We'd love to hear your trail stories if you've got time to join us."

"I'd like to hear your stories, too," I said. "I'll get us some coffee."

I rounded up two mugs of hot brew and filled Rocky's with an insane amount of sugar as he liked it, and we joined the young couple at their table. Over the next quarter hour, they ate their weight in potatoes, grits, and biscuits, while Rocky regaled us with tales of his long-ago hike with two high-school buddies, one of whom tried to scare the others by saying he'd seen a Wendigo in the woods, that it had possessed him, and that he felt Wendigo psychosis coming on.

Cole held a loaded forkful of pancake aloft. "What's Wendigo psychosis?"

Rocky filled us in. "It's when a person craves human flesh and resorts to cannibalism."

"Oh yeah?" Cole crammed the pancake into his mouth, making the rest of us laugh.

I looked from Cole to Sammie. "What are your plans once you finish the trail?"

Sammie said, "We studied computer programming at Bates College. We've got jobs with a company in Boston. They hired several graduating seniors. Most of them started work in June, but we arranged to delay our start date until January so we could hike the A.T. We figured if we didn't do it now, we might never get the chance."

Rocky raised his coffee mug for another sip, but first asked, "What are your trail names?"

Cole stuck out his chest and beamed unabashedly. "I'm Hard Drive."

"I'm Software," Sammie said. "Together, we're a complete system."

The names were cute and appropriate for the two young programmers. Sammie and Cole finished every bite of their breakfast. Just in time, too. The busboy from the Greasy Griddle came back a final time to claim the remaining dishes and trays.

As we stood from the table, Cole asked, "Is there a place nearby we can get provisions?"

"Fred's," Rocky and I said in unison. Fred's General Mercantile had been around since the late 1970s. A combination grocery, hardware store, gift shop, ski shop, and café, Fred's could fulfill all your needs on the mountain.

Rocky tossed back his coffee. "I'll give y'all a ride over. Got a few things I need to pick up myself."

Before he could go, I said, "Sasha asked to have brighter lightbulbs installed in her bathroom. Can you put in some with a higher wattage?"

"Wattage is a measure of power," he replied. "Light output is measured in lumens."

"Thanks for illuminating me," I said dryly, making him chuckle.

"We don't have any bulbs on hand, but I can pick some up at the store. She might feel like she's in the spotlight, though."

I fought the urge to snort. "I'm pretty sure that's what Sasha is going for."

CHAPTER 9

Just living is not enough, said the butterfly. One must
have sunshine, freedom, and a little flower.
—Hans Christian Andersen (1861: *The Butterfly*)

Misty

Over the course of the day Monday, Brynn and I cleaned
the guest rooms. She took the east wing, and I handled the
west wing. As Sasha left her room to the housekeeper, she
called back, "Be sure to put everything back where you
found it!"

Though Brynn said nothing with her mouth, her eyes
bored holes in the back of Sasha's head. Sasha's rude behavior was getting old fast. Thank goodness the rest of her
group were nothing like her—well, other than Kendall, that
is. Still, while Kendall copied Sasha's style of dress and
some of her mannerisms, she hadn't adopted Sasha's arro-
gance, thank goodness.

The yoga students filtered in and out of the lodge. Their
classes were scheduled primarily in the morning and late
afternoon to leave midday open for other activities.

I rapped on the door to Madman Maddox's room, called
out "Housekeeping!", and leaned in to listen for a response.
Hearing none, I unlocked the door and wheeled my cart inside. A couple of beer bottles sat on the coffee bar. I slid

them into the recycle bin on my cart and emptied his trash cans. After wiping down the surfaces and disinfecting the bath, I turned to the bed. One side of the king-sized bed was rumpled, the pillow askew and covers thrown back where Madman had climbed out of it this morning. The bedding on the other side lay flat, as if no one had slept there. But I wasn't fooled. On the other pillow was a telltale hair—a long, dark one that could only belong to Sasha. Looked like Madman had given in to temptation, and tried to hide it by smoothing down the covers. The Rookie of the Year was Jerk of the Year in my opinion. Perhaps it was petty of me, but I skipped folding one of his fresh towels into a bear. If he wanted a towel animal, he could watch a YouTube tutorial and do it himself.

I was sitting at the desk later when Heike wandered into the great room. Rocky had since returned from Fred's and upended Brynn's housekeeping cart in the lobby so he could fix the rattling wheel. As he turned the screwdriver, Heike reached out and grabbed him by the shoulder, digging her fingers into his flesh. "Aha! I feel tension. Come. I give you deep tissue massage."

As Heike dragged him away, Rocky looked back and mouthed *Help!*

Shortly thereafter, several students set up on the deck, ready for another class. Kendall claimed a spot in front. According to the schedule, Sasha was supposed to lead the group in something called Vinyasa Flow. She came down the hall just as the class was to begin. Her focus was on her cell phone as her thumbs typed away. She made her way out to the deck, where she placed her phone near her mat. She started the class with the lovely sound of the singing bowl.

Halfway through the class, as she led the group from the cobra position up to downward dog, her phone blared a raunchy Cardi B hit. The students froze in place, awaiting instruction on their next move as Sasha consulted her screen. She picked up her phone, stood, and waved Glenn forward, pointing down at her mat, silently signaling him to take over the class. He cast her a disapproving glance as she passed him, but she was too focused on her phone to notice. She put the device to her ear. "Hey, babe! I miss you like crazy. Miss me, too?"

Sounds like Sasha has a boyfriend. Of course, that fact hadn't stopped her from pursuing Madman Maddox. She flounced past the desk and down the hall to take her call in her room.

An hour later, I was reading a book at the desk when Rocky returned from his visit with Heike, moving his arms and legs like a loose-limbed marionette. "That woman unkinked muscles I didn't know I had." To prove his point, he raised his arms and twisted side to side, moving his hips as if working a hula hoop. "Go let her work her magic on you. I've covered it."

"Really? Wow. Thanks, Rocky." *Catch me if I swoon.*

I ventured down to the hall and knocked on Heike's door. She opened it and stepped back to allow me in. She'd closed her shutters, creating a dark, private space in which her clients could better relax. A single candle provided dim light. From somewhere in the room came the soft, serene sounds of a string instrument. Heike directed me to undress behind a portable room-divider screen. Though Heike might be used to people stripping in her presence, I hadn't been naked in front of anyone but Jack or my doctor in years. My discomfort expressed itself in idle chitter-chatter. "Have you been with Third Eye long?" I asked over the divider.

"Little while," Heike said.

"This music is pretty. What type of instrument is that?"

"Zither."

Her clipped answers told me she wasn't one for conversation.

I spent the next hour facedown in only my panties being pummeled and pulverized by Heike's powerful hands. When she wrapped them around the base of my neck, a frisson of fear skittered down my backbone. *This strong woman could easily snap my spine.* Fortunately, my primitive thought was quickly replaced by a more rational one. *Even if she could hurt me, what reason would she have?* She applied her thumbs to the nape of my neck, working my cervical vertebrae. She went on to work every muscle and bone in my back. When I finally rose from her massage table, I felt ready to turn cartwheels. Rocky was right. Heike worked wonders.

Late that afternoon, Glenn was performing tai chi on the lodge's lawn and I was sweeping leaves off the walkway when Sasha slunk out the door and groaned with enough drama to be nominated for an Emmy. Glenn slowly turned away and exhaled loudly. The movement and breath could be part of his practice, but I suspected they were signs of pent-up frustration.

I paused my chore. "Everything okay, Ms. Ducharme-Carlisle?"

"Kendall is . . . *a lot*." Sasha raised her hands, fingers splayed, and gestured as if pushing someone away. "I can't get a second to myself! She even got upset with me for locking the door between our rooms." A breeze blew our way and Sasha's nose wriggled. She threw her head back and issued a series of dainty sneezes. *Snit-snit-snit!* "Ugh! The ragweed here is the worst!" When she recovered from her sneezing fit, she said, "I need more towels. Right away."

"I'll have Brynn put some in your bathroom."

She didn't bother to thank me, but instead pulled her phone from a pocket on her yoga pants, tapped the screen, and mused aloud. "Seven thousand steps to go."

"Got one of those fitness apps?" I asked.

She held up her wrist, indicating the black band she'd worn since she stepped off the bus. "The tracker sends data to my phone. Workouts. Recovery. Sleep data. Everything. It's the best one on the market."

Glenn shifted position on the lawn, his arms going skyward before one bent and came down to form what appeared to be a number four. He looked at Sasha. "We need to address your phone call during sun salutations this morning." He shifted to another position. "It's essential to be mentally present during practice. Cell phones are a distraction and disruption. We don't allow students to bring them to class. The same rule should apply to instructors."

Sasha issued an indignant snort. "I'm not just an instructor, Glenn. I'm the *owner* of Third Eye. The studio would have closed if I hadn't come along. Have you forgotten that?"

"No," he said. "I remember." He came out of position to stand straight and address her directly. "But there are certain expectations and traditions—"

Before he could finish his thought, Sasha squeaked and

bolted to the trailhead beside the lodge. Through the window on the front of the lodge, I saw Kendall in the lobby. She looked around as if searching for someone. Sasha must have seen Kendall and run off to avoid her.

Kendall strode to the door and poked her head out. "Is Sasha out here?"

Glenn and I exchanged a knowing look. Though I didn't want to lie, nor did I want to upset Sasha by telling Kendall where she'd gone. I settled on glancing around and saying, "I don't see her."

Kendall's face fell. "She said she'd text me, but she didn't."

I felt sorry for her. She seemed to lack a sense of self, to be codependent on Sasha. But her obsession wasn't healthy. Maybe I could direct her to another activity as I'd done with my sons when they were bored. "There are books on the shelf in the lobby. Puzzles and games, too."

Glenn straightened and offered her a serene smile. "Monopoly is too pro-capitalism for a guy like me, but I'll challenge you to a round of Scrabble if Sanskrit words can count."

She brightened and Glenn walked past me, aiming for the door, a knight in batik armor.

That evening, Glenn wheeled his gong onto the deck. The students carried their mats outside and set up for their meditation practice. Two were notably absent—Sasha and Kendall. Was Sasha still avoiding her big blonde shadow? Was Kendall holed up in her room, refusing to attend without her bestie?

I decided to join in, and rounded up a cushion from a

deck chair to use as an improvised mat. Glenn gave me a welcoming smile. Just as Sasha had started her class with the lovely sound of the singing bowl, Glenn began his meditation by lightly applying the cloth-covered mallet to the gong. The sound was deep, low, and soothing, not a crash like a cymbal, but a pleasant reverberation sending good vibrations through the lodge and adjacent woods. He bowed his head to his students. "Tonight, it seems especially appropriate that here, in the midst of nature, we chant the Panchakshari mantra." He ran his gaze over the group, stopping on me and providing a quick lesson that seemed primarily for my elucidation. "The mantra is a tribute to Shiva, the Hindu god of transformation that represents one's highest self. The five syllables are understood to represent the five elements of nature—earth, sky, water, air, and fire." He closed his eyes and softly chanted. "Om Namah Shivaya. Om Namah Shivaya. Om Namah Shivaya."

I closed my eyes, too, and joined in with the group. Though it felt awkward at first, I soon lost myself in the soothing sounds and felt the tension seep from my body. I could see the attraction of mantra meditation. *Too bad Brynn didn't stick around. She'd enjoy this.*

When the session ended, Rocky and I set the furniture out again so the group could enjoy the beautiful evening on the deck. Rocky suggested we enjoy it, too. He retrieved two bottles of hard cider from his room and we claimed a table in the corner for ourselves. Voices filled the air as the students returned. A few minutes later, Cole came out onto the deck alone.

"Hey, there," Rocky said. "Where's your better half? She tired of you already?"

"Sammie's resting. Figured I'd give her some peace and quiet." Cole walked over to the railing to watch the sunset. His hand tightened on the rail and worry lines creased his forehead, quite a change from the carefree kid who'd traipsed through the doors of my lodge the evening before. I couldn't help wondering if he'd gotten bad news.

Shortly thereafter, Sasha and Kendall came outside. Once again, Kendall carried a bottle of expensive wine and the two glasses from her room. The women were in the middle of a conversation, but the context told me they were talking about the young mother with the sick kid.

Sasha huffed. "Can you believe she had the nerve to request a refund of her retreat fee? I would've brought someone else if I'd known she'd bail and run back home for nothing."

"Someone else?" Kendall set the bottle and glasses on a table. "Was there a waiting list?"

"Well, *no*!" Sasha snapped as she flopped into a chair. "But that's not the point."

Glenn returned from taking his gong back to his room, and held a steaming mug of tea in his hands. He stopped in the doorway and glanced over at Sasha and Kendall before turning around and taking a seat by the hearth inside the great room instead. Kendall had opened the bottle of wine. Like the night before, Sasha seemed intent on drinking more than her share. She held up her glass and ordered Kendall to "Fill it up!"

Kendall did as she'd been directed, though she seemed to have a harder time hiding her irritation tonight. "Maybe we should pace ourselves."

"Um, hello, Kendall?" Sasha waved a hand in her friend's

face as if to verify that she was conscious. "We came here to have fun, remember?" Even in the twilight, the pink stain that rushed to Kendall's cheeks was clear. What wasn't clear was whether it was an embarrassed blush or an angry one. Sasha glanced around. "Where's Madman?"

While many of the guests were enjoying the evening on the deck, the NASCAR star had opted not to make an appearance this evening. Was he avoiding Sasha, regretting their roll in the hay? She picked up her phone and tried calling him, frowning when she got no answer. She left the table and went inside. We heard her knock on Madman's door and call, "Hey! It's Sasha! You in there?" She returned alone, her face crestfallen. "He must've left the lodge."

Kendall's expression turned smug. She seemed to enjoy seeing her "bestie" being slighted, getting a taste of her own medicine.

Cole came over to our table. "Is there a computer I can use to check the weather?"

Though I'd seen him with a cell phone, the devices were not as user friendly as computers when it came to searching websites. "You can use the computer at the check-in desk." He followed me as I went inside and logged into the system. As Cole took a seat on the stool, I left him to his browsing and rejoined Rocky outside.

Evening turned into night and the students retired to their rooms. Eventually, Rocky and I were the only ones left. Rather than get up early tomorrow morning to clear the deck, Rocky and I moved the furniture aside that night. We parted ways in the now-empty great room.

His gaze caught mine and held for a moment. "Good night, Misty," he said softly.

His wistful tone wasn't lost on me. Dare I think he found my company as appealing as I found his? Or was he simply tired after a busy day? I feared it was the latter but hoped it was the former. Even so, his stay here would only be temporary, until the lodge was fully booked on a regular basis, something I was doing my best to make happen. *How's that for irony?* My voice came out soft, too. "Good night, Rocky."

CHAPTER 10

As if you could kill time without injuring eternity.
—Henry David Thoreau (1854: *Walden*)

Misty

BONGGGG! The note resonated through the darkness, waking me from my slumber and echoing in my foggy mind. *Weird.* The anniversary clock's chimes hadn't woken me since we'd first bought the thing years ago. My brain usually recognized the tones as nonthreatening and allowed me to sleep through them. *Why would the clock striking one have woken me tonight?*

Yeti must have heard it, too. She stood on the pillow beside me, her body rigid as she stared at the door. She rotated her ears like tiny, furry parabolic microphones, a feline spy. My gaze moved past her to the clock on the night table. The bright red LED readout told me the time was 2:37. *Why had the anniversary clock struck one, then?*

The fog cleared and I sat up, trying to make sense of things. That noise couldn't have been my anniversary clock. Besides the fact that it wasn't one o'clock, I'd removed the batteries so the chimes wouldn't bother Vera and Vivian next door. The noise that woke me had been something else and, judging from the way Yeti stared at the door, it had come from inside the lodge. Cold fingertips of fear crept up my spine much like Heike's warm fingers had worked my back earlier.

I climbed out of bed, bringing my phone with me in case an emergency call was necessary. The clock on the microwave blinked brightly in the dark room. 12:00 . . . 12:00 . . . 12:00. The oven didn't have a battery backup like the alarm clock did. The flashing readout told me the lodge had temporarily lost power while I'd been sleeping. Outages were not uncommon here, where electricity was delivered by aboveground poles and wires rather than an underground system. Winds, snow, and ice could wreak havoc, causing downed lines at worst, or mere temporary flickers. The winds were indeed gusty tonight. The trees rustled and the windows creaked, ratcheting up the eerie feeling in my bones. I grabbed a hiking pole from my closet. If someone had broken into my lodge, I might need to defend myself.

I turned the lock as quietly as I could, but the sliding deadbolt split the silence with a *CLICK*. Taking a deep breath, I peeked my head out into the dimly lit hallway. It was empty and quiet. Yeti pushed past my ankles and eased into the hall, as curious about the noise as I was. As she padded softly along the hall, I tiptoed behind her, hiking pole at the ready.

As we entered the great room, an elongated shadow in the east wing stopped me in my tracks. My heart leaped into my throat. It was a person, their silhouette cast by the dim light over the exit door at the end of the hall. *Is it an intruder, or merely a guest with insomnia stretching their legs?* Another shadow appeared below the first and answered the question for me. The second shadow had a square-shaped head, four legs, and plenty of fur. *Molasses.*

Exhaling in relief, I lowered the hiking pole and continued through the lobby. Yeti trotted along beside me. Rocky emerged from the hall, a claw hammer clutched in his fist. His hair was mussed, spikes sticking up, and his features were soft with sleep. Stubble extended from his beard along the usually clean-shaven part of his jawline. Though he was sexy from the neck up, the neck down was a different story. He wore a classic red union suit, complete with a button flap on the rear. He looked like Pa come to life from the pages of *Little House in the Big Woods.*

But I supposed I couldn't fault him for his choice in sleepwear. Mine wasn't exactly the type you'd find at Victoria's Secret. My roomy nightgown made sure all of Victoria's secrets were well kept. My sons had bought the garment as a gift. It was lightweight red and blue flannel, with a hemline that came clear down to my ankles and sleeves all the way to my wrists. The neckline was high, the lace edging stretching all the way up to my chin.

Rocky strode over to me in his bare feet, his gaze running up and down my nightgown. "Wow, you look . . ."

He seemed to be searching for a word, so I supplied one to my liking. "Amazing?"

"Amish."

I brandished my hiking pole. "Don't make me whack you. Besides, you've got some nerve making fun of me. You're not exactly *People* magazine's sexiest man alive in that oversized onesie." *Though the tousled hair and stubble are definitely working for me.*

He looked down at himself. "My girls gave me these pajamas for Father's Day."

"Really? My boys gave me this nightgown for Mother's Day." I supposed the coincidence shouldn't be a surprise. Sleepwear was a go-to gift idea.

A grin played about his lips as he fingered the satin bow at my throat. "Our kids want to cover us up." He raised his gaze to meet mine. "But it'll take more than the world's ugliest nightgown to hide your charms."

I broke out in a full-body blush as I brandished the hiking pole again. "I'm not going to fall for your flattery." *Not yet, anyway.*

"Can't blame a guy for tryin'." He scratched his head. "Why'd we come out here again?"

"The noise."

"Oh yeah. Sounded like something hitting metal." He glanced around, his gaze stopping on each of the doors and windows. "Nothing looks out of place."

I looked around, too, mentally reviewing the metal things in the lodge. The washing machines and dryers. The fireplace poker. The pole lamp in the back corner. None of those things would make the type of chime noise we'd heard. Well, the lamp might, but it was upright now, no sign of it having fallen over. After a short, whispered discussion, Rocky and I decided the noise had probably come from outside. With no guests seemingly disturbed by it, we returned to our respective rooms. I fell asleep with visions of Rocky in his union suit dancing in my head.

I was at the front door of the lodge at six thirty Tuesday morning, the late-night sound forgotten in my haste to help

Patty inside. Rather than bring a helper and carry the food in her arms, she'd loaded the trays onto a wheeled service cart today. I followed her as she rolled the food over to the buffet table, and helped arrange the trays in the electric warmers.

Once everything was in place, she turned to me. "What did your guests think of my breakfast yesterday? Other than the skinny, snooty one, I mean. She made her opinion clear."

I recalled Sasha recoiling in horror when she saw the heavy fare. She'd been the only one, though. Cole had stuffed himself silly and Sammie had eaten far more than I'd thought she could hold, too. "The other guests loved your food. I'm so glad we made this arrangement."

"Me too," Patty said. "It gave us some breathing room in the diner."

We proceeded to set up the coffee urns, juice dispensers, dishes, and silverware, the arrangement going much faster today now that I was getting the hang of things. As Patty left to return to the diner, Rocky's truck rolled into the parking lot. *Where in the world had he gone this early?* I quickly poured him a cup of coffee, added sugar, and met him at the door with it.

As he took the steaming mug, he gave me a just-as-warm smile in return. "I could get used to this."

"Don't. I took care of a man for twenty years. I have no intention of taking care of another."

"Understood. You're playing hard to get." He slugged back a gulp of the brew.

I lifted my chin to indicate his truck, cooling off in the lot outside the window. "Where have you been at this ungodly hour?"

He responded in kind to my earlier jest. "I answered to a woman for three years. I have no intention of answering to another."

"Understood. But you better answer to *your boss*."

He angled his head. "You're sexy when you're assertive."

I crossed my arms over my chest and skewered him with my gaze, waiting for an answer I wasn't sure I was entitled to. After all, he wasn't on the clock yet. Or was he? We'd only agreed that he'd provide maintenance services on an as-needed basis.

He relented. "You win, boss. I was taking the lovebirds back to the trail."

"Sammie and Cole?"

"Yep. I was outside letting Mo do his business about an hour ago and they came out of their room with their packs on. When they saw me, they asked if I could give them a lift."

"That's strange. When they checked in Sunday evening, they told me they'd be staying three nights. They only stayed two." What's more, they hadn't informed me or said goodbye.

Rocky studied my face and must have sensed I felt hurt. "Don't take it personal. Sammie asked me to express their apologies for cutting out without notice. My guess is they would've stayed another night if Cole hadn't gotten antsy. Seems it was his idea to hit the trail again."

While I would have liked to see the two off, they still had a long way to go before they'd finish the trail. I couldn't blame them for feeling anxious and changing their minds.

Rocky rubbed his tummy. "Can I take you to breakfast? I know a good place. It's not far." He held out his hand to indicate the buffet.

We filled our plates and took seats at a table in the great room. The enticing smells of food and coffee lured many of the guests from their rooms, too. Kendall selected both a banana and an apple from the fruit bowl today, though her eyes again cut longingly to the pancakes, potatoes, and biscuits.

Glenn emerged from his room carrying his rolled-up mat tucked under his arm. After preparing a mug of herbal tea, he jerked on the string of the tea bag as if playing with a yo-yo, dunking it in the hot water to steep it. He was still dunking the bag when he stopped at our table. "My apologies if you've had any noise complaints. I got up in the middle of the night to use the bathroom and bumped my knee on my gong in the dark." He cringed in contrition.

Looked like the mystery of things that go *bonggg* in the night was solved. "No worries," I told Glenn. "No one's said a word." No point telling him the noise had woken me and Rocky. I didn't want him to feel bad. It would be easy to become disoriented in a dark, unfamiliar room.

"Glad to hear it." With that, he carried his tea out to the deck.

There were fewer students today, some opting to sleep in rather than greet the sun, but most of them were in place on the deck by seven o'clock for the scheduled sun salutations. Their instructor, however, was nowhere to be seen. She didn't call the desk for help today, either.

The students stretched on their mats. Glenn glanced inside several times with increasing levels of concern. Kendall did the same, though her looks were perturbed. She seemed to be tiring of Sasha's inconsiderate behavior.

Maybe that was a good thing. Maybe Kendall would move on and find a true friend.

I walked to the French doors and quietly addressed Glenn. "Want me to call Sasha's room and let her know the class is ready for her?"

"I'd appreciate it."

I strode back to the registration desk, picked up the phone, and dialed Sasha's room. *Rrring! Rrring! Rrring!* I held for ten rings before hanging up. Glenn was watching me. I shook my head, pointed down the hall, and cocked my head in question. He nodded. I scurried down the hall to Room 19 and knocked on the door. *Rap-rap.* No response came from within. I knocked again, harder. *RAP-RAP-RAP.* Still nothing. I put my ear to the door to listen. No television noise. No sound of the shower running. *Hmm.* Even if Sasha were hungover, it seemed she'd hear her phone ringing and me knocking at her door. A nervous wriggle tickled my gut.

I walked back down the hall and across the great room. Both Glenn and Kendall waited at the French doors, expectant looks on their faces. I raised my palms. "She's not responding."

Kendall's lips pursed. Though she said nothing, I guessed what she might be thinking. *Sasha's sleeping off my pricey bottle of wine.*

I looked to Glenn. "Should I use my master key to check on her?"

"No need," Glenn said. "Sasha sometimes . . ." His eyes cut to Kendall, and he seemed to censor himself. "Sometimes she can't make her classes. I'd be happy to lead the sun salutations." He dismissed me with a nod, moved his mat to the front of the group, and began the practice.

Brynn came in the door a half hour later, calling out "good morning!" as she headed for the housekeeping closet to round up her cart. I returned the greeting. She pushed her cart past me into the east wing, the wheel blissfully quiet today thanks to Rocky fixing the loose fitting.

Ten minutes later, a high-pitched shriek came from outside. I turned to see Norma Jean pointing down at the deck, her curls bobbing as she shook her head in disbelief. The others gathered around her. Joaquín dropped to his knees, put his palms to the deck, and bent his head down. *What the heck is going on?*

As I rushed outside, Joaquín lifted his head from the deck, revealing the knothole he'd been peering through. "It's Sasha! She's in corpse pose!"

That nervous wriggle in my gut now felt like a snake in a pillowcase. "What?!"

He simply pointed down at the hole. I lowered myself down and took a look. At first, all I saw was the pipe Rocky had installed to divert the water. But then my gaze was drawn by something pink. My mind screamed *Don't look!* But I knew I had to. It was a white toe with a pink-painted nail. My gut clenched. *That toe must be connected to a body.* My gaze shifted to take in the rest of the person to whom the toe belonged. There, under the deck, lay Sasha Ducharme-Carlisle. She was on her back, dressed in her pink satin pajamas. Her pose was unnatural, her shoulders up and arms crooked at the elbow, as if she were performing a hoedown on her back. The odd positioning implied that someone had put their arms under hers and dragged her there. Her face was shiny, evidencing a generous dollop of moisturizer that must have been applied at bedtime. A wispy white goose feather was stuck to the goop on her cheek, having escaped her down pillow. Her sleep mask lay askew across her face, one bloodshot, lifeless green eye looking up at me, as if seeing me from the great beyond. I yanked my head back and gulped.

The class burst into chatter.

"How'd she get down there?"

"Is she drunk?"

"Is she dead?"

I rose, ran to the doors, and hollered into the lodge. "Rocky! Come quick!" I wasn't sure what I expected of him. He was a handyman. Though he could fix a lot of things, this situation wasn't one of them. Still, my head was spinning and I couldn't think straight. He was a level-headed guy. He'd know what to do.

Rocky came running. "What's wrong?"

"It's Ms. Du—" I stopped myself. No need for niceties now, and her formal name was too long to get out quickly. "It's Sasha! She's under the deck. I think she's hurt! Or . . ." *Worse*.

"What?" His eyes flashed in alarm and confusion. I pointed and he moved to the railing, bending over to try to look under it. To discourage guests from walking along the dangerous precipice, he'd installed no steps from the deck down to the cliffside, so there was no easy way down. Next thing I knew, he'd flung a leg over the railing and dropped to the rocky ledge. He got down on all fours and scrambled under the deck. His movements were visible through the narrow spaces between the boards. He stopped under the knothole. Though I could only get thin slices of an image, my guess was he was checking the woman's vitals. I was just about to ask if she was okay when he hollered, "Call nine-one-one! Get the police out here, now!"

CHAPTER 11

It is the peculiar nature of the forest, that life and death may ever be found within its bounds.
—Susan Fenimore Cooper (1850: *Rural Hours*)

Misty

Rocky emerged from under the deck. The group went quiet, waiting to hear what he'd discovered. His face was tight as his gaze met mine. "I don't feel a pulse. Her skin is cold, too, and hard."

In other words, rigor mortis had begun to set in. The once-flexible yoga instructor had gone stiff.

I turned to Glenn. "Does she have a medical condition?"

His head shook slowly, as if on its own accord. "She never mentioned one to me."

My eyes sought out Kendall in the crowd. "What about you?" I asked. "Did Sasha tell you about any health issues she was having?"

"No!" Kendall shook her head frantically. She clutched her fists to her chest as if to cover the eye on her tank-top logo so it couldn't see the horrible truth. "Sasha seemed fine when she went to her room last night. Totally fine! I can't imagine what happened!"

Kendall unclutched her fists and moved her hands to her own eyes now, as if to shut out the scene. She burst into sobs and began to sway on her feet. I rushed over to steady her while Glenn retrieved a rocking chair from the back of the deck. Together, we managed to lower the sobbing woman into the seat.

The group was still gathered on the deck when a police car arrived a few minutes later. A thirtyish male officer emerged from the driver's seat. I rushed to the front door and directed the officer to the back of the lodge.

"Be careful!" I cried as I skittered along after him. "There's not much space between the lodge and the drop-off." He was obviously familiar with the mountain and didn't need cautionary warnings from me, but he wasn't much older than my sons and my protective motherly instincts were impossible to turn off.

Rocky stood on the cliffside, one hand on a support post to stabilize himself. The yogis were gathered at the rail on the deck above, looking down. Below them, under the deck, Sasha lay with her head downhill.

The cop bent down to assess Sasha, stretching out an arm to feel for a pulse. A moment later, he turned his head to look up at Rocky and me. "You folks work here, I take it?"

"I'm the owner of the lodge," I said. "Misty Murphy." I gestured to Rocky. "Mr. Crowder handles maintenance."

The officer cut his eyes to the group above, who were all staring down at us. "What about them?"

"Yoga students," I said. "On a retreat."

He angled his head to indicate the body. "Any idea what happened to her?"

"None," I said. The only clue was the goose feather, and all that told us was that whatever happened to her took place after she'd applied her face cream and gone to bed.

He pulled a radio from his belt and pressed the button to contact dispatch. "This is Officer Hardy. I've got a body here. Can you get me some help from the sheriff's office?"

While the local police were fully capable of handling most serious matters, it wasn't often a person was found dead of unknown causes in this small town. The Watauga County Sheriff's Department would have people specially trained to handle this kind of situation.

Officer Hardy looked up at the crowd and motioned toward the lodge. "You folks go inside. Stay in the lobby until we figure out what's happened here. Nobody goes back to their rooms. You hear me?"

The group murmured in assent.

The officer, Rocky, and I circled back around to the front of the lodge. While the cop went to retrieve cordon tape from his cruiser, Rocky and I went back inside, stopping at the registration desk, away from the students.

Fortunately, Glenn had taken control of the situation, insofar as the yoga class was concerned. He raised his palms. "We've just had an emotionally challenging experience. Why don't we all take a seat and I'll lead some breathing exercises to calm our nerves."

While Glenn dealt with the class, I looked up into Rocky's face and whispered, "What do you think happened to her? Could someone have hurt her intentionally?"

He raised his shoulders, uncertain. "Wish I could tell you. I didn't see any signs of injury, but it seems strange that she'd go under the deck on her own."

Even though her position told me such a scenario was highly improbable, I asked, "Could she have tripped and rolled under the deck?"

"I suppose it's possible," he said. "But why would she be wandering around outside in her pajamas with her sleep mask still on?"

I hoped that, whatever had happened to her, it had been either natural causes or an unfortunate accident. I didn't have a stomach for violence, and a homicide wouldn't exactly be good publicity for my lodge. I felt a twinge of guilt at the thought. It was selfish to be thinking of the effect of Sasha's death on me. I speculated aloud. "Maybe she took one of those sleeping pills that make people do kooky things. She could've wandered outside with her sleep mask on and hit her head." A sleeping pill mixed with all the wine she'd drunk would have been a very dangerous combination.

"Could be," Rocky said. "Maybe there's something in her room that'll help the sheriff's department figure things out."

My heart performed a fresh flip-flop. *Sasha's room could be a crime scene!* Brynn had gone down the east wing to clean. Had she started with the rooms closest to the lobby, or the ones at the far end? "I'll be right back." I hurried around the corner and into the hall.

Vroooooom. The vacuum roaring, Brynn backed out of Sasha's room at the end of the corridor, pulling the appliance with her. When she spotted me rushing at her, she used her foot to depress the pedal and turn the device off. Her brows formed a deep V. "Everything okay?"

Things couldn't be further from okay! "Sasha was just found outside!"

The V grew even deeper. "How is that a problem? Isn't

she supposed to be outside, teaching her class? The schedule said she was leading sun salutations this morning."

I hadn't been clear enough. "Sasha was found . . . *deceased*."

Brynn simply stared at me for a long moment before giving her head a hard shake. "Are you saying Sasha Ducharme-Carlisle is dead?"

"I am," I said. "She is." *She got the woman's name right this time.*

Her eyes widened. "What happened? Did she have an accident?"

"We have no idea. All we know is that she ended up under the deck in her pajamas."

"Pajamas? So, something happened to her during the night?"

"It looks that way."

Brynn glanced back into Sasha's room. "I thought it was odd that her yoga bag was still sitting on the sofa, but her singing bowl is gone."

"It is?"

"Yeah. I figured she'd taken it with her to the class. I thought maybe she didn't need a mat for whatever she had planned this morning."

How does Brynn know about singing bowls? No better way to find out than to ask. "You're familiar with singing bowls?"

"Sure," she said. "They sell them at the metaphysical supply store where I shop." Her tone was matter of fact, as if everyone shopped at a metaphysical store for their everyday tarot card and magic crystal needs. She went on. "Yesterday,

Sasha left a small jewelry case on her dresser, too, right next to the bowl. I didn't see the jewelry today, either. I assume she locked it in the safe."

"She might have done the same with the bowl. Apparently, it was quite valuable. I'm sure the sheriff's department will sort all of that out. They're on their way."

Brynn glanced through the open door and grimaced. "I just finished cleaning her room. They won't be happy about that."

I bit my lip. I hoped she hadn't inadvertently disturbed anything that might have been helpful to the investigation. But that was water under the bridge now. I told her my theory, that Sasha might have taken a sleep medication, that it could have reacted badly with the wine. "Did you happen to notice if she had any sleeping pills?"

"I found a pill on her floor when I was vacuuming. The machine made a rattling noise, so I turned it off right quick to see what it had sucked up. I was afraid it might be an earring, or maybe even that little nose ring Sasha wears. Turned out to be a round blue tablet. I figured she might need it, dirty or not, so I put it in the empty water glass on her night table. I didn't see any pill bottles or boxes of medication or blister packs, though, if that's what you're asking. She's got a zipper bag for toiletries on the bathroom counter. There could be pills in there, I guess. I saw some pills in Kendall's room yesterday, though. I didn't check the label on the bottle to see what they were, but I noticed they were blue, too. They were on her coffee bar."

I supposed law enforcement would take a look at Sasha's things, including the blue pill, and figure out if sleeping medication had been to blame. They might even run a blood test on her. Seemed like that would be standard pro-cedure in a suspicious death with no obvious cause. "The police officer wants everyone to wait in the great room for the time being. It's best if we leave everything as is for now."

Brynn left the vacuum and her housekeeping cart in the hallway, and followed me back to the lobby. The retreat par-ticipants had spread out around the space, filling the sofas, chairs, and tables. Several eyed the breakfast buffet, and at least one stomach rumbled. But they held back, seeming to fear it would appear insensitive to indulge in a hearty breakfast so soon after their yoga instructor was found dead underneath them.

The phone buzzed on the registration desk. I picked up the receiver and recited the practiced greeting that had now become automatic. "It's a beautiful Blue Ridge day at the Mountaintop Lodge." I put a palm to my forehead. *Sheesh.* How tactless of me. At least the person on the other end of the line wouldn't be aware of my blunder. Or so I'd thought. "How may I help you?"

Patty's voice came over the line. "What's going on over there? I see a police car in front of your place."

I glanced out the front window of the lodge and across the parking lot. I could see Patty standing inside the door to her diner, looking my way. I raised a hand in recognition and whispered, "The yoga instructor was just found dead under the deck out back."

She responded exactly how I had. "What?!"

"I couldn't believe it, either."

"Which instructor was it? The bald hippie or the skinny, snooty one who turned up her nose at my food?"

I covered the mouthpiece with my hand and lowered my voice even more. "It was her. The skinny, snooty one."

"What happened? Did she starve to death?"

"We don't know yet. The sheriff's department is on its way to figure things out."

"I hope they get to the bottom of things quick. My customers are curious. They keep asking if I know anything. Everyone's speculating. Won't be long until the rumors start to fly."

My eyes shifted from Patty to the other windows of the diner. Sure enough, the glass was filled with the faces of diners looking at the lodge.

She lowered her voice. "This must have thrown you for a loop, Misty. How are you holding up?"

It was sweet and thoughtful of her to be concerned with my feelings. Her empathy brought tears to my eyes. "Honestly?" I said. "I'm trying to hold it together, but I'm a mess on the inside. I feel responsible for my guests. The fact that one of them ended up like this . . ." Strangled with fresh emotion, I couldn't even finish my thought.

"I'm on my way." *Click.*

In the few seconds it took me to return my phone to the cradle, Patty was already marching across the parking lot with a mug in her hands. She came inside, walked over to the desk, and set the mug in front of me. "Chamomile tea," she said. "It'll settle your nerves."

"Thanks, Patty," I said, though I feared it would take gallons of it to calm me down completely.

She turned to Brynn, who'd settled on the other stool. "How about you? Need a cup?"

"Thanks, but I'm good." Brynn reached into the pocket

of her gauzy dress and pulled out a small glass vial. "I've got my calming oil." She pulled out the stopper, waved the vial back and forth under her nose as she inhaled deeply, then turned and held the vial out to me. "This stuff works wonders. Dab some on your pulse points. It's got ylang-ylang, patchouli, citrus, and blue tansy oils."

I had no idea whether the oil would work, but it couldn't hurt. Besides, the concoction smelled divine. I dabbed a few drops on each wrist and the sides of my neck before handing it back to Brynn. I closed my eyes and inhaled deeply. Sure enough, it felt as though my racing heart was starting to slow. Of course, it could merely be a placebo effect.

Patty glanced out the window. "I'd better get back to the diner." She reached out to give my hand a sympathetic pat. "If there's anything I can do, don't hesitate to call, okay?"

"Thanks, Patty," I said.

As Patty returned to her restaurant, a large SUV from the Watauga County Sheriff's Department pulled up under the overhang. The door opened and a wisp of a woman in uniform slid down from the driver's seat. The petite officer made Sasha look like an Amazon. Her hair hung down her back in a long salt-and-pepper ponytail gathered in an elastic every four inches or so. She plunked a standard sheriff's campaign hat atop her head and glanced around, surveying the area, her head moving in ticks as she seemed to be making mental notes. Though her small size made her look young, her purposeful movements and her salt-and-pepper hair showed she was seasoned and self-confident. Having assessed the outside of the lodge, she strode to the entrance.

Rocky and I met her there, opening the door for her. The

name badge on her chest read Deputy Sheriff Highcloud. Her name and features indicated she was of Native American descent, possibly Cherokee. What remained of the area's tribe was now centered on a reservation in the southwestern part of the state but, before most of the people had been forcefully relocated via the Trail of Tears, they'd once spread across the region. The shallow crow's feet etched around the deputy's dark, hawklike eyes said she'd been on the earth a little longer than I had, and the piercing look in them told me she was perceptive. Her rigid posture, one hand resting on her tool belt, was guarded. Dealing with criminals must make one constantly wary.

She looked from Rocky to me. "Who's in charge here?"

"I am," I said. "I own the lodge. I'm Misty Murphy."

She offered her hand for a shake. "Deputy Yona Highcloud."

Rocky introduced himself, too. "I'm in charge of maintenance."

Now that Rocky and I had exchanged introductions with the deputy, her focus shifted to Brynn. My assistant sat quietly behind the counter, waving her vial of oil under her nose as if administering an additional emergency dose of tranquility. *Did the deputy's arrival cause her additional stress?*

"Ms. O'Reilly," the deputy said, her voice emotionless as she gave the housekeeper a nod of acknowledgment.

Brynn's voice was equally cool when she responded with a nod of her own. "Deputy Highcloud."

Clearly, these two would not be discussing boys over a bottle of prosecco while painting each other's toenails any time soon.

The deputy's gaze moved upward and roamed about as she seemed to be searching for something. When her eyes stopped, I followed her line of sight to the wood support beam at the bottom of the truss that spanned the lobby's ceiling. Mounted on the bottom of the horizontal beam were two black dome-shaped security cameras, one aimed down the east wing, the other aimed down the west wing. Their fish-eye lenses provided a 180-degree range. Placed back-to-back, together they provided a full, 360-degree view of the interior of the lodge.

That said, the clarity of the images varied greatly depending on the distance from the lens. I'd pulled out the manual a few days ago to familiarize myself with the system. While Yeti had been clearly identifiable when she'd strutted through the lobby, she'd dissolved into a grainy mass of grayish pixels as she'd reached the end of the hall and turned into the open door of our room. Still, the video footage could tell us what happened to Sasha.

The deputy waved for me to follow her outside, where we could talk in private. When Rocky started to come along with us, she put up a palm to stop him. "Just Ms. Murphy for now."

Rocky stepped back, but a frown flitted across his face. He looked to me, as if seeking reassurance that I could face an interrogation alone. I bit my lip. *What choice did I have?* The deputy had already told him he wasn't welcome to join in our discussion.

Once the deputy and I were outside and out of earshot of anyone else, she said, "Give me the rundown."

"Okay." I wasn't sure how far back to start, but I figured it couldn't hurt to begin with the group's arrival. I told her

about Sasha bringing students up from her studio in Charlotte for a retreat, how the young woman had led the students in sun salutations yesterday, and how she'd failed to
show up to lead the ritual this morning as scheduled. "I
tried calling her room, but she didn't respond. She didn't respond when I knocked, either."

"Did you try unlocking the door?"

"No. I didn't want to invade her privacy and risk upsetting her. She was rather . . ." *Quick, Misty. What's a nicer
way to say* 'demanding'*? Does anyone use the word* per-
snickety *anymore? Fussy, maybe?* I finally found the right
word. "Particular. Ms. Ducharme-Carlisle was a particular
guest."

"Mm-hmm." The deputy's head tilted slightly. "What did
you do when you didn't get a response at her door? Did you
check to see if her car was in the parking lot?"

"No. She doesn't have a car here. None of them do. The
group rode up together on a charter bus. It's coming back
to pick them up on Sunday."

She mused aloud. "That explains why your parking lot
is relatively empty, despite all the guests at your lodge." She
cast a glance through the window at those guests before returning her attention to me. "How did her students react
when she didn't show up for her class?"

I thought back. "No one seemed especially surprised
or upset. The other instructor took over for her. I got the
impression Sasha hasn't been the most reliable teacher." I
cringed, feeling guilty speaking ill of the dead, but also
wanting to tell the deputy anything that might be helpful. I
told her the group was in the middle of their sun salutations
when one of the students spotted Sasha through a knothole

in the deck. "She's lying under it. Rocky crawled under the deck to check her vital signs, but she was already gone."

Though the deputy's head didn't move, her eyes shifted again to look through the window at the crowd gathered in the great room. "Anyone else touch the body?"

"Just the police officer."

"How'd the class react when she was found?"

I kept my voice low when I told her they'd speculated Sasha might have been under the influence of alcohol. "Sasha drank quite a bit of wine on the deck last night. She was weaving when she headed back to her room. Some of the others must have noticed it. Kendall McFadden was the most upset when Sasha was found. She's a student, but she and Sasha were also friends of sorts."

"Of sorts?" Her eyes narrowed. "What do you mean by that?"

I told her about Sasha's surreptitious escape from the lodge the day before, how she'd been desperately trying to ditch her clingy companion so she could have some alone time. "Their friendship seemed to be somewhat one-sided."

"I see." She mused aloud again. "Kendall might have a problem with respecting boundaries. Of course, she's not the only one."

"What do you mean by that?"

"Ms. O'Reilly," she said, cutting her gaze to my assistant inside. "She's got a problem respecting boundaries, too. I arrested her for trespassing not long ago. She and her co-ven were performing a ritual for the summer solstice out by Grassy Gap Creek. Problem was, they were on private property. The owner didn't realize they were there until they lit a fire. He called in a report when he saw the flames through the trees."

While I was relieved to know that Brynn's transgression wasn't serious—after all, trespassing was a relatively minor crime—I wasn't sure what to make of her Wiccan ways. I knew little about the pagan practice. Before I made a judgment, I'd educate myself on the subject. At least now I understood why she'd asked to take the autumn equinox off from work. Apparently, the seasonal changes were Wiccan holidays, just as they were in many other spiritual or cultural practices.

The subject of trespassing and boundaries had me thinking of another situation involving a person encroaching on another's space. "When I was cleaning Madman's room yesterday, I found a long, dark hair on his pillow."

"Madman?" she repeated. "Are you talking about Dax 'Madman' Maddox? The NASCAR driver?"

I nodded. "He came with the group for the retreat."

"Huh," she said. "I thought he was dating what's-her-name. The Honey Bee."

"As far as I know," I said, "he still is." A breakup between the two would have been big news, but I'd seen nothing about a split pop up online.

"Do you have reason to believe the hair belonged to Sasha?"

"She's the only guest with dark hair that long." Lest I bear false witness, I added, "She made it clear she was interested in Madman Sunday evening. She invited him to sit at her table on the deck and made some obvious advances." I remembered her laying her head on his shoulder and batting her eyes shamelessly. "I got the impression that her attention made him uncomfortable." I told her how he'd shrugged Sasha off and looked around to make sure nobody had been recording video of the incident. "When he left, she winked at him and said, 'See you later.'"

"Do you know what she meant by that, exactly?"

"No." Given the wink, I'd assumed she might have been referring to a private rendezvous planned for later. But maybe all she'd been referring to was the fact that she'd see him at the yoga and meditation classes, or around the lodge.

The deputy continued to grill me. "So, all you saw was the hair on the pillow? You didn't see an article of Sasha's clothing or anything else of hers in Madman's room, or see her actually enter or leave his room?"

"No, I didn't."

"Have you seen the two of them together since?"

"Only during the scheduled classes, but the other students were present then, too. He didn't come out to the deck last night like he did on Sunday. She tried calling him and went down to his room, but he didn't answer his phone or the door. I figured he might have been avoiding her."

"Was he in his room when she knocked?"

"I can't be certain," I said, "but I believe he was. I didn't see him leave the lodge after their last class, and I didn't see him return before everyone went back to their rooms for the night. Of course, he could have gone in and out the side exit without me seeing."

The deputy pulled a notepad and pen from a zippered pouch on her tool belt and jotted some notes. When she finished, she said, "I'll want to take a look at your security footage. I saw your two cameras in the lobby. How many others have you got?"

"That's it."

"No exterior cameras?"

"No."

She frowned, making me feel inept. My failure to install exterior security cameras could make Sasha's murder more difficult to solve. Did it also mean I'd failed to deter a killer? My gut shrank into a hard ball of guilt and nerves. I'd wanted to provide my guests with an enjoyable, memorable experience. I might have not succeeded in the former, but I'd certainly accomplished the latter. They'd probably never forget their visit here. Neither would I. *Could I be partly to blame for Sasha's death?* Maybe. Maybe not. But on the remote chance my actions had any effect on the outcome, I vowed to myself to do whatever I could to help law enforcement solve the case.

The deputy glanced over at the Greasy Griddle. "Looks like the diner's got exterior cameras. I'll take a look, see what they picked up. Of course, they'll only show the front of the lodge."

With Sasha's room being on the back side of the lodge, the diner's cameras wouldn't have picked up any activity at her back window, or her killer dragging her body and leaving it under the deck. But it could show whether someone had approached the lodge from the front, or accessed her room through the side window. The video camera footage might help determine whether Sasha had been killed by a fellow guest, or someone from outside the lodge. I wasn't sure which possibility scared me the most, the idea that a stranger could access my lodge and attack a guest while she slept, or the idea that a killer might be staying under my roof, that I might be changing sheets and crafting towel bears for a murderer.

The deputy rocked back on her feet and raised her brows. "Anything else you know?"

"Brynn already cleaned Sasha's room this morning. The schedule for the retreat shows that Sasha was supposed to lead the sun salutations this morning, so Brynn assumed the guest room would be vacant for a while and that it would be a good time to clean it. Brynn said that a small jewelry box she'd seen on the dresser yesterday wasn't there today. Sasha's singing bowl wasn't on the dresser, either. Apparently, it was a valuable one, some kind of antique. Brynn said she thought Sasha had taken the bowl with her to the sun salutations, but now we're wondering if maybe she'd put the bowl and her jewelry in the room safe."

"You haven't checked the safe, then?"

"No," I said. "We figured it was best to leave things as untouched as possible." It had probably been a moot point in light of the fact that Brynn had already touched nearly everything in the room as she cleaned it, but at least it showed we'd tried to preserve the evidence, right? "Brynn also told me she sucked up something in the vacuum. She heard it rattling around, so she checked the filter. She thought it might be something valuable, like a small piece of jewelry, but it turned out to be a round blue pill. She wasn't sure whether it was a critical medication, so she put it in the empty water glass on the table next to Sasha's bed."

"Is the pill still there?" the deputy asked.

"It should be. Everything else should be back in place, too. Brynn is an experienced housekeeper. She'd know not to disturb a guest's belongings any more than necessary. Besides, Sasha specifically told Brynn yesterday to put everything back where she found it. Brynn knew Sasha didn't want her things moved."

The deputy gave me strict orders not to access the security camera footage yet, and instructed me to go back inside and keep everyone corralled in the great room. While the deputy went out back to talk to Officer Hardy and take a look at the body and crime scene, I returned to my roost at the desk next to Brynn. Rocky had taken a seat across from us, on the bench next to the rack of brochures for local attractions. He stood and his eyes sought mine, as if to make sure I was all right. I wasn't, of course, but I had to hold it together for now for the sake of my guests.

Glenn had taken a seat on the stone hearth and continued to lead the group through a calming meditation. "Inhale for eight counts," he said. "One, two, three . . ."

Sitting on my stool, I performed the breathing exercise along with the others. Every nerve in my body was on edge. I wasn't sure if deep breathing would help, but it couldn't hurt. Unlike the others, though, I kept my eyes open. As I inhaled, I saw the deputy outside the back window. She walked up to chat with the police officer for a moment or two before she disappeared from sight.

Glenn spoke in that practiced slow and soothing voice of his. "Now, raise your arms slowly . . . palms up to the sky . . . elbows straight and away from your ears. Take another deep breath. One . . . Two . . . Three . . . Four."

As Glenn switched to another exercise, Rocky stepped over to the desk and whispered, "How'd it go with the deputy?"

I raised my shoulders. "I told her what I know, which isn't much."

Brynn leaned in toward us and discreetly gestured to Glenn. "You think Zen Glenn, you know?" She went into mime mode, looking down while forming a circle with the fingers of one hand near her mouth and angling the other in front of her chest.

I ventured a guess based on the position of her hands. "Are you asking if I think Glenn plays the saxophone?"

Rocky interpreted Brynn's mimicry in a totally different way. "Or if he uses a sight to survey properties?"

Brynn gave us a sour look, annoyed that we'd misinterpreted her Oscar-worthy dramatic performance. "I was miming smoking a bong."

"A bong?" I raised my palms. "How was I supposed to know that?"

Brynn said, "Didn't you see those old Cheech and Chong movies?"

"I was too young when they were released." I gave her a sour look of my own. I didn't admit that I'd rented the movies on VHS from Blockbuster and watched them with friends a few years after their initial run in the theaters. Those days were so long ago I'd forgotten much about the movies other than that the actors spoke with accents and expelled a lot of smoke and laughter.

I rejoined Glenn's exercise, inhaling once more. *Five . . . Six . . . Seven . . . Eight.*

We were all holding our breath and counting silently to ourselves when the deputy entered the lodge again and came up to the desk. "The medical examiner is on the way. In the meantime, I'd like to see what I can gather from the group. Who's that other instructor you mentioned? Glenn?"

With all of the students seated and silent, holding their breath, it was no longer obvious who was leading their exercise.

I expelled my breath. "Glenn is the guy in the T-shirt and striped pants sitting on the hearth."

As she looked his way, he said, "Exhale," and released a loud, long breath. *Hoooooooo.*

She walked over to the edge of the rug and addressed the class. "I'd like to talk to each of you, one at a time, starting with Glenn. If you could come outside with me, sir." She angled her head in invitation.

As he stood up from the hearth, Heike came down the hall. In all of the craziness, I'd forgotten about the woman. Knowing he was in for a nice scratch, Molasses stood and walked toward her. She stopped and bent over to put a hand on either side of his head, ruffling his ears. Though I didn't speak German and had no idea precisely what her words meant, it was clear from the universal high-pitched doggie voice that she was singing Mo's praises. After greeting the dog, she stepped up to the breakfast buffet and picked up a plate before seeming to realize the room was abnormally still and quiet. She looked up to see all eyes on her, including Deputy Highcloud's.

"Who are you?" the deputy asked.

"I'm Heike Richter." Heike glanced around, her forehead creasing in confusion. "There is some problem, *ja*?"

Glenn stepped over, took her gently by the shoulders, and bent over to look her in the eyes. "Sasha is gone, Heike."

"Gone?" Heike looked from Glenn, to the students, to the deputy, and back again. "She left the lodge?"

"No," Glenn said. "I mean she's passed away. She was just found under the deck. Dead."

"Dead?!" Heike's mouth fell open and her plate slipped from her hand, hitting the floor and exploding into shards. *Crash!* She blinked her wide eyes as they filled with emotion. "But she is young and healthy! How can she be dead?"

"We don't know yet." Glenn gave her shoulders a comforting squeeze before lowering his arms. "That's what the deputy is here to find out."

A wail burst from Heike, coming from someplace deep and primal. I could understand her being upset by her boss's death, but this level of grief surprised me. Glenn put a hand on her lower back and guided her over to one of the chairs, where she flopped down and buried her face in her hands, her shoulders shaking as she sobbed. It was a toss-up whether she or Kendall was more expressive in their grief.

Deputy Highcloud turned to me. "Are there any more guests who aren't gathered here?"

"A few." I scanned the faces and racked my brain to identify the missing students. Luckily, Glenn helped me out. "Vera and her daughter aren't here. Neither is Madman Maddox."

While Vera and her daughter were likely sleeping in, the absence of Madman could be more intentional. *Is he purposely avoiding the group? Does he have something to hide?*

Rocky's eyes darkened and his forehead crinkled like corrugated metal. "Don't forget Sammie and Cole."

"That's right!" I turned back to the deputy. "Two guests departed first thing this morning. A newlywed couple who are hiking the Appalachian Trail. Rocky drove them back to an access point so they could continue their hike."

"Oh yeah?" The deputy turned to him. "What time did you drop them off and where?"

Rocky said, "Around six, near the Mountaineer Falls Shelter."

"*Six?*" The deputy's eyes narrowed slightly. "That's awfully early. That means they got up well before dawn." Her eyes narrowed a bit more as she jutted her chin to indicate my handyman. "You did, too."

"Didn't have a choice," Rocky said. "Molasses woke me up for a potty break."

The deputy pointed to the dog. "I take it the furry fellow is Molasses?"

"Yes, ma'am," Rocky said, though there was no real need for him to respond. The dog had already answered the question himself by wagging his tail when he heard the officer say his name.

I filled in the information gaps. "Sammie and Cole left earlier than they'd originally planned. When they checked in Sunday night, they told me they planned to stay three nights and leave tomorrow to continue on to Georgia." But they couldn't have anything to do with Sasha's death, could they? The very idea that the young lovebirds could have done something sinister seemed ridiculous. Then again, maybe only one of them was involved. *The one who'd looked anx-*

ious yesterday evening. But what reason would Cole have had to hurt Sasha? Had the two even interacted?

The deputy looked from me to Rocky. "Did they tell either of you why they cut their stay short?"

I shook my head.

Rocky said, "Cole made some noise about the stop here putting them behind schedule, and wanting to finish up as soon as possible so they could get settled in Boston. They've got jobs there starting at the beginning of next year."

The deputy counted the months off on her fingers. "September, October, November, December. Next year is nearly four months off. If they're heading south, they've already completed most of the trail. They'd have four or five weeks left, at most." In other words, their impatience to get back on the trail seemed unnecessary.

Though I was inclined to agree, maybe they had simply missed the romance and adventure of the trail and wanted to get back to it. *But if that is the case, why not just say so?*

Officer Hardy had finished cordoning off the exterior of the lodge and came inside. Deputy Highcloud instructed Heike to wait in the great room with the rest of the group and asked the officer to round up the remaining guests. After the deputy and Glenn went out the door to talk, Brynn grabbed a broom and dustpan from the housekeeping closet and swept up the jagged remnants of the plate Heike had dropped. She'd just finished when Officer Hardy escorted Madman, Vera, and Vivian into the great room to join the others. All three appeared disheveled, like they'd been rousted from bed and forced to dress quickly. While Vera and Vivian took seats near Norma Jean and Chugalug, Madman aimed directly for Kendall, pulling up a chair beside her and leaning in to speak quietly with her.

With the two of us alone at the desk, Rocky looked into my eyes again. "You okay?" he asked softly.

"Not at all." I took a shuddering breath, bit my lip to keep it from trembling, and blinked back the tears threatening to form in my eyes.

He reached over the counter and took one of my hands in his, giving it a supportive squeeze. "Don't worry, Misty. Deputy Highcloud will sort things out."

I hoped so. And I hoped she could do it quickly. If word spread that someone was murdered at the Mountaintop Lodge, only creeps and ghosthunters would want to stay here.

As the guests continued to wait, they cast furtive glances at the breakfast buffet, their hunger becoming more acute. Stomachs rumbled and growled. One of them moaned and groaned in elongated notes like a whale call.

Finally, Madman stood from his seat on a sofa and broke the impasse. He raised his palms. "Don't get me wrong. I'm sorry Sasha's dead and all, but a man's gotta eat."

I couldn't blame him for being hungry. Food was a fundamental human need, after all. Kendall rose, too, murmuring a similar sentiment about how Sasha would have wanted her to keep her strength up so she could help solve the questions surrounding her death. She followed the NASCAR champ to the buffet and piled her plate high with all of the things she'd denied herself while Sasha had been alive. Grits. Biscuits. Gravy. Hash browns. Soon, the entire group was digging into the food and speculating further about what had happened to their yoga instructor. Kendall wolfed down her hash browns as if trying to fill the hole Sasha had left with potatoes and grease. *Could she have something to hide?*

CHAPTER 12

Heaven is under our feet as well as over our heads.
—Henry David Thoreau (1854: *Walden*)

Yeti

Earlier, a man had wrapped a long strand of wide yellow
tape around the trees out back, tearing it with his teeth and
tying off the ends. Yeti crouched and watched as the end of
one of the pieces waved in the wind like a streamer. If not
for the window glass containing her, she'd have run over
and pounced on the strip.

Two other people walked past her window now, rolling a bed on wheels and aiming for the deck. She saw
them bend down to look underneath it, just as the others
had done earlier. After a few minutes, these two pulled a
woman out from under the deck, laid her atop the rolling
bed, and strapped her down. They covered her with a white
sheet before rolling her past Yeti's window and disappear-
ing around the corner. Yeti would have enjoyed pouncing
on the sheet, too. She liked playing the sheet game when
Misty made their bed each morning.

After a few minutes passed with no one else going out
back, she decided the fun must be over. *Might as well take
a nap.*

CHAPTER 13

Man's heart away from nature becomes hard.
—Chief Standing Bear (1928: *My People the Sioux*)

Misty

While I wondered about Kendall, my mind played back the preceding evening, when Cole had seemed anxious and asked to use the computer to check the weather reports. The young couple's early departure bothered me. *Could they have been trying to get moving before an incoming storm hit?* I hoped that was the case.

I logged on to my computer and pulled up the browsing history. *Uh-oh.* Not a single weather site appeared on the list. What I found instead were several sites detailing poison berries and plants found in the Blue Ridge Mountains.

A sick feeling slithered into my stomach as I pulled up the first site. The page contained information on *sambucus canadensis*, otherwise known as American elderberry, which produced dark purple berries. While the berries themselves were not poisonous, the site noted that other parts of the plant contained calcium oxalate, a toxin. Even small doses of oxalate caused intense burning sensations in the mouth and throat, as well as swelling, hypersalivation, and choking. Though death from this toxin was rare, it could cause airway obstruction, with potentially lethal consequences. *Yikes.*

The browsing history showed that Cole had also researched pokeweed. The site he'd referenced stated that pokeweed poisonings had been common in the eastern U.S. during the nineteenth century, when people made tinctures as antirheumatic preparations or ingested the berries or roots, which were often mistaken for parsnip, Jerusalem artichoke, or horseradish. Again, the site noted that fatalities were uncommon, but at least one child had died after consuming juice made from crushed seeds. The site also noted that the berries were commonly cooked into pies or jellies, and that the cooking process inactivated the toxins. Another site he'd searched noted that people sometimes mistook poisonous hemlock for its benign lookalike, Queen Anne's lace or wild carrot.

Why in the world would Cole have been researching poisons? I consulted the browsing history again. Before running these searches, he'd been on WebMD researching symptoms of poisoning.

Rocky leaned against the counter, one elbow crooked up on it. "Hey," I whispered. When he turned, I motioned for him to come around the desk.

Brynn leaned over from her stool and eyed my screen. "What are you looking at?"

We huddled our heads and I told them that the site was one Cole had looked at the preceding evening after asking to use the computer to check weather reports.

I looked from one of them to the other. "Do you think Cole could have something to do with Sasha's death?"

Rocky said he'd seen no signs of injury on Sasha, so death by poison seemed a real possibility. But Cole had appeared to be a nice young man, full of life and adventure— at least until last night, when he'd seemed anxious and riddled with angst. A horrifying thought gripped me. *Could Cole have attempted to poison Sammie?* He said she'd been resting last night when he came out to the deck. Had he administered something to her and been waiting to see the results? Had Sasha somehow ingested the poison, too? If so, how? My gaze moved to the Greasy Griddle's coffee urn and juice dispensers, before moving on to the water cooler I supplied for my guests. I quickly dismissed them as sources of poison. Juice was only available during breakfast hours, and more guests would be sick—or dead—if the coffee urn or water cooler had been poisoned.

Maybe Cole had somehow poisoned Sasha also to throw suspicion off himself. Like Sasha, Sammie was thin. She was much taller than Sasha, though, and could possibly survive a dose that might kill Sasha. Maybe, once Sammie had survived, Cole had decided to get her back on the trail where he could finish the job under less suspicious circumstances. Or maybe he'd changed his mind and decided not to kill his new bride. *What reason would he have had to do away with Sammie in the first place?* The two appeared hopelessly, and hopefully, in love.

After I shared these rambling thoughts with my staff, I said, "What do you think? Am I way off base?"

Rocky exhaled sharply. "Hard to say. Maybe Cole has a hidden dark side. The trail changes people, some for better, some for worse." He proceeded to tell us a story about a man who went by the trail name Mostly Harmless. Most people who had met him on the A.T. thought he seemed like a nice, laid-back guy. When he was later found dead in a tent, his body emaciated, a group even raised the funds to pay for a DNA test in the hopes that it would help law enforcement identify the man so that his loved ones could be informed of his demise. When he was positively identified and his real identity had been released, the group was shocked to learn he had a dark and violent past. Several women claimed he'd abused them, and he'd been estranged from his family. The folks who knew him from the trail had a difficult time reconciling the kind, calm man they'd met with the troubled brute he'd been before.

Brynn ventured a guess, too. "Maybe something drove Cole over an edge and he snapped and killed Sasha. Even normal people can lose their minds if they're triggered by something."

She had a point. "But what would have triggered him?" I asked. "What could have pushed Cole over the edge?"

None of us knew the young man well enough to have an answer for that. Sasha's behavior could be extremely arrogant and irritating, but had she even interacted with Cole?

Rocky rubbed his chin thoughtfully. "A man can be very protective of the woman he loves. Maybe Sasha said something rude to Sammie, insulted her in some way, and Cole decided to get revenge."

It was a plausible theory, but one we had no direct evidence to support.

Brynn gestured to her computer. "Let's take a look online,

see if we might find something out about them that would give us a clue."

While Brynn typed Cole's name into her browser, I did the same for Sammie on my computer. All we found were photos they'd posted of themselves on social media, nearly always in the outdoors. At Acadia National Park in Maine. White Mountain National Forest. The northern end of the Appalachian Trail at Mount Katahdin in Maine four months ago, looking fresh-faced, ambitious, and, while by no means overweight, remarkably heavier than they'd been when they arrived at the lodge Sunday evening.

When I commented on their slighter appearance, Rocky said, "I dropped eighteen pounds when I hiked the A.T. I've heard hikers who complete the trail from start to finish lose around thirty pounds on average."

Gee. All I'd have to do to reach my goal weight was hike 2,200 miles. *Easy-peasy.* While I was on my computer, I figured I might as well see if I could find out anything about the blue pill Brynn had seen in Sasha's room. I typed "blue sleeping pill" into my browser. The search returned several results. The first link detailed a sleeping aid named Eszopiclone that was blue in color. Over-the-counter Unisom sleep gels were blue. One of the results, Donormyl Blue, even had the word blue in the name. There were several others as well. I turned my monitor so Brynn could view it. "Do any of these images look like the pill you saw?"

She ran her gaze over the screen as I toggled between them. "It wasn't a gel capsule, and it wasn't oblong. It was round and lighter blue in color."

I ran another search simply for *blue pill.* One of the

results that popped up was for illegal drugs being produced by a Mexican drug cartel. The pills were intended to look like Oxy 30, but contained fentanyl. Several people had died from taking the pills. *Could Sasha have been hooked on opioids?* As sad as I felt for people who became addicted to drugs, I also realized that if Sasha had died of an overdose, or a bad reaction between a drug and the wine, it would be an easy determination for the medical examiner, and would mean a murder hadn't taken place at my lodge. Cole could have simply been looking up plants to avoid on this section of the trail. As I considered the possibility, I wondered why, if an overdose had indeed killed Sasha, she hadn't died in her bed. Why and how, if she were doped up, would she have climbed out her window and crawled under the deck to pass on? Then again, drugs could make people do strange things.

Glenn came back inside a few minutes later. Through the doors, I could see the team from the medical examiner's office load Sasha's body into the back of their vehicle. Covered by a white sheet, her tiny body looked almost childlike lying on the gurney. Though I hadn't much liked the woman, she was someone's daughter. If she had indeed been murdered, I owed it to her mother, as one myself, to do anything I could to see that justice was done.

The two medics spoke briefly with the deputy before climbing into their SUV and driving off. The deputy stepped to the door and motioned Officer Hardy outside. The two ducked their heads for a brief, private huddle, then came back into the lodge.

Before the deputy could summon another person outside,

I raised a finger to get her attention. Her brows rose as she walked over to the desk. Officer Hardy came with her.

I kept my voice low so the guests wouldn't overhear. "I just found something. You'll want to come around and take a look at this."

Rocky stepped out from behind the desk and held the swinging gate open for Deputy Highcloud and Officer Hardy. The two came around to the back of the desk, stepping over Molasses, who'd decided to lie down for a nap in the normally low-traffic space behind the counter. While Rocky resumed his seat on the bench across the lobby, the law enforcement officers took spots on either side of my stool and looked over my shoulder.

One by one, I brought up the websites. "Cole searched these sites last night. He'd asked to use the computer to check the weather, but there's no weather sites in the browsing history. You think it means anything?"

The deputy frowned. "It means the medical examiner should check the deceased for these particular poisons." She pointed at the screen. "Print off the pages he looked at."

I did as she'd asked. The printer under the counter whirred to life and spit out paper, complete with colorful images of poisonous berries and plants. She retrieved them and handed them to Officer Hardy. "Take pics of those and text them to the M.E. Tell him a guest here ran a search on those sites last night."

He gave her a nod and spread the printouts across the counter so he could snap photos.

While he snapped the pics, I gave them a quick rundown

of my search on blue pills. "Do you think Sasha could have overdosed?"

"If that's the case," Deputy Highcloud said, "the M.E. will let us know. But I'd like to go take a look at that pill." She crooked a finger at Brynn. "You're up, Ms. O'Reilly."

Brynn followed the deputy down the east wing to Sasha's room at the end. I climbed off my stool and stood at the far end of the counter, leaning forward to watch as they went down the hallway. Brynn handed her master key to the deputy, who used it to open the door to Sasha's room. Although they'd opened the door, the two remained in the hall rather than going inside, probably to avoid further contaminating what could be a crime scene. Brynn spoke softly, gesturing as if pointing things out in the room. The deputy pulled a pair of blue booties from her pocket and entered the room. She came back out a moment later with a small baggie. I suspected it contained the blue pill.

The deputy returned to the desk, where she handed the baggie off to Officer Hardy. "Send a pic of that pill to the medical examiner, too. Make sure the print on the pill is visible." Her orders issued, she backtracked to Sasha's room.

I surreptitiously watched the officer as he worked to ensure he captured a good image of the pill. When he enlarged the image on his phone to check the clarity, I noticed the pill was imprinted with the identifier C5. His job done, he tucked the bagged pill into a zippered pouch on his tool belt. He returned to the great room, where he stood like a sentry over the guests. I, of course, immediately typed "blue pill C5" into my browser while keeping an eye on him lest I be caught sleuthing. The search produced a link that told me the pill was a five-milligram Clarinex, a prescription allergy drug classified as an antihistamine. The list of side effects included drowsiness, dizziness, and trouble sleeping. *You're not supposed to drink alcohol when taking an antihistamine, are you?* Seemed like I'd heard that someplace before. I ran another search, this time typing "Clarinex and alcohol" into my browser. Sure enough, several sites popped up, all of them warning that someone taking Clarinex should refrain from drinking alcoholic beverages. Had Sasha died from a combination of the allergy drug and liquor? Why would she drink so heavily when she was taking the allergy medication? Surely her doctor had warned her against it.

As footsteps came up the hall, I closed the window and returned to my home screen. The deputy and Brynn stopped at the desk.

Deputy Highcloud addressed me. "Ms. O'Reilly says she can't open the room safe. You didn't give her the override code?"

"No," I said. "I'm the only one who knows it." I'd reset the override code on each of the safes myself. I figured the fewer people who knew the code, the better. After all, hotel housekeepers were constantly accused of pilfering property from guests, and I wanted to limit my liability by limiting my employees' access to guests' valuables. Of course, there was little I could do if the guests didn't take steps themselves to protect their property. I was surprised Sasha hadn't put her jewelry and the singing bowl in the room safe when not in use yesterday.

The deputy gestured to the stack of sticky notes on the desk. "Jot the code down for me."

I jotted down the number, 1427. My sons J.J. and Mitch had been born on May 14 and October 27, respectively. Probably not the toughest code to crack, but one I could easily remember.

"Wait here," the deputy told Brynn. "I'll be right back." She went down the hall again and disappeared into Room 19 for a few seconds before returning empty-handed. Though she said nothing, I could only assume she'd found the safe empty. She walked past the desk, asking Brynn to come along with her. The two went outside to Brynn's Prius. Through the window, I saw my assistant dig into her pocket and hand the deputy a set of keys. The deputy opened the door and began to search Brynn's car. *I wonder what that's all about.* The deputy had raised the trunk lid and was taking a look inside when Patty came over with one of her kitchen staff to collect the warming trays and dishes.

Patty stopped at the registration desk, took a look at my anxious guests, and leaned in to whisper, "I saw the deputy going through your housekeeper's car. Do they think she did it?"

"Deputy Highcloud is probably just being thorough. The only things I know are that there was an allergy medication in Sasha's room, and that one of my guests ran an internet search for poisons last night."

"Poisons?" Patty gasped and the head of every guest in the great room snapped in our direction. She grimaced and whispered, "Sorry!" When they turned their attention away again, she eyed the group discreetly from the corner of her eye. "Which guest was it?"

"None of the ones still here," I said. "It was a young man named Cole. He and his wife left the lodge before dawn this morning." I told her that they were recent college grads hiking the A.T. while they had a chance before joining the working world as computer programmers in Boston.

"That adorable couple?" Her face scrunched in confusion. "I saw them coming and going from your lodge yesterday with Rocky. Looked like nice kids to me. They even helped pick up some napkins one of my takeout customers dropped in the parking lot."

"Cole's internet search could have absolutely nothing to do with Sasha's death," I said, willing my words to be true. I didn't want any of my guests to be guilty of such a heinous crime, but especially not a young man fresh out of school with so much promise and a bright future ahead of him. "I don't see any obvious reason for him to want her dead. I don't know that the two even said a single word to each other while they were here. But it's odd that Cole and Sammie left early without letting me know in advance. Seems like they took off in a hurry."

Patty issued a suspicious *hmm*. "Where'd they go?"

"Back to the trail. Rocky dropped them off his morning."

Her brown eyes widened. "He might have been alone in his truck with a killer? Maybe two killers?"

I raised my palms. "Who knows?"

Patty backed away from the desk. "I better collect the dishes. We'll be gearing up for the lunch rush soon. You let me know how this all plays out."

"I will." I grabbed the empty mug and handed it to her. "Thanks again for the tea. It helped a lot." That was a lie. My nerves remained frazzled. But what did help was knowing I had a new, caring friend just across the parking lot.

Patty and her staff had just left with the trays and bins when Brynn and Deputy Highcloud returned to the lobby. While Brynn came around to her stool, the deputy stopped at the counter to speak with me. "How many sets of keys are there for each room?"

"Three," I told her. "An original key for each room is locked in the safe." The safe was bolted to the floor and enclosed in a locked cabinet below the counter. "We keep two sets for guests in this locked drawer here." I unlocked the drawer and pulled it open to show her.

"Did Sasha have both sets of keys to Room Nineteen?" The deputy stood on tiptoe to look over the counter, but even on her toes she was too petite to get a good look into the drawer.

"No," I said. "She was the only one staying in the room, so there didn't seem to be any need to give her more than one set. The second set is still here."

When I reached for the second set of keys to show her, she stopped me with a raised palm and a "Whoa. We don't want any prints that might be on the keys or chain disturbed."

"I cleaned all of the keys with disinfectant before these guests arrived," I said. "And I'm the one who checked Sasha in. If there are any prints on those keys at all, they should be mine." I'd wanted everything clean and sparkling at my lodge, right down to the room keys.

She circled around to the back of the desk, looked down

into the drawer, and crouched to take a look at the lock. She turned her face up. "Who all has a key to this drawer?"

"Just me and Brynn." I hiked a thumb to indicate my assistant, who sat on the other side of the deputy.

The deputy asked whether either of us had lent anyone our keys or given anyone access to the drawer. Neither of us had. She had me check the hotel's safe to make sure the original key to Sasha's room was still there. It was. She pulled a small plastic bag and a pair of tweezers from the plastic toolbox she'd left on the counter and used them to retrieve the second set of keys from the cabinet and place them in a clear plastic evidence bag. Using a marker, she jotted the date and other pertinent information on the bag to identify the contents. When she finished, she tucked the marker into the breast pocket of her uniform. "I'll need to get your prints, Ms. Murphy." She cast a glance at Brynn. "We've already got Ms. O'Reilly's on file."

She proceeded to pull a small device from a zippered pouch on her belt. She set it on the counter and motioned for me to give her my right hand. After placing each finger on the small screen at the end of the device and collecting the prints, she repeated the process with my left hand. She slid the device back into the pouch and angled her head to indicate Brynn. "Ms. O'Reilly showed me her master key. I assume you've got one, too. Who else has a master key? Mr. Crowder?"

"Yes," I said. "He's got one, too."

While the inspector I'd hired before buying the place had performed a thorough inspection of the lodge, his focus had been on structural items in need of repair, not cosmetic issues. After Rocky and I had agreed for Rocky to stay on at the lodge and take care of maintenance issues, I'd given him a master key and asked him to perform a cosmetic inspection of all the rooms and do what he could to make the lodge look its best. He'd made sure the furniture, doors, windows, and blinds were in good working order, and touched up the paint and wood stain where needed. No scratched paneling, cockeyed drawers, squeaky hinges, or wobbly beds here.

Rocky's master key would have given him access to Sasha's room, but he couldn't have anything to do with her death, could he? My gut clenched, but only for the briefest of moments. Sure, he'd been in the hallway outside Sasha's room last night just after that odd chime sound, but so had I. Like me, he'd been drawn by the noise, nothing else. I knew it in my heart. I knew it in my mind, too. After all, he'd had Molasses with him. No way would he have taken the dog with him to commit a murder. Molasses would've only gotten in the way, shed all over the crime scene, and made a quick getaway impossible. The enormous dog was never in a hurry. He had one speed and it was slower than, well, Molasses. *So that's how he got his name!* I could only hope I'd have similar epiphanies where this death investigation was concerned.

I filled in the deputy. "This probably has nothing to do with Sasha's death, but I heard a sound last night, like a chime, or metal. At first, I thought my anniversary clock had struck one, but then I remembered I'd taken the batteries out of the clock so the chimes wouldn't bother my guests. I came out of my room to investigate. Rocky did, too. We spoke briefly in the lobby."

The deputy's gaze slid in his direction before returning to my face. "Which room is his?"

"Twenty."

Though she said nothing out loud, her thoughts were clear. *His room is directly across the hall from the victim's.*

Before I could tell her about Molasses being with him, and thus exonerating my maintenance man, the deputy turned to Rocky and called, "Mr. Crowder? You're up."

As the deputy and Rocky stepped outside to speak, Brynn leaned over to me and whispered, "You think Rocky killed Sasha?"

"Absolutely not!"

"Really?" She quirked her nose. "Because you kind of threw him under the bus."

"I did no such thing!" Or at least I hoped I hadn't. "I only told the deputy the facts." Of course, I hadn't gotten around to mentioning that Molasses was with Rocky when we met up, but the deputy would see the three of us on the security camera footage when she watched it. That would clear up any confusion.

"Well, at least I'm in the clear," Brynn said. "I wasn't in the lodge last night, and my car was in the parking lot at my apartment from the time I arrived home from work yesterday until I left for work again this morning. My neighbors would have seen it. They'll vouch for me."

It seemed a defensive and odd thing to say but, then again, Brynn was a little odd. Maybe her telling me that she had an alibi was simply her musing aloud. *Or maybe she's trying to throw me off her scent. . . .* I doubted she was the culprit, and I felt bad that I had even the tiniest suspicion.

After all, she'd put in a lot of effort over the last two days to make sure the experience my first guests had at my lodge was a good one. She'd even offered to do some of the less-appealing, backbreaking cleaning work, such as snaking the shower drains to ensure they were clog-free and cleaning the accumulated gunk and lint from under the vending machines, washers, and dryers.

All of us in the lodge sat awkwardly, casting suspicious glances at one another, wondering if someone in the group could be responsible for Sasha's death. Most of the guests had left their cell phones in their rooms when they'd come for the sun salutations, and they didn't seem to know what to do with themselves. As I'd done the day before when Sasha ditched Kendall, leaving the clingy blonde adrift, I suggested they might be able to pass the time with one of the books, games, or puzzles. I walked over and pulled the things from the bottom shelf, wondering whether I should gather up the Third Eye merchandise Sasha and Kendall had placed on the shelves above. I decided to leave that decision to Glenn. After all, he worked for the studio.

I spread the books and games on a table, and several of the guests wandered over to take a look at the selections. Vera and her daughter invited Kendall to join them at their table, where they planned to tackle a 4,000-piece world map puzzle. I'd bought the challenging puzzle for my boys when they were in junior high, figuring they might learn something about geography while also having fun.

I returned to my perch at the registration desk. Brynn sat next to me, fidgeting with nervous energy. Though the constant motion was a little irritating, I couldn't much blame her. Every nerve ending in my body was on edge, too, and I'd nearly chewed through my lip. One by one, the deputy brought the remaining guests outside. Most of the interrogations were quick, lasting only a few minutes. I surmised that the yoga students either had no helpful information to give, or didn't want to divulge anything that might point a finger at themselves. Highcloud's interview of Madman Maddox lasted slightly longer. No doubt the others had spoken of Sasha's repeated attempts to seduce the NASCAR star, perhaps even wondered if he'd taken her up on her not-so-subtle offers of a romantic romp. *Could he have succumbed to her wiles, only to have lost his temper again for one reason or another?* He was relatively young, more subject to impulsive behavior, as evidenced by his shoulder-bump attack on that other driver. Had he feared Sasha might screw things up between him and his Honey Bee? His career had already suffered a bobble. Maybe the thought of romantic strife, too, was more than he could deal with right now.

After the deputy had interviewed everyone, including Heike, she asked for my master key. After I handed it over, she stepped to the front of my desk, stood next to the police officer, and addressed the guests. "Just to be thorough, we're going to take a quick look in the guest rooms. Everyone okay with that?"

"Of course," Glenn said. "Whatever you need."

Most of the others murmured their assent, but I noticed two mouths stayed firmly shut—Kendall's and Madman's. Kendall began to rise from her seat as if to protest the intrusion on her space, but seemed to think better of it and sat back down. Madman openly scowled, his eyes narrowing and his square jaw flexing.

Evidently noticing their responses, the deputy said, "Ms. McFadden? Mr. Maddox? Any objections? If so, now is the time to say something. Otherwise, you've given consent to a search."

Maddox cocked his head. "What if I say no? What then?"

The deputy said, "Then I'd get a search warrant. I'm only asking for consent to save us all some time. I know you all must be eager to get back to your rooms."

Maddox didn't seem to like the insinuation that he could be a suspect. His reputation was already soiled by his unsportsmanlike behavior at the racetrack. Maybe he thought he'd be unfairly accused because of it. But, in the end, he said, "Go ahead and look in my room. I got nothing to hide."

Kendall's eyes were wide and wild, but she gave a vigorous nod, giving her consent. Was she afraid they'd find something in her room, or was she simply emotionally overwhelmed by her friend's death? Maybe she didn't like the idea of someone rifling through her personal items. I didn't much like the thought of law enforcement looking in my panty drawer, either, but it was a small price to pay to be ruled out as a suspect.

Over the next two hours, the deputy and the police officer searched each guest room, including mine and the one that Sammie and Cole had vacated. They also took photos of Sasha's room and collected evidence from it, bagging all of her things, including her water bottle and down pillow, and taking them out to the deputy's vehicle.

The deputy returned to the desk and quietly said, "Come with me. I need to show you something."

Uh-oh. What can it be?

CHAPTER 14

Men argue. Nature acts.
—Voltaire (1764: *Philosophical Dictionary*)

Yeti

A man had come into her room, unannounced and uninvited. When she'd told him in no uncertain terms with an arched back and hiss that he wasn't welcome here, he'd ignored her. *How dare he!*

He'd rummaged through all of the cabinets and drawers, but seemed annoyed when she'd climbed into them herself to conduct an inspection. *Hypocrite.* He'd looked in the closet and under the bed. He'd even peeked into Yeti's bags of food and litter. *That's none of your business, sir!*

She'd finally run him off, swiping her claws at the back of his leg as he'd gone. Unfortunately, all she'd gotten was fabric, no skin. To make the situation more embarrassing, her claws had stuck in the material, rendering her an unwitting captive. The man had to reach down and free her claws from his pants. She'd never felt so inept and humiliated. She turned and skittered under the bed to hide her shame.

CHAPTER 15

Be an opener of doors . . .
—Ralph Waldo Emerson (1867: "The Preacher")

Misty

What could Deputy Highcloud want to show me? Had she found the murder weapon? A clue? Something definitive that would put this horrid matter to rest right away? I hoped with every fiber of my being that it was the latter. The quicker Sasha's mysterious death was solved, the quicker both she and the matter could be put to rest.

My heart pounded, sending blood rushing through my veins like roaring rapids as I followed the deputy down the east wing. Although I thought she was taking me to Sasha's room at the end, she surprised me by stopping at Room 17, the one Kendall occupied. She used my master key to open the door and entered, motioning for me to follow her. She closed the door behind us and walked over to the door that adjoined Rooms 17 and 19. The door was designed with two deadbolts, one on each side, so that the parties in both rooms had to unlock it from their own side in order for it to open. On the side of the door opposite each deadbolt was a flat metal plate rather than a knob. The gold tone plate was shiny, Brynn having cleaned it to a gleam the preceding day. I noted that the deadbolt was locked on Kendall's side. *Is it locked on Sasha's side as well?*

"What do you know about these marks?" The deputy pointed to a spot on the trim about six inches above the deadbolt and immediately next to the flat plate marking the location of the deadbolt in Sasha's room. Small gouge marks marred the trim with thin, light-colored scratches where the wood had been damaged through the stained top layer.

I stepped back as a horrifying thought hit me. *Had Kendall been able to force Sasha's deadbolt open from this side? Had she entered Sasha's room and killed her?* "I don't believe those marks were there when Kendall checked in. Rocky went through all of the rooms and repaired any cosmetic damage before the yoga group arrived."

"Are you certain?"

While the damage seemed obvious now that the deputy had pointed it out to me, the marks were thin and the gleam of the shiny circular plate could have helped to mask them from some angles. *Would Rocky or I have necessarily noticed these gouges?* "I'm not a hundred percent sure. Rocky might be able to give you a definitive answer."

She opened the door to the hall. "Round him up for me, please."

I went down the hall. Rocky looked up from his seat when I reached the lobby. I waved him over, and he followed me down the hall and into Room 17.

We gathered at the door adjoining Kendall's and Sasha's rooms, and the deputy pointed again to the gouge marks. "Do you know whether these marks were there before Kendall checked in?"

"I do know," Rocky said, "and they weren't. I checked all of the trim around the windows and doors to make sure none of it was loose, and I looked for any signs of damage. I buffed out the smaller scratches with sandpaper and used wood filler on the deeper nicks and scores. I filled in the marks with one of those handy stain pens."

The deputy's brows lifted. "You're one hundred percent certain this damage wasn't here?"

Rocky said, "To quote Voltaire, 'Doubt is not a pleasant condition, but certainty is absurd.'"

The deputy grunted impatiently. "And?"

"It may be absurd, but yes, I'm one hundred percent certain." He crouched and examined the lower trim for a moment before pointing at a spot. "See here? I sanded and stained this spot. I did my best to match the existing stain and it's as close as I could get, but it's not exact." He pointed out another spot. "I sanded and stained this piece of trim, too." He shifted his focus from the trim back to the deputy. "I looked all the rooms over carefully. I wanted to impress my new boss with my attention to detail."

My cheeks warmed a little. If I hadn't been so discombobulated by the morning's events, I would've been even more flattered by his remark. "You did impress me," I said. "You do solid work."

The deputy glanced from Rocky, to me, and back again, a thoughtful expression on her face.

Rocky backed away to let the deputy take a closer look at the repaired trim. I bent down to look, too. Sure enough, on close inspection, it was clear that the spots on the trim lower down had been freshly sanded and stained.

If the scratches hadn't been there before Kendall and

Sasha checked in . . . "Does this mean Kendall killed Sasha?" I asked.

"Not necessarily," the deputy said. "It only means someone might have tried to access Sasha's room through this door."

"Someone?" I repeated. "It would have had to be Kendall, right?" After all, nobody was bunking with her. She had the room to herself.

"Not necessarily," the deputy said again. "You, Ms. O'Reilly, and Mr. Crowder here all have keys to this room. Maybe it was one of you. Or maybe it was someone Kendall invited into her room. Or maybe someone used Kendall's keys, or the second set to this room. Or maybe someone scratched up that trim to implicate Kendall."

"That's a lot of uncertainty." Rocky issued a mirthless chuckle. "No chance you'll ever feel absurd, is there?"

"I gotta go with Voltaire right now." She rocked forward onto her toes. "It's my job to consider all of the possibilities, not just the obvious ones. Like you, I want to impress my boss with my attention to detail."

He gave her a respectful nod. "Point taken."

The three of us returned to the lobby, where the deputy took the second set of Kendall's keys into evidence before summoning the woman. "Ms. McFadden, come to your room, please." She motioned for Officer Hardy to accompany them. My guess was she thought things could get ugly, maybe even physical, if Kendall were indeed the killer and didn't comply when confronted.

We all waited in hushed silence for them to return. I wondered if Kendall would be in handcuffs when they did. I also wondered if she'd confess, or if we'd hear some sort of scuffle, or if Kendall would simply surrender silently and let her defense lawyer work things out later.

After a few minutes, the three came back up the hall. Kendall was unshackled, though her terrified expression said the interaction had not exonerated her. While Kendall joined the others in the great room, the deputy asked to take a look in the crawl space and attic.

I had no objection to her taking a look at those spaces, but it seemed a waste of time given that there was no access to the attic or crawl space from the guest rooms. When I inquired, she said, "Just being thorough. Sometimes you find something surprising in the place you least expect it."

It was true. I'd expected to find serenity and solitude here in the mountains, but I'd also found a new friend and, just maybe, some male companionship.

Rocky stood from the bench. "I can help you with that." He rounded up a hammer from his toolbox and led the deputy down the east wing.

I left Brynn at the desk and went with them. Rocky reached up and used the claw hook on his hammer to grab the handle on the pull-down door in the corridor's ceiling. The door led to the east wing attic. Once the door had dropped down, he extended the fold-up ladder attached to it. The deputy climbed the ladder, pulled the dirty string attached to the bare bulb in the ceiling, and disappeared into the attic. She must have turned on her flashlight for extra illumination, because we could see its beam bouncing around. Her voice was muffled and echoed in the large space. "Nothing looks out of order up here." She stepped to the opening and looked down at Rocky and me. "Tell me if you think different."

Once she'd climbed down, she handed Rocky her flashlight. He ascended the ladder and looked about, too. "I haven't been up here before, but I can't say anything looks out of the ordinary." He climbed down the rungs.

The deputy turned to me, her head cocked in question.

"I've been up there," I said. "I had the place looked at before I bought it, and the inspector took me up there to point out places where the roof had been patched in the past." He'd also told me that the repairs had been done properly, and the leaks appeared to have been fixed. "Same with the attic on the east wing. Brynn and I cleaned them before the guests arrived, too."

The deputy swung a finger. "Up you go, then. Tell me if anything's changed."

I took her flashlight, climbed the ladder, and poked my head up through the opening, glancing about. There was little to see. The lodge had both an indoor storage closet and an outdoor storage shed that were spacious and much easier to access, so nothing was stored in the attic. Because the ceilings were coffered—supported from underneath by the decorative rustic beams—there were no ceiling joists dividing the expansive, flat floor. There was no ductwork, either. Air conditioning wasn't needed on the mountain, where summer temperatures rarely exceeded the low seventies, and heat was supplied by electric baseboard heaters in each room.

As far as I could tell, everything looked the same. The same wooden panels that formed the ceilings of the guest rooms formed the attic floor, this side of the wood left rough and unfinished. The same red pipes ran in parallel lines on either side of the attic opening, ready to douse the lodge with water in the event of a fire. The same dusty pink insulation lay along the perimeter. The same slivers of light slanted through the air vents under the eaves, and the same slightly musty smell met my nose, courtesy of the damp mountain climate. There were no telltale footprints that I could see, but that wasn't a surprise. Brynn had suggested we sweep out the attics before the guests arrived, so there was no dust in which a footprint could be left.

I tugged the string and the light turned off with a *click-click*. I climbed down the ladder and handed the flashlight to the detective. "Nothing caught my eye."

Rocky folded the ladder back up into place and pushed the hinged door up until it closed.

We returned to the great room, where Deputy Highcloud addressed the guests. "I'm going to ask all of you to wait out on the deck while Officer Hardy and I wrap things up. That includes you two, Rocky and Brynn. We'll let you know when we're done."

The guests and my staff complied, shuffling en masse to the French doors and onto the deck. Kendall, the last one out, cast a tearful, anxious glance back at the deputy as she shut the doors behind them.

Once the door closed, Deputy Highcloud turned to me. "It's the moment of truth. Let's take a look at that camera footage and see who lied to me."

CHAPTER 16

Nature will bear the closest inspection. She invites us to lay our eye level with her smallest leaf, and take an insect view of its plain.

—Henry David Thoreau (1839: *Natural History of Massachusetts*)

Misty

Deputy Highcloud and I sat on the two stools, while Officer Hardy dragged over a chair from one of the tables in the great room.

I was dying to know what Kendall had said about the scratches. "What did Kendall say about the damage on the door trim?" If she'd said it was there when she arrived, we'd know she was lying. She'd certainly appeared scared when she'd come back from discussing the matter with law enforcement earlier.

"She said she hadn't noticed one way or another, but that she and Sasha had carried things back and forth between their rooms, and could have inadvertently scratched the trim with a hairbrush or nail file, or even a bracelet or the buckle on her fitness tracker."

It seemed unlikely any of those items would produce such deep gouges by merely brushing against the trim. What's more, what were the odds that the scratches would occur directly next to Sasha's deadbolt? I wasn't buying it. The skeptical expression on the deputy's face told me she wasn't buying it, either. But she hadn't arrested Kendall yet. *Does she need more evidence?*

The deputy pointed at the screen. "Start the footage the last time Sasha was seen alive."

The last time I'd seen Sasha was when she'd left the table on the deck after drinking copious amounts of wine in short order and wobbled back to her room. That had been around nine thirty or so. I started the feed at nine fifteen. The screen was split, showing the two camera feeds side by side but together providing a complete image of the lodge's interior in a slightly distorted fish-eye display. The deputy directed me to play the footage at four times the real-time rate. "We'll slow it down when we see something."

At 9:43, according to the time stamp, Sasha came in the back door. Kendall trailed along behind her like a lost puppy. The deputy reached out and clicked the feed to slow it down. We watched as the two made their way down the hall, growing less defined and more pixelated the farther they went from the camera. By the time Kendall turned to go into her door, she was merely a blurry blonde blob. If I hadn't known it was her, I wouldn't have been able to identify the person as Kendall.

The same went for Sasha. She took longer with her door, appearing to fumble with her key. When she stepped into her room and closed the door behind her, a small dark spot appeared on the floor.

"Wait." I pointed. "What's that? Did she drop her keys?" The dark spot could be the pine cone keychain.

The deputy and police officer leaned in. He squinted. "Hard to say. Could be."

At ten o'clock, the hallway lights, which were on a timer,

dimmed. Not long thereafter, the footage showed others coming in from the deck and returning to their rooms. Cole. Glenn. The joggers. Rocky and I came inside last and said our good nights. He walked down the hall to his room at the end and disappeared inside. As the detective watched, she jotted notes on her pad.

We sped the feed up until 10:30, when Norma Jean emerged from her room halfway down the hall with her little dog on a leash. She walked him down to the end of the hall and took him out the wing door, which was just past the door to Sasha's room. They returned only thirty seconds later, the dog having done his business in record time. I supposed a tiny dog like that had a small bladder. As Norma Jean made her way along the hall, the spot in front of Sasha's door moved along ahead of her.

The police officer pointed to the screen. "Looks like she kicked Sasha's keys."

She probably hadn't realized she'd kicked the keys because the tags on her dog's collar were jingling, too. Norma Jean's foot hit the keys a second time, sending them skittering even farther up the hall, clearly visible now. They ended up against the baseboard between two rooms.

We sped up the feed. The hallway stood empty for more than two hours, but at 12:41, the door to Sammie and Cole's room opened and Cole emerged.

The deputy pointed her pen at the screen. "Who's that?"

"Cole."

Her head bobbed as she seemed to recollect the name from earlier. "The one who lit out of here this morning."

Cole tiptoed down the hall and across the lobby to the laundry room. A few seconds later, he emerged, a bag of pretzels in his hand. *Looks like he came out to get a midnight snack from one of the vending machines.* The screen flickered, as if the electricity had faltered again for a microsecond, not long enough for things to turn off completely, but long enough that it was noticeable to the human eye. Cole seemed to have noticed it, too. He stopped in his tracks and glanced around before continuing on into the lobby. He'd tiptoed most of the way back to his room, but had not yet passed the keys on the floor, when the screen went black.

"That must've been when the power went out," I said. Unfortunately, when the electricity went down, it took the Wi-Fi down with it. Without internet access, the security camera couldn't supply a video feed. The screen returned to life only a second or two later, but according to the 1:16 a.m. time stamp on the screen, it was actually thirty-four minutes later. The keys were no longer on the floor. *Had Sasha's killer taken advantage of the power outage to sneak into her room undetected? Had Cole found Sasha's keys in the hallway and used them to access her room while the camera feed was down?* We wouldn't know unless her keys turned up.

There was no more movement in the hallway until 2:37, when a fuzzy red blob appeared at the end. *Rocky, in his union suit.* An even fuzzier black blob appeared at his knees. *Molasses.* Rocky stood stock-still for a few seconds, probably listening to see if the chime sound that had woken us would come again. I emerged from my room, hiking pole at the ready. Yeti and I sneaked down the hallway. Rocky padded toward me in his bare feet, Molasses moseying along with him. On screen, Rocky and I reenacted our little talk in the lobby. When he reached out to finger the satin bow at my throat, the deputy turned to me. "Something going on between you two?"

My first inclination was to say no, but I quickly thought better of it. Denial would seem disingenuous, and could make her suspicious of both me and Rocky, make her wonder if we'd been fully honest with her. "We met recently when I hired him to make some repairs. We're not in a personal relationship, but things sometimes get a little . . ."

I was still searching for the right word when she supplied it for me. "Flirty?"

A hot blush rushed up my neck. "Yeah."

"You could do a lot worse." She offered a conspiratorial smile, the first sign that there was a real woman behind her detached, professional exterior. But any spark of camaraderie was quickly doused when she added, "Unless he's the killer."

"He's not," I insisted.

"Oh yeah?" She angled her head with interest. "How do you know that?"

Because he's a nice, reliable guy. Because he's made me feel less alone up here in the mountains. Because he's had my back, helped me make my dream come true. But I couldn't very well say those things. Instead, I shared the thought I'd had earlier. "Because no killer takes a slow-moving mountain dog along to the crime scene."

Her head straightened. "You might have a point. But I'm not ready to write him off just yet."

We started the feed again. On screen, Rocky and I returned to our rooms.

As we continued to watch, there were a few more flickers on the screen, but no people appeared. The flickering stopped as the winds calmed, and all was still until 5:11, when Rocky and Molasses emerged from their room. Rocky had traded his union suit and bare feet for his usual jeans, lightweight flannel shirt, and work boots. Rocky led Molasses out the front door to relieve himself. A minute later, Cole and Sammie exited their room and walked to the registration desk. They read my sign instructing guests with needs after hours to use the house phone to contact me. They exchanged words, but without audio or the ability to lip-read, I had no idea what they'd said to each other. When Rocky and his dog walked back through the door, the young couple turned and went over to him. They handed him their room keys and engaged in a brief conversation while Molasses took advantage of the stop to plop his hindquarters down on the wood floor and scratch behind his ear with his back paw. Rocky motioned for Sammie and Cole to follow him, and everyone went out the door, including the dog.

At 6:30, I came hustling down the hall to let Patty in the door with the items for the breakfast buffet. Rocky returned to the lodge at 6:42. The yoga students and Glenn wandered out of their guest rooms, through the lobby, and out onto the deck to get ready for their sun salutations. Glenn and Kendall glanced back into the lobby several times. After consulting with Glenn, I tried calling Sasha's room, then went down the hall to knock on her door, returning to tell him there'd been no answer. The deputy, Officer Hardy, and I continued to watch until I rushed outside after hearing the guest's shouts of horror when Sasha's body had been spotted under the deck.

When the deputy directed me to stop the feed, I asked, "Did you glean anything from the footage?"

Her eyes narrowed slightly as she appeared to ponder my question. "I'd hoped to see someone entering Sasha's room through the door. That would've given me something definitive to go on. What the footage tells me is that someone either entered Sasha's room another way, or they entered through her door while the electricity was out."

We had no way of knowing what transpired in the lodge during the lapse. *If only there were some way of seeing what had gone on in Sasha's room* . . .

She slid off the stool. "Most crimes are crimes of opportunity. Sasha's keys in the hallway had opportunity written all over them."

She didn't spell it out further, but she didn't have to. Cole had been in the hallway where the keys lay, waiting to be discovered. As much as I hated to think Cole could have killed Sasha, his internet search for poisons and their effects had me feeling suspicious of him. Add in the lapse in camera footage occurring when he was in the hall, and my nerves buzzed with suspicion. *Could he have poisoned Sasha, then tried to dispose of her body?* From the location of her body, I surmised that whoever dragged her outside had intended to roll her off the cliff, but realized that doing so would pose a danger to themselves. Besides, with the thick forest on the slope behind the lodge, the body wouldn't roll more than a few feet before ending up against the trunk of a tree. Anyone on the deck would have been able to look down and spot her body. What's more, I could think of no reason Cole might want to kill Sasha. *Other than that empty wallet of his* . . .

I offered a possibility, one that didn't implicate the young honeymooners. "Maybe one of the other guests found Sasha's keys."

Her expression was dubious. "Officer Hardy and I verified that any keys we found in the rooms fit the door of the room we were in. We also patted everyone down prior to their interview and checked that the keys matched their door locks. If anyone had still had Sasha's keys on them, we would've found them. The killer would have to be pretty stupid not to have gotten rid of them."

She directed me to play the feed starting with the group's arrival on Sunday. Again, while there was some activity in the lodge that night, nobody entered or left any room other than their own. So how had Sasha's hair ended up on Madman's pillow? Had she climbed in through his window, just like the killer seemed to have climbed in through hers? We continued watching at nearly warp speed until Rocky walked down the hall and used his key to let himself into Sasha's room.

The deputy reached out and stopped the feed. "What's he doing?"

"Replacing the light bulbs over the bathroom mirror," I told her. "Sasha complained that they weren't bright enough." I pointed to the screen. "See? He's carrying a pack of bulbs."

We watched again until Brynn entered Sasha's room with an armful of towels. When the deputy paused the feed again, I said, "Sasha requested extra towels, too. With all the exercise she was doing, she probably needed to take more than one shower a day."

"She seems to have had all of your staff in her room."

It was true. "She was a high-maintenance guest."

We watched the rest of the video until we reached the point at which we'd originally started, the last time Sasha had been seen alive, when she staggered back to her room.

The deputy frowned. "Any idea which of your guests was aware that the singing bowl was valuable?"

"I assume most of the students knew. If they didn't know before they came up for the retreat, they might have overheard Kendall mention it at sun salutations. She told me to be careful when I was arranging Sasha's things on the deck. She said that that Sasha had paid five thousand dollars for it."

"What about Sammie and Cole? Did they hear Kendall say how much Sasha had paid for the bowl?"

"They weren't up yet. They didn't come out for breakfast for another couple of hours, and they didn't spend a lot of time talking to the other guests. They spent their day shopping for provisions and washing their laundry."

"Maybe they had their window open Monday morning and heard Kendall through the screen."

"Maybe." My head swam and my gut churned. "None of this makes any sense to me."

The deputy's lips pursed. "Violent crime has never made sense to me either. But once the medical examiner determines the cause of death, we should be able to start piecing things together. In the meantime, I'm going to have signs posted along the A.T. telling Sammie and Cole to get in touch with me and asking anyone who's seen them to contact law enforcement. I'll have officers try to intercept them at access points and road crossings, too. With their hasty departure this morning, they've left a lot of questions behind." She slid down from the stool. "Don't tell anyone what was—or wasn't—on the video. If the killer knows they weren't caught on camera, they'll be less likely to confess. I'd rather make them think I've seen something, have them sweat it out."

"Understood." I mimed locking my lips and tossing the key over my shoulder.

"Call me if you think of anything else."

"I will."

I slid down from my stool, too, and Officer Hardy and I followed the deputy as she walked over to the French doors and opened them to address the crowd. "It's my understanding that y'all planned to stay here at the lodge until Sunday when your charter bus will return to take you home. We've collected a good deal of evidence, and I feel confident we'll be making an arrest soon." She paused as if to let her words sink in and ran her gaze over the group, appearing to make direct eye contact with several of them, including Madman and Kendall. "In the meantime, I'd appreciate it if you folks would stick around in case we have further questions."

Vera popped up off the chaise lounge on which she'd been perched. "My daughter and I are not going to stay here and risk getting murdered in our sleep!"

I couldn't blame the woman for wanting to go home. I'd feel the same. I'd been so thrilled to fill the rooms for this entire week, and now I was at risk of losing all of their business. I couldn't very well charge them a cancellation fee under the circumstances, either. Glenn and Heike seemed to realize they were in the same boat. The studio could be forced to refund the retreat fees, and Glenn and Heike could be out an entire week's earnings. They exchanged glances.

The deputy said, "I understand your concerns, and I definitely advise all of you to take precautions. Return to your rooms before dark, and always take a look through the peephole before opening your door. Keep your windows closed and locked, and valuables out of sight. Lock your jewelry in the safe in your closet." She raised a hand in goodbye. "Y'all take care now."

With that, she and Officer Hardy strode across the great room, left the lodge, and headed across the parking lot to the Greasy Griddle. I thought about calling Patty to give her a heads-up, but decided against it. By the time I could dial her number, the officers would already be at her door.

On the deck, Glenn stood and held up his palms to calm the crowd. "Before anyone makes a decision on leaving, let's talk things through as a group."

Madman stepped to the open French door and skewered me with a look. "You owe it to us to tell us what you know."

"Yeah!" Vera cried, seconding his motion. "What did you see on the security camera footage?"

"I'm sorry," I replied. "I'm not at liberty to discuss the contents of the video."

When the group erupted in angry murmurs, Rocky put his fingers to his mouth and issued a loud whistle to quiet them. "The most the camera would show is someone coming or going from Sasha's room. That doesn't mean they're necessarily the person who killed her."

Rocky seemed to have thought things through. As a handyman, he could be expected to study equipment and angles, to know how things worked and attempt to solve a problem with a mechanical analysis. So why did his words send a little frisson of fear slithering up my spine? Not with regard to him, of course. I'd already ruled him out. But was it possible that, when Brynn had gone into Sasha's room with the extra towels, she'd unlocked the back window so that she could climb through it later that night to steal the jewelry and singing bowl? I'd heard that it was a good idea to check window locks after any service provider had been in your home for that very reason, that an unscrupulous one might unlock a window to gain access later to burglarize the place.

Norma Jean cuddled her little dog to her chest and said, "What about those young honeymooners? They never came to breakfast and they're not here now."

Because the deputy hadn't asked me to keep mum about Sammie and Cole, I supposed it was okay to share about them with my guests. Still, I wanted to make sure I was being fair and not misleading anyone. "Deputy Highcloud hopes to intercept them on the trail so she can take their statements."

Norma Jean held her dog even tighter. "She thinks they did it, then?"

My gut clenched. "The deputy has some questions for them, that's all. Just like she had questions for all of you. They could be perfectly innocent."

Vera harrumphed. "Or they could be perfectly guilty."

The group erupted in speculation.

Madman shook his head. "All that time in the wilderness must've messed with their heads."

Vivian's lip curled up in disgust. "Remember how dirty they were when they arrived? You'd have to be crazy to want to live like that."

Joaquín chimed in, too, his gaze surveying the group. "It

had to be them, or else some random stranger. The rest of us know each other from the studio. None of us would have done it."

I'd heard that most murder victims were killed by someone they knew personally rather than a random attacker, but there seemed to be no sense in pointing out that fact. They might all turn on one another and things could get even uglier. "Deputy Highcloud said that once the medical examiner determines a cause of death, it will help pinpoint the person responsible."

Now that I was done speaking, Heike and Glenn stood to make their case for remaining at the lodge.

Heike dabbed at her eyes with a napkin she'd snatched from the breakfast table. She gulped back fresh sobs as she spoke. "I agree with Joaquín." *Gulp.* "I believe the killer has moved on and that it is safe for us to continue our retreat." *Gulp.* "I do not want you all to miss out on the services you signed up for." She held up her sign-up sheet. Nearly every space was filled. The conflicted faces told me the retreat participants were thinking about the relaxing massages they'd be passing up if they went home now.

Glenn followed up with, "I'm planning to stay. The bus is already arranged. We'll be safe if we follow the deputy's suggestions. Besides, after what has happened, we all need to relax and meditate more than ever."

I toyed briefly with the idea that maybe Glenn or Heike had something to do with their boss's death. Working for a pushy, insensitive woman like Sasha had to be exhausting and infuriating. But I quickly dismissed the idea, at least where Glenn was concerned. He had well-developed coping techniques to deal with stress. Besides, he was one of those gentle souls who didn't get easily ruffled, blessed with the unflappable demeanor of the Buddha. Heike, on the other hand, wore her emotions on her sleeve and seemed far less in control of them. Could she have tired of Sasha's boorish behavior and used her strong hands to end the woman's life? While it seemed possible, if either she or Glenn found they couldn't tolerate working for Sasha, it was more likely they'd have simply found new work and quit their jobs at Third Eye, like reasonable people do. Not liking your boss didn't seem enough reason to kill her, especially when killing her while still employed by her would mean putting yourself out of a paycheck. There would have to be something more, some bigger reason, for me to think either of them was guilty.

The guests exchanged glances and arguments both for and against remaining at the lodge. Eventually, they all agreed to stay on-site and continue their retreat as originally planned. Glenn said he'd take over Sasha's scheduled classes.

Vera's lips pursed. "As per usual."

Several of the others offered reluctant nods, coupled with a cringe here and there.

Vera took their agreement as an implied prod to go on. "I've always liked Glenn's classes better anyway. Yoga is supposed to be about quiet reflection and the mind-body connection. Sasha always turned her practices into a pep rally."

Her words elicited more nods of agreement coupled with yet more cringes.

The matter settled, Glenn said, "I'm glad you all have decided to stay. I'll see you on the deck later for our deep-stretch class." He turned to me. "You should join us, Misty. Deep stretch is especially beneficial for us folks with a few years under our belts. Older bodies tend to lose flexibility."

A few years under my belt? I felt an urge to kick the leader of the morning's sun salutations where the sun doesn't shine. But instead, I forced a smile and said, "A stretch class sounds lovely."

CHAPTER 17

Then higher on the glistering Sun I gaz'd
Whose beams was shaded by the leafy tree,
The more I look'd, the more I grew amaz'd
And softly said, what glory's like to thee?
Soul of this world, this Universe's Eye,
No wonder, some made thee a Deity:
Had I not better known, (alas) the same had I.
—Anne Bradstreet (1650: *The Tenth Muse Lately
Sprung Up in America*)

Misty

Their discussion complete and the decision to remain made,
I returned to my desk. The joggers donned their running
shoes and left the lodge. Madman Maddox headed out, too,
a NASCAR ballcap on his head. Kendall hustled out the
door, too. The strap of her crossbody purse angled across
her chest from one direction, while the strap on her water
bottle crossed from the other. The two formed a distinct X
on her chest, as if marking her as a target. It struck me as
odd that Kendall seemed willing to venture out on her own
now, when a killer was on the loose, when previously she'd
been reluctant to take a single step without Sasha by her
side.

The phone on my desk rang with a call from outside the
lodge. I recognized the area code as Charlotte. I decided to

forgo the "beautiful Blue Ridge day" schtick, and simply said, "Mountaintop Lodge. How may I help you?"

The caller identified himself as a reporter with a television station in Charlotte. I supposed I shouldn't be surprised that he had contacted me by phone rather than driving all the way up here to get the scoop. By car, it would've been a four-hour round trip. "What can you tell me about the body that was found at your lodge? I understand the deceased was Sasha Ducharme-Carlisle, the owner of Third Eye Studio and Spa based here in Charlotte."

I didn't want to risk slipping and saying something I shouldn't, nor did I want to say "no comment" and sound suspicious or defensive. The mere thought that my lodge would be mentioned on the news in Charlotte in association with a murder caused my gut to twist. Charlotte and the surrounding suburbs were home to around a million people, many of whom came up to the mountains for vacation. Any negative publicity associated with my lodge could scare off potential guests and be devastating to my bottom line. Sasha's killer hadn't just taken her life, they might have taken my livelihood, too. After some quick thinking, I simply said, "Unfortunately, we know very little right now. But my heart goes out to her family and friends."

He confirmed the lodge's address and asked me for some basic facts. When the group had arrived. How long they planned to stay. How many people had come up for the retreat. I told him what I could and he thanked me for the information.

Once I was off the phone, I summoned Rocky and Brynn to the housekeeping closet for a surreptitious staff meeting. "This murder could put the lodge out of business," I said. "Especially if it isn't resolved quickly." I needed to get their thoughts, find out what they knew or had seen, do anything I could to help Deputy Highcloud solve the case. But it wasn't just my business interests that had me wanting to solve the case. Determining who the killer was would be a challenge, and I was always up for a challenge. Besides, being on-site at the lodge gave me an advantage the deputy didn't have. I was at the crime scene, quite possibly with the killer. "Do either of you have any thoughts? Suspicions? Theories?"

Rocky offered a paraphrased quote, which he attributed to Aristotle. "Every action is due to one of seven causes—chance, nature, compulsion, habit, reasoning, anger, or appetite."

"Okay," I said. "Which one of those reasons do you think made someone take Sasha's life?"

"Could be a combination of them," Rocky said. "A chance to fulfill an appetite."

"Meaning what, exactly?" I asked.

"Burglary," Rocky said. "Someone wanted her valuables and saw a chance to take them."

Brynn concurred. "I'm with Rocky. Someone went into Sasha's room to take her jewelry and the singing bowl, and something went wrong."

I pondered aloud. "That could make sense. After all, if someone had planned to kill her, there would have been easier ways to do it."

The killer could have followed her down the trail yesterday afternoon and taken her life in the woods. It would have been easy to hide her body somewhere on the forested mountainside. It might not have been found for days, if ever.

In light of this fact, it did seem more likely that the motive, at least initially, had been theft. There was just one problem . . .

"But none of the guests appears to be hurting for money," I said. None of the *current* guests, anyway. Anyone who could afford the studio's $1,700 retreat fee plus lodging and meals had to be reasonably well off. Sammie and Cole had been the only guests who weren't flush with cash. The mere thought broke my heart again. *Cole can't be the killer, can he?*

Brynn said, "You can't always tell when someone's got money troubles. Sometimes they fake it."

She had a point. Many people who appeared wealthy ended up in bankruptcy.

I realized then that maybe I'd put the cart before the horse. Here we were talking theories and motives, when we should be first collecting facts. "Did you notice anything awry in Sasha's room when you went in to clean it? Other than her missing jewelry and singing bowl?"

"Plenty," Brynn said. "She'd put recyclables in her trash bin again, for one. I had to sort them myself."

I couldn't quite keep the irritation from my voice. "I meant anything to do with her death, Brynn."

"Oh. Right. Well, her down pillow was on the floor and there were feathers everywhere. My first thought was that she and Kendall must've had a pillow fight." She rolled her eyes. "Those two are like teenagers."

She had a point. Both Sasha and Kendall seemed superficial, immature, and self-centered, all aspects of the typical teen.

Brynn continued. "There were smudges on the inside of

her back window, too. It looked like whoever opened it had her face cream on their hands. The weird thing was that there weren't any prints on the outside of the glass that I could see. The sun was coming up and shining through the window, so if there were prints on the outside, they should have been visible. I'd already cleaned the inside of the windows in her room before I knew anything was wrong. While I was talking to Deputy Highcloud, the policeman dusted for prints inside and out on both windows. He didn't seem to find any. There were also some crushed leaves and dirt on the floor just inside the back window. Of course, I'd cleaned that up already, too."

Hmm. "Leaves and dirt inside the room would indicate that someone had entered the window from outside and tracked the debris in." But how could they have come in from the outside without touching the outside of the window and leaving fingerprints? The only ways I could think of was if they'd worn gloves or if the window was already open.

Brynn had reached the same conclusion "My guess is Sasha had left her window open when she fell asleep, so whoever killed her was able to get in without having to open it themselves. The policeman emptied the contents of my vacuum into an evidence bag, too, dusty feathers and all."

I supposed they'd take a look at the matter, see if there was anything in it that might shed some light on the situation. But even though an open window would explain things, with Sasha suffering from a ragweed allergy I couldn't imagine her leaving her window ajar, especially on a windy night that was sure to stir up the allergen. *Could*

Brynn have wiped the glass clean in order to throw suspicion off herself?

Rocky ventured another theory. "Could be that someone went out their own window to pay Sasha a visit, and she let them into her room through hers. Someone who didn't want to be caught on a security camera going into the hotel room of another woman."

Though Rocky hadn't offered a name, it was clear who he was referring to, and I said the name aloud. "Madman."

Rocky's theory seemed viable. Even though Madman had rebuffed Sasha's advances in front of the others, he might have decided a midnight rendezvous didn't sound so bad. After all, the black hair I'd seen on his pillow said the two might have already engaged in intimate relations. Maybe he'd snuck out his window, made his way outside the lodge down to her room, and rapped on her glass until she woke, opened it, and let him in. Or maybe he'd phoned or texted her to arrange a booty call.

Could he have lost his temper again? Maybe hit her with something? If she'd threatened to reveal their tryst, he might have been driven to violence. Rocky said he hadn't noticed any injuries on Sasha, but she'd been wearing long-sleeved satin pajamas that covered most of her body. She could have had an injury that didn't show, maybe an abdominal wound.

"Sorry," Brynn said, "but that theory doesn't fly. Both of Sasha's windows were closed and locked when I went into her room."

The only way Sasha's windows could have been locked was if her killer dragged her outside, then returned to her room and left by a door, either the room's main door that

GETAWAY WITH MURDER   165

opened onto the hallway or the interior door that adjoined
Room 17, Kendall's room. After all, the killer couldn't have
locked Sasha's window from the outside. Those facts increased the possibility that someone staying at the hotel
had accessed her room. The obvious person was Kendall,
as she could make an easy, undetectable escape through
their adjoining door. The scratches we'd seen on the trim
on Kendall's side of the door might have been from her trying to lock Sasha's deadbolt and hide her own guilt. But, if
the killer wasn't Kendall, why would they have used Sasha's door and risked being caught on camera if going in
and out of her window was an option? Could they have
made the connection that the power being out would dis-
able the Wi-Fi and thus interrupt the camera feed, allowing
them to use Sasha's door without being caught on video?
Cole might have known. After all, he was a computer sci-
ence major. *Hmm.*

Locking the window had been a blunder, pointing fingers at the guests rather than a random homicidal maniac
who'd slipped in Sasha's window. Then again, Brynn was
the only one who could verify that the windows were truly
locked when she entered the room to clean it this morning.
Maybe she was lying about the windows being locked to
throw suspicion off herself. Maybe she'd come over to the
lodge last night, snuck in Sasha's window, and killed the
yoga instructor. Again, I considered the possibility that
she could have left the window unlocked after cleaning
the room yesterday, or after bringing the extra towels Sasha
had requested.

Still, even though this scenario was possible, it too
seemed far-fetched. Brynn had made her feelings about

Sasha clear. She considered the woman to be an insufferable twit. But Sasha would have been gone at the end of the week. There'd be no need to kill her. And if Brynn had planned to kill Sasha for some other unknown reason, such as in an attempt to steal her valuables, wouldn't she have tried to hide her disregard for the woman? And wouldn't she have refrained from pointing out that she'd noticed the bowl and jewelry were missing?

"Anything else?" I asked.

"No," Brynn said. "That's all I noticed."

When I looked to Rocky, he simply shrugged to indicate he knew nothing more, either.

"Are we done here?" Brynn asked. When I replied in the affirmative, she took a step backward. "I'm going to round up some sage and smudge the lodge. This place needs to be cleansed ASAP."

Rocky went out to his truck and drove off to take care of a client who needed a storm door installed. I'd given him my business credit card and asked him to stop at the building supply store for exterior security cameras and additional outdoor lighting. I hoped the cameras would serve as a deterrent if the killer was thinking about striking again. Worst-case scenario, the cameras might record the killer making a second attempt to steal from my guests or take a life. It would be much more difficult now that everyone had their guard up and had moved their valuables into their room safes.

While I swept and dusted the great room, Brynn burned her sage again. She waved the feather and smudge stick around like a fairy who'd traded her magic wand for an oversized cigarette. As before, she tapped the ash into her smudge bowl. Unlike last time, though, this time there were guests to witness her ritual. Norma Jean watched Brynn from her spot on the sofa, her expression equally intrigued and apprehensive. Glenn, on the other hand, closed his eyes and breathed deeply, inhaling the sage. I supposed it couldn't hurt him. The smoke wasn't thick. Joaquín did the same, though he took things further, raising his hands and emitting a low, elongated hum in what appeared to be his own personal meditation session.

After she'd finished smudging the lodge, Brynn rounded up her housekeeping cart to clean the vacant rooms. I did the same. I'd completed two rooms when a *knock* made me look up at the door of Vera's room, which I was currently dusting. Patty stood in the doorway. "Hey, Misty." She glanced around the space, her head bobbing in approval. "Spick and span. Getting the hang of things?"

"Slowly but surely," I replied. "I can now strip and remake a bed in two minutes flat."

She glanced down the hall in both directions before whispering, "I figured you'd want to hear about my conversation with Deputy Highcloud."

Would I ever! I especially wanted to know about the Greasy Griddle's security camera footage. *Could it solve Sasha's death?* "You figured right."

Leaving the cart in the room, I exited and waved for Patty to follow me to my room at the end of the hall where our conversation could take place without anyone else overhearing.

As we stepped inside, Yeti stood up from the windowsill, stretched, and hopped down, walking over to her food bowl and looking up at me. I knew she wouldn't give me a moment's peace until I served her a snack, which she might or might not turn up her nose at. The moody little beast was finicky and unpredictable. I rounded up her box of treats and shook a few into the bowl. She sniffed at them, paused for a moment to consider whether or not they suited her, and evidently decided she'd deign to eat them today. While she crunched her way through the snacks, I asked Patty about the security camera footage from the diner. "What did it show?"

"A few deer wandering through the parking lot and a car that made a U-turn and headed back onto the parkway in the opposite direction."

"That's it?"

"That's it. Until Rocky came out with Molasses while it was still dark and then left with the newlyweds."

"You're sure? I was hoping for more."

"The resolution wasn't crystal clear," she said, "but between the lights on my diner and the lighting along the front of your lodge, we would've easily seen movement if someone walked past or came out one of the front windows. A few of your guests opened their windows, but the only thing that went in or out was air."

"What about the doors at the end of the wings? And the windows along the sides?"

"From the camera angle, we could see the door and windows on the east wing, but not the west. Other than the white-haired lady with the little dog, nobody came out of the east wing door all night."

Though it would have been more conclusive if the camera had provided footage along the west wing, too, it seemed improbable someone would have entered or exited on that side given that Sasha's room was all the way at the other end of the lodge. It would have been a long way to walk. *Criminals prefer to be quick, don't they?*

I mulled over what Patty had told me. The lack of movement along the front of the lodge meant that none of the guests in the rooms that faced the parking lot had come out of their window to get to Sasha's. Madman's room was on the front side of the lodge. So were Glenn's, Vera's, and both of the joggers, as well as several others who'd raised no suspicion. Rocky's room was on the front, too. Patty's video affirmed that the man could be trusted, just as I'd thought.

I remembered the long, dark hair I'd seen on Madman's pillow when I'd cleaned his room on Monday. "What about Sunday night? Did y'all watch the video recorded then?"

"We did," she said. "It was the same thing. We saw some of the windows being opened in the rooms on the front of the lodge, but no one climbed in or out of them."

I considered the ramifications. The fact that nobody had snuck out of a window on the front of the lodge increased the likelihood that the killer was a guest with a room on the backside. The room Sammie and Cole had occupied was on the back of the lodge. So was Joaquín's. Heike's, too. I pondered again Heike's extreme reaction to Sasha's death. It would be normal to feel shocked, but she'd been nearly inconsolable. *Could her intense reaction be the result of guilt?*

I looked to my new friend. "Be extra careful closing up at night. The killer took some of Sasha's valuables. If they're after money, they might try to hit your diner next."

Patty patted the pocket of her bright red apron. "If they come, I'm ready for them."

"Oh yeah?"

She reached into the pocket and pulled out a pointy, two-pronged meat fork. "I figured this was my best choice of weapon. It's lightweight and versatile. Depending on how I wield it, I could take out an eye, jab the killer in the throat, or disembowel him." She demonstrated the three moves like an expert fencer, bringing the fork down for the eye, up for the throat, and straight ahead for the gut.

The thought that Patty might have to use the weapon made my stomach queasy. Still, I was glad she'd made some sort of preparations.

"What have you got to defend *yourself* with?" she asked.

"I've been so busy trying to figure out who the killer might be, I haven't even considered a weapon."

"Take this, then." She handed the meat fork over to me. "I've got four others just like it back at the diner."

I clutched the fork to my chest. "Thanks for looking out for me, Patty."

She lifted a shoulder. "That's what friends do."

"Let me return the favor," I said. "If you find yourself alone at the diner late at night, you call me. I'll come over and make sure you get to your car safely. There's safety in numbers."

"It's a deal."

I reached an arm out and gave her an awkward, sidewise hug so as to avoid poking her with the meat fork.

After Patty left, I lay the meat fork within easy reach on top of the cart, and finished cleaning Vera and Vivian's room. The next room up was Madman's. Though I knew now that he hadn't snuck out of his window to get to Sasha's room, there was still the possibility that he'd taken advantage of the power outage to scurry unrecorded down the hall and kill her. He had what seemed to me to be a good motive. If the two had indeed slept together, as the hair on his pillow would suggest, Sasha could blow things up between him and his girlfriend if she spilled the beans. As pushy as Sasha was, maybe she'd given him some type of ultimatum. He might have felt trapped, overreacted out of desperation. *Who knows?*

I took advantage of my time in Madman's room to poke around for clues. I wasn't just housekeeping, I was house*creeping*. Nothing caught my eye. It wasn't a surprise. If there had been any incriminating evidence in here, Deputy Highcloud would have seized it.

I continued on my rounds, skipping my own room, which I cleaned on my own time. Eventually, I'd made my way to the room Sammie and Cole had occupied. I unlocked the door with more than a little trepidation. Though the two were long gone now, just the thought that a possible killer had stayed in this room last night felt like bad juju. *I'm starting to sound like Brynn and Glenn.*

I left the door open, which was standard procedure for hotel housekeepers, both for their own safety and to let guests see that they were not rifling through personal belongings. However, I left the cart in the doorway to prevent anyone else from entering the space.

As I went to empty the trash and recycling bins by the coffee bar, I noted that, unlike Sasha, Sammie and Cole had properly sorted their refuse items. Their consideration seemed like an omen. *They're good kids,* I told myself.

They can't possibly have anything to do with Sasha's death. Once they were located, they'd have a perfectly good explanation for Cole's suspicious internet search and their early departure, right? But even as I tried to convince myself, a cloud of doubt settled over me.

I wiped down all of the surfaces in the room, returned the television remote control to the bedside table, and spritzed the mirror and window glass, wiping them until they gleamed. After changing the bed linens, I walked into the bathroom.

I gasped. There, on the counter, lay a white plastic pregnancy test stick with a blue tip. The word in the indicator box provided both the results of Sammie's test and a motive for Cole to have taken Sasha's property—*Pregnant.*

Chapter 18

The woods are lovely, dark and deep,
But I have promises to keep,
And miles to go before I sleep,
And miles to go before I sleep.
> —Robert Frost (1923: "Stopping by Woods on a
> Snowy Evening")

Misty

When Jack and I had learned I was pregnant with our first child, Jack was initially elated, as was I. Though he remained excited, I noticed a marked change in him over the ensuing weeks. He became more serious about his work, feeling the pressure of providing for his growing family. The baby was a blessing, of course, but J.J. was also a responsibility, and one Jack didn't take lightly. Cole likely felt the same way. The pregnancy would explain why he'd looked so serious when he'd ventured out onto the deck last night. It would also explain why Sammie had gone to bed early. Pregnancy could be exhausting.

Had Cole snuck down to Sasha's room with the intent of taking her valuable bowl and jewelry? He'd seen Sasha on the deck, drinking glass after glass of wine. Maybe he'd thought he could slip easily in and out of her room without her knowledge, but then she'd awoken and confronted him. He could have killed her to cover his tracks. He could have snuck in her window—if indeed she'd left it open—then returned to his room via the hallway while the power was out. Or, if he'd discovered the keys on the floor in the hall, he might have tried the keys in the various doors, hoping to sneak in and grab some valuables while the guest slept, unaware of the intrusion. Cole could have discovered the keys worked on Sasha's room and slipped inside, a crime of opportunity as Deputy Highcloud had theorized. If only the keys would turn up, the crime lab could check them for prints. I wondered whether Cole even knew that Sasha's singing bowl was valuable. If Kendall hadn't told me how much the thing cost, I certainly wouldn't have guessed it was worth so much.

The fact that a wadded-up tissue and the packaging for a new tube of toothpaste were also on the counter told me that law enforcement had upended the trash can on the counter to search its contents and were already aware of this pregnancy test. It seemed they'd reached the same conclusion I had, that the positive result could have provided a motive for the theft and murder. Had Deputy Highcloud seen the test? I assumed so, though I wondered why she hadn't taken it into evidence. No detail seemed to get past her but, just in case it had been an oversight to leave the test behind, I slid it into one of the small plastic bags used to line the trash bins. I'd stash it in the safe in my room until I could speak with her about it.

The thought of Jack and me learning of my first pregnancy reminded me that I had yet to contact him and tell him what had happened here. Better he learn it from me than hear about it on the news and freak out. Same for the boys, though I knew they paid little attention to their news feeds. Unless something came across Instagram or TikTok, they wouldn't hear about it, especially in the insulated worlds of their college campuses.

I sent a text to Jack and the boys. *A woman was killed at the lodge last night. I'm fine. Sheriff's office is investigating. Looks like a robbery gone wrong.* I didn't tell them it could have been an inside job by one of the other guests—a guest that remained in my lodge. No sense making them worry any more than they already would. *Don't worry,* I added. *I'm taking precautions.*

I'd barely hit SEND when my phone rang with an incoming call from Jack. I gave him a quick rundown.

"I'm coming up to the lodge," he said. "I don't want you there alone."

"I appreciate the offer," I told him. "But you've got your job to do." Admittedly, there was also a part of me that didn't want Jack to meet Rocky. I was afraid Jack might sense that there was some sort of vibe between me and my handyman. Stupid, really. Jack and I were divorced now. I had every right to a romantic attraction, to engage in a bit of innocent flirtation. Still, it would be awkward. And, as a divorced woman, I needed to learn to stand on my own two feet—or at least to get by without the help of my ex. "I'll be okay. I'll keep a hiking pole by my bed. Besides, the killer would be crazy to try anything again. Everyone's on alert now."

Jack debated the usefulness of a hollow pole as a defensive weapon, as well as my risk assessment, but eventually he acquiesced. "If you change your mind," he said, "just call. I'll come right up."

"Thanks, Jack."

Texts came in from my sons, too. *Who knew they could*

actually respond so quickly? It usually took them hours, if not days, to reply to my messages.

J.J.'s came in first. It included an emoji of a head exploding along with the words *Be careful!*

Mitch's text read *HOLY @^#*!*

I'd heard of potty mouth. But was there such a thing as potty keyboarding? I supposed I couldn't get on to him for cussing when he'd merely used symbols.

I finished with Sammie and Cole's room, stashed the pregnancy test in the safe in my room, and cleaned the remaining guest rooms in the west wing. I was rolling the cart back up the hall when Madman returned to the lodge. He stopped to talk to Joaquín in the lobby. According to their conversation, he'd spent the afternoon drinking iced tea, eating apple pie, and discussing all things NASCAR with local fans at the Greasy Griddle. When he turned to come up the hall, his gaze locked on me, bearing more heat than an engine after a race. I offered him a smile, but he brushed past me without a word. It was unsettling. I decided to chalk his demeanor up to immaturity and the strange mood permeating the lodge now that Sasha had been found dead here.

Brynn had already finished the east wing and was watering the plants in the pots out front. Thirty minutes remained in her shift, but there were no other immediate tasks requiring attention, and the day had been difficult and exhausting. She'd also had to work extra hard to clean the graphite fingerprint powder off the windows and shutters in Sasha's room. It had taken quite a bit of scrubbing.

"You can go on home," I told her when she walked back

inside. "I can handle anything that comes up in the next half hour."

"Be careful tonight," she warned. "I'm sensing an evil energy here that the smudging couldn't eradicate. I'll bring my crystals tomorrow and try some spells."

"But you're not scheduled to work the next two days," I reminded her.

"I know," she said. "Don't worry. I won't consider it work time and expect to be paid for it. But I have to do something. I want you, Rocky, and the guests to be safe. Myself, too."

While I didn't think Brynn's pagan magic could truly protect the lodge or the people within, I supposed it couldn't hurt anything, either. I could understand her wanting to help. What more could she offer than a plea to a higher power or an incantation or two? I wanted to feel like I was doing something to help with the matter, too. That's why I was trying to put the clues together on my own.

Then again, maybe I *could* offer more. After all, I had always been a problem solver and a sleuth of sorts. Whenever Jack or one of the boys misplaced something around the house, I was the one to find it, piecing together the minutes before they'd last seen the item to determine where it had been left. When my boys tried to hide the naughty things they'd done, such as sneaking a sugary snack before bedtime, I literally followed the crumbs to their secret stash of Oreos secreted behind their favorite sci-fi series on their bookshelf. And when J.J. accidentally spilled bleach on the black cummerbund he was required to wear along with a tuxedo for the school orchestra concert, I'd improvised with my Spanx waist cincher. No one had noticed the switch. Well, no one but my son, who had trouble mustering enough breath to blow his horn with the fabric squashing his organs.

Once Brynn had gone, I returned to my room, gave Yeti some attention, and warmed up a bowl of soup in the microwave for my dinner. I ate the soup while watching the news. The cable station, which was based in Charlotte, provided only a brief report of the murder. The anchor stated that the owner of the Third Eye Studio & Spa had been found deceased on a yoga retreat at a mountain lodge, but he didn't provide the name of the inn, thank goodness. The developing story would be updated as details became available.

After I'd eaten, I changed into a T-shirt, flip-flops, and a pair of yoga pants I'd bought for lazy-day comfort, not exercise. Glenn was right. A deep-stretch class would do me good and, after fretting about the murder all day, I could use a positive distraction. I didn't have any of the equipment I'd need, though, so I tucked my credit card into the small pocket on my stretchy pants. I knew Heike had one of those phone attachments to skim my card for payment. I'd seen it in her room when she'd given me my massage. *Had that only been yesterday?* It felt like eons ago now. So much had happened since then. So much had gone wrong.

It was nearing seven o'clock and the students were starting to set up outside as I walked down the hall to Rocky's room and knocked. He opened the door and ran his eyes over my clothing. "You doing the class?"

"Yeah. I was hoping maybe you'd join in, too."

"I suppose it couldn't hurt me none. Give me two minutes to change into something more comfortable, and I'll meet you out there."

He closed the door to get changed, and I walked down the hall to wait for him in the great room. I rounded up two yoga mats from the pop-up store Sasha and Kendall had stocked and found the price on the sheet they'd posted. *$75 each? Ouch.* The price tag seemed a bit high, but I wasn't about to haggle over it with Glenn. I knew it was Sasha who'd set the price, not him.

Glenn walked up the hall with his boho bag slung over his shoulder. His mat peeked out of it as if it were an oversized newspaper and he were an overaged paperboy.

"Rocky and I are going to join your stretch class." I held my credit card out to him. "This is for our mats."

He waved a dismissive hand. "I can't take that in good conscience. The markup on those mats is excessive. Sasha ordered them in bulk and they cost only a small fraction of what the studio sold them for. Consider them my gift to you two."

Glenn turned to the shelf and pulled out two foam blocks, two long woven straps, and two blankets. "You'll need these things, too. In fact, I think I'll offer all of this stuff to the class. After what's happened, I can't imagine that whoever buys the studio will continue to use a logo with Sasha's eye in it."

So, I had been right. The green eye in the Third Eye Studio & Spa logo was hers. "Thanks, Glenn." I took the other items from him. "This is very generous of you."

He continued out to the deck, where he advised the class to help themselves to the remaining merchandise. "It will give you all a memento to remember Sasha by."

The group came inside and solemnly selected items from the shelves before returning to the deck.

Rocky came up the hall in a pair of classic gray sweat-pants and a T-shirt advertising a brand of tools. Molasses trod along with him. I handed him the mat, block, blanket, and strap.

As he took them from me, he said, "I didn't realize yoga required so much equipment." He unrolled the strap. "I don't even know what this stuff is for."

"You'll see." Though I didn't attend yoga class on a reg-ular basis, I'd gone to a practice here and there, and knew a little about how things were done.

We walked out to the deck and set up at the back of the group. Mo flopped down on the deck nearby, but kept his head up to watch us. Heike took a space next to the dog, reaching out a hand to chuck his furry chin in greeting. The deck was full tonight, everyone in attendance. *Everyone, that is, except Kendall.*

I hadn't seen Kendall since she'd hurried out the door late this morning, alone, with just her water bottle and purse. Had she returned while I was cleaning, and was now holed up in her room? I glanced over at the back of the east wing. No lights were on in the second room from the end, or any of the other rooms, for that matter. The sun had slipped behind the trees and the back of the lodge was in full shade. The shutters were closed inside her window, too. If Kend-all had returned, she was sitting in very dim lighting.

Once we were all seated with our legs crossed on our mats, Glenn greeted the group in that slow, near-hypnotic voice of his. "Welcome, everyone. Today we lost our friend, our teacher, a fellow traveler on life's journey. I suggest we dedicate this practice to Sasha. Let's all close our eyes and spend a moment in silence to offer her spirit a safe passage to its next destination."

As I sat with my eyes closed, the hair on the back of my neck stood on end. I felt the uneasy sensation of being watched. I opened my eyes to mere slits. *Yikes!* My instincts hadn't been wrong. Madman Maddox stared at me from across the deck, his eyes wide open, his lips pressed into a firm line. *If looks could kill . . .*

My eyes snapped open of their own accord, and our gazes locked for a few seconds. What was the guy angry about and why did he seem to be directing that anger toward me? My mind went back to Rocky's earlier quote from Aristotle, the one that said every action has its roots in chance, nature, compulsion, habit, reasoning, anger, or appetite. While Madman seemed angry at me now, other than a persistent glare he'd taken no action yet. *Would he?* If so, what would the action be and when might he take it? Had he been angry at Sasha for some reason, too? Had that anger caused him to do something vile and violent?

When a loud rustle of the trees drew Madman's fiery gaze away, I closed my eyes again and thought things over. Nature, compulsion, and habit seemed to be interrelated to me, as well as appetite. If it was in someone's nature to kill, they'd be compelled to do it, maybe make a habit of it, have an appetite for it. Madman's confrontation with his fellow driver after the race could indicate a violent nature that might compel him to act aggressively, even brutally. But, as far as I knew, he'd had only the one conflict at the track, so his aggression didn't necessarily seem to be a habit. Of course, there could be a lot more going on behind the scenes than had been revealed. It wasn't unusual for celebrities and people in positions of power to engage in cover-ups, to keep sordid details out of public knowledge.

I wasn't aware of anyone else in the group who had a violent or thieving nature, who was compelled to kill or steal, who made a habit of hurting or taking things from others. Then again, I didn't know this group well at all. Could Sasha's death have been the result not of an appetite for valuables or violence, but something sexual in nature? Had her death been some type of erotic game gone wrong? The thought made my skin crawl and filled my stomach with acid.

There was also the possibility that someone had killed Sasha by chance, that the crime was one of opportunity as Deputy Highcloud seemed to suspect. Someone could have come upon her keys and seen them, quite literally, as an opening to rob Sasha of her riches. If that was indeed the case, which of my guests had found the keys and seized the chance to access Sasha's room?

Glenn ended the moment of silence and led us through a series of stretches on our mats. Though my muscles were tight, they rejoiced with the poses and movements as if awakening from a long slumber, and I could feel a positive energy flowing back into my body. I would direct that positive energy to finding Sasha's killer.

When the class ended, I glanced once again at Kendall's window. *Still dark*. My guts squirmed. Earlier I'd been suspicious that she'd been gone so long, but now I'd begun to worry about her. What if she wasn't the killer, but was instead another potential victim? What if the killer had gone after Kendall, too? What if she was lying dead somewhere in a ditch? And why, when we worry that someone has died, do we always assume they end up in a ditch?

Rocky seemed to sense my upset. He stepped closer as the class filtered back inside. "What's wrong, Misty?"

"It's Kendall," I said. "She left earlier with just her purse and a water bottle, and I don't think she's come back yet. There are no lights on in her room."

Rocky glanced over at her window, too, his jaw flexing when he saw that it was dark.

I wouldn't forgive myself if I didn't do everything in my power to stop another tragedy. "I'm going to call her room."

We gathered up our things and Rocky followed me to the registration desk, where I dialed her room. There was still no answer after five rings. I pulled up Kendall's personal information on the computer and dialed her cell. It rang three times and went to voicemail. I left her a message. "Hi, Kendall. It's Misty Murphy from the lodge. I haven't seen you since late morning and just wanted to make sure you're okay. Give me a call back when you get a chance. Thanks."

Having returned their mats to their rooms, the guests ventured back into the great room. I asked each of them whether they'd seen or heard from Kendall since she'd left the lodge earlier. None had.

When I posed the question to Joaquín, he ran his fingers thoughtfully over his mustache. "Maybe she's in police custody."

Though Kendall had left the lodge on her own, I knew

that Deputy Highcloud's decision not to arrest her didn't mean the deputy thought she was innocent. It only meant that there wasn't enough evidence—perhaps, *yet*—to provide grounds for making an arrest. Of course, that could have changed after Kendall left the lodge. Maybe the deputy had called Kendall and arrested her somewhere off-site. But wouldn't I have been notified? Maybe not. Maybe they were still interrogating her, or hadn't finished booking her yet.

I gave it another hour before I repeated my attempts to contact Kendall. As before, there was no answer from her room, no answer when I called her cell. I looked to Rocky, who sat in the great room reading the latest amusing release from North Carolina author David Sedaris. *I'll have to borrow it from him when he's done.* Rocky had stuck close by me this evening, seeming to realize I could use the moral support. He looked up from his book.

I pointed down the hall. "I'm going to check Kendall's room." I doubted she'd snuck back into the lodge unseen, but it was possible. Besides, there might be something in her room that would tell me where she'd gone, maybe one of the tourist brochures or a note she'd jotted down somewhere.

Rocky followed me down to Kendall's room. I rapped on the door. "Kendall? It's Misty." I leaned in to listen. There was no sound. Just to be sure I didn't accidentally walk in on her, I tried a second time. Still no response. Using the master key, I opened the door and switched on the light. The room looked like the ones in the west wing had today when I'd gone in to clean them. Not quite the natural state a person would leave their guest room in, but rather with some of their items purposefully arranged on the tops of dressers or tables to be examined or photographed by law enforcement.

To my surprise, Kendall's cell phone sat on her bedside table. She must have placed it there before coming to sun salutations. She'd probably been so emotionally discombobulated when she left the lodge later this morning that she'd forgotten to take it with her.

A pill bottle stood on her dresser. I went over and read the label. It was Clarinex, the same drug that had been found in Sasha's room. I knew it was a popular allergy medication, so I supposed it wasn't surprising both women would have a prescription for it.

Seeing pamphlets on top of her table, I strode over to take a look. They were fanned out across the tabletop, but the one on top was for the Blowing Rock. The fabled mountaintop rock sat above a valley known for a strong upwind. As legend had it, when a heartbroken Cherokee brave had leaped from the rock, the wind blew him back up into his lover's arms. People had even reported seeing snow falling upward at the rock. It was a beautiful, mystical place, and the legend of the brave being given a second chance at life could have drawn Kendall to it. But the rock was twenty-eight miles and a forty-five-minute drive from here. She would've needed a way to get there. I didn't see a car pick her up at the lodge. How could she have summoned a ride later when she'd forgotten to take her phone with her?

Her phone lit up as it received a notification. *Is she getting a text from someone? An alert of some sort?*

I walked over and read the screen. It was a push notification from her fitness tracker, telling her she'd climbed three stories, taken 15,378 steps, and walked over seven miles today. "She's alive," I told Rocky. "And she's making a run for it!"

CHAPTER 19

All things in nature occur mathematically.
> —René Descartes (1640: Letter to Pere
> Marin Mersenne)

Misty

The instant the significance of the notification hit me, I dialed Deputy Highcloud and gave her the news. "Kendall McFadden is on the run! She's heading down Beech Mountain Parkway."

"How do you know that?"

I explained about the push notification her fitness tracker had sent to her cell phone. The information indicated that Kendall had climbed only three floors, yet walked thousands of steps and several miles. The lodge sat just past the pinnacle of the mountain, a short way down the backside. The data showed that she'd walked from the lodge to the top of the mountain where the business district sat—three floors' climb—then continued past the town on Beech Mountain Parkway, which wound its way downhill in that direction. If she'd tried to escape down the less developed backside of the mountain, she would have climbed more than three floors, as the roads here went up and down at various points on their more gradual descent.

The walk couldn't have been an easy trek for her, either.

The parkway was a narrow, two-lane road with no shoulder, dangerous to travel on foot. She'd have to keep an eye out for cars, some of which tended to swing into oncoming lanes when taking the curves too fast, or she'd have to pick her way along the edge of the steep woods. Of course, these facts accounted for why it had taken her so long to cover the distance. I knew from walking with friends back in Raleigh that it took only about twenty minutes to cover a flat mile. If we weren't up a mountain, Kendall could be long gone by now.

The deputy seemed to perform her own mental calculations. "If you're right, she'll be coming up on Highway 105 soon. That puts her in Avery County. I'll get in touch with their sheriff's department and see about rounding her up before she decides to hitch a ride with someone. I already had some more questions for her myself."

"You did?"

"The blue tablet that was in Sasha's room is a prescription allergy drug called Clarinex."

I'd already puzzled that part out on my own, but I didn't admit it. I didn't want her to realize I'd surreptitiously watched as Officer Hardy had snapped pics of the pill to send to the medical examiner.

The deputy said, "You're supposed to avoid alcohol when you're taking it, so I wasn't sure if Sasha's drinking was just her being reckless or whether someone might have given the drug to her to try to knock her out. I found Sasha's health insurance card in her wallet and contacted her carrier. She's never been prescribed Clarinex. But you know who has?"

"Kendall."

"That's right. Either she gave Sasha some of her prescription pills, which is a drug violation, or she used them herself to either kill Sasha with the drug-alcohol combination, or to sedate her so she'd be easier to kill."

"The medical examiner still hasn't determined the cause of death then?"

"They've narrowed it down. Preliminary results showed bruising inside Sasha's lips and around her nose. That, plus the bloodshot eyes and the feather on her cheek indicate she was likely smothered with her pillow."

What a horrifying way to go. Yet, while the manner of death was horrible, it was also unexpected. "So, she wasn't poisoned?" *Could Cole be in the clear?*

"We can't rule that out yet. We're still waiting on the bloodwork. We're expecting to see high levels of carbon dioxide, which is a sign of asphyxiation, but only the tests will show whether Sasha had Clarinex or poison in her system."

I mulled things over for a moment. "For what it's worth, Kendall seemed to be legitimately trying to stop Sasha from drinking so much last night." Of course, at the time I'd assumed she was annoyed that her friend was hogging her expensive wine, but could she have also been afraid Sasha might come to harm with a bad drug interaction? In my mind, I could see the two of them sitting on the deck, Sasha raising her glass, the fitness tracker on her wrist . . .

Oh my gosh! Sasha had told me that her tracker provided sleep data. She'd been wearing it with her pajamas Monday morning when she'd handed me her mat, water bottle, and the singing bowl through her door and asked me to set them up for sun salutations. *She would've been wearing it last night, too, then, right?* "Sasha has a fitness tracker, too. The exact same kind as Kendall, except Sasha's is black. She told me it records her sleep data. If she was wearing it last night, it could tell us when she was attacked."

If she'd been attacked during the time the Wi-Fi and camera feed were out, the information wouldn't be helpful. But if she were attacked at a different time, it could help us figure out what might have happened. And if her data showed activity at precisely the same moment that Kendall's also reported activity, we could identify the killer! I shared my thoughts with the deputy.

"There's just one problem," she said. "Sasha wasn't wearing a fitness tracker when we took her body in. We collected everything from her room and there wasn't a tracker there, either."

Had the killer purposely removed it? Maybe the killer thought that by hiding the tracker, they could cover their tracks. Because Kendall wore the exact same type of device, it would seem she'd be the most likely to be aware of it. But if she'd kept her head together enough to take the fitness tracker off Sasha, you'd think she'd have the sense to remove her own when she decided to flee from law enforcement. I suggested that the tracker data might still be revealing. "Maybe even knowing when it was removed would be helpful."

"You've got a point," the deputy agreed. "I'm going to see if I can locate Kendall, then I'll swing by the lodge to pick up her cell phone. Once we get the details on the type of tracker they had, we'll take a look at Sasha's account and see what activity it reported."

We ended our call. Though Rocky had heard my side

of the conversation and pieced most of the discussion together, I filled him in on the medical examiner's preliminary findings. "It looks like Sasha was smothered with her down pillow."

"Whoa." He took a shaky breath. "That's brutal."

"It seems odd that Deputy Highcloud didn't find her fitness tracker. I'm thinking maybe the killer took it off her." I glanced over at the pillows on Kendall's bed and narrowed my eyes in thought. "Unless Sasha was already unconscious, I'd suspect she'd try to fight off whoever was holding the pillow to her face. The tracker could've come off then." I continued to think aloud. "But if that's how it played out, Officer Hardy and Deputy Hightower would have found it in her room. Hmm. Maybe it got loosened while she fought off her attacker, and fell off afterward, while she was being dragged to the deck."

Rocky said, "Let's take a look. I'll round up a flashlight."

We left Kendall's room. After Rocky grabbed a flashlight from the toolbox in his room, we stepped across the hall to Sasha's door. My master key at the ready, I hesitated just a brief moment, recoiling at the thought that we were about to enter a murder scene. Seeming to sense my horror, Rocky put a hand on my shoulder. When I looked up at him, he said, "You can do this, Misty."

Buoyed by his faith in me, I inserted the key into the lock and turned it. *Click.* I pushed the door open and switched on the light. The room was far less eerie and intimidating than I'd expected. With all of Sasha's personal items removed and Brynn having thoroughly cleaned it, it resembled any other guest room. The only difference was the scent of sage, which still hung heavy in the air. Brynn must have spent extra time smudging this space.

Rocky and I took a moment to double-check around the bed to make sure law enforcement hadn't overlooked the fitness tracker somewhere. They hadn't. It wasn't stuck between the bed and the wall, or shoved between the mattress and box spring. Rocky walked over to the window, pulled the shutters back, and unlocked it. He slid it open, letting in the cool evening air, removed the screen, and stuck his head out, shining the flashlight down on the ground. I walked over and stood shoulder to shoulder with him, my gaze moving along with his flashlight as it played back and forth across the dirt, rocks, and grass. A few feet from the lodge, the rhododendrons and fresh dirt covered the pipe. The narrow channel drain could not be covered by dirt, of course, as rainwater needed to be able to flow into it to be properly diverted. Rocky had painted the metal brown so that it would blend in with the surroundings and not draw the eye. It wouldn't have caught mine if I hadn't known it was there.

I pushed the window up as far as it would go and climbed out. Rocky came after me. I walked over to the channel drain and peeked down inside. A few dead, dark leaves had made their way into it, lying in a wet layer at the bottom. But there, barely visible on top of them, was a black strap with a broken clasp. *Sasha's fitness tracker!* Thank goodness it hadn't rained today or the device might have been washed through the new pipe and off the cliff.

"We'll need something long and thin to fish it out," Rocky said. "I'll go get a screwdriver."

"No need," I said. "I've got something better. I'll be right back." Rather than crawl through the window, I used the door at the end of the east wing to go back inside. I hustled down to the housekeeping closet and retrieved the meat fork Patty had given me. Utensil in hand, I rushed back outside. It took a little trial and error, but we finally managed to insert a tine into one of the small holes on the strap and finagle the tracker out between the narrow slits in the drain. The only question now was, would this little strap be the key to solving Sasha's death?

Though some of my guests gathered on the deck tonight, the mood was dark and somber, not light and jovial like it had been the night before. People were quiet, sipping their drinks and staring out at the dark woods or up at the sky as if looking for answers neither could provide. I walked over to the Greasy Griddle and bought three pies for the group in an attempt to lift everyone's spirits, but even copious amounts of sugar, vanilla, and fruit filling seemed incapable of offering the smallest consolation. I'd hoped this group would make happy memories on the mountain, but they'd be going home with horrid recollections instead.

Rocky took me aside. "If you're frightened, Molasses and I would be happy to sleep in your room with you tonight. I could bunk on the foldout."

I bit my lip. It was a thoughtful offer, but we hardly knew each other. It would be awkward. Not to mention potentially fraught with sexual tension.

My thoughts must have been obvious, because he said, "I know what you're thinking. This isn't a come-on. I'd never be able to perform with you wearing that god-awful nightgown." A roguish grin tugged at his lips.

I crossed my arms over my chest and gave him a sour look. "Thanks a lot."

His face became more serious. "If you change your mind, you know where to find me. I was pretty good at comforting my girls when they were scared. All it took was a few bedtime stories and some cuddling to distract them."

I had to admit, the cuddling sounded tempting. When I said "Thanks" this time, it was sincere. Rocky seemed to have a protective nature. While I liked to think I could take care of myself, it was nice to know someone was there for me if I needed him. I returned to my desk and he retook his seat in the great room. Molasses flopped belly-down in front of the fireplace, furry legs fully splayed to enjoy the cool stone floor.

I was sitting at the desk a half hour later when Molasses raised his head and looked to the front of the lodge, his ears pricked. I turned to see the Watauga Sheriff's Department SUV pull to a stop outside the doors. Deputy Highcloud was in the driver's seat. Another deputy sat in the passenger seat, and Kendall sat in the back. Her head was down and she was weeping so hard the front of her shirt was soaked. When Deputy Highcloud entered the lodge, several in the group sat up and took notice. They erupted in whispers, some even going to the front windows to get a better look at their classmate sitting in the vehicle outside.

I slid off my stool and circled around the desk to meet up with the deputy. "Where'd you find her?"

"Just past the turnoff for Sugar Mountain. I half expected her to make a break for it, but she looked almost relieved when I pulled up. She might have just been tired from all that walking. She's probably got blisters. As soon as I got her into the SUV, she burst into tears. She said her friend's death is her fault."

My mouth dropped. "She confessed?"

"Seems that way, but she's blubbering so hard we can't understand her. I told her to hold her thoughts until we get to the sheriff's department so we can do things right. I'd like to get her on video in case she changes her mind later and tries to recant."

While I was sad to know that the friendship between the two women had reached a tragic end, I was glad to know that this case might soon be put to rest. Maybe then my guests could enjoy the rest of their retreat. "Rocky and I found Sasha's fitness tracker in the drain out back. It must have fallen off while she was being dragged to the deck. I'll go get it for you."

I scurried to my room to retrieve both the tracker and the pregnancy test from my in-room safe. Yeti opened her eyes to see what I was doing, but didn't find my actions interesting enough to warrant lifting her head from her comfy pillow. Of course, she had no idea my hands held evidence in a murder investigation. I returned to the lobby. As I handed the items over to the deputy, I said, "I saw the pregnancy test in Sammie and Cole's room when I was cleaning. I bagged it and set it aside for you. I've been wondering why you didn't take it into evidence. I thought it could be important."

"It could," she said. "But there were two of them. Sammie must've wanted to make sure she didn't get a false positive, so she took the test twice. I was running low on evidence bags, so I just took the one. But thanks for rounding it up." She pointed down the hall. "Is Kendall's phone still in her room? I need to take it into evidence, too." She offered a mirthless chuckle. "She might need it to call a defense attorney when I'm done with it."

We walked down the hall and I used my master key to let Deputy Highcloud into Kendall's room. She gathered Kendall's phone and charger, and tucked them into the pocket of her pants. On our way back to the lobby, she said, "By the way, the keys I seized this morning were squeaky clean, not a single print on them." She pulled the keys from a pouch on her belt and handed them to me. With a quick "Take care now," she exited the lodge, climbed back into her SUV, and drove off.

The other guests had all gathered in the great room to watch Kendall be driven away. They erupted in speculative chatter now, just as they had when they'd learned Sammie and Cole had left the lodge before daybreak and were under suspicion.

Vera shook her head. "I suspected Kendall all along. She had a weird obsession with Sasha."

One of the joggers grimaced but concurred. "She's got codependence issues."

Joaquín ran his fingers thoughtfully over his mustache. "She's definitely been sort of stalker-y, but I'm still having trouble seeing Kendall as a killer. I've never seen her lose her temper. She rarely sticks up for herself and she was easily cowed. Sasha treated her like a doormat, and she just let it happen."

Vera was undaunted. "Maybe that's why she snapped. Everything built up until she couldn't take it anymore."

Vera's explanation made perfect sense, and she could very

well be right. Deputy Highcloud seemed to think Kendall was guilty, too. Heck, Kendall had even claimed responsibility for Sasha's death, apparently. So, why, then, did I not feel more relieved?

CHAPTER 20

Not for ourselves alone are we born.
—Marcus Tullius Cicero (44 b.c.: *De Officiis*)

Yeti

It had been a strange and lonely day. Misty had only come in once to say hello and give Yeti a snack, and she'd stayed in the room just a short time. There'd been none of the usual snuggles and nose boops. No murmured words telling Yeti what a beautiful, wonderful, and loved kitty she was. No scratches on her lower back, just at the base of her tail, that caused her to lift her furry little derrière in the same way those people on the deck had stuck theirs in the air earlier during their class.

But Misty was here now, so Yeti hopped up on the sofa, strolled across it, and placed her paws on Misty's soft belly. She flexed her toes and dug her claws in as she kneaded Misty's flesh, her purr like a feline mantra, the repetitive motion and soothing sound making Yeti feel calm and content. Misty made a soft sound of protest—*Ouch!*—but she did nothing to stop Yeti's ministrations. Once the cat tired of kneading Misty's belly, she stepped up onto it, circled around once to weave her body into a tight ball, and plopped down. *This is the life.*

CHAPTER 21

I took a walk in the woods and came out taller than the trees.

—Henry David Thoreau (1854: *Walden*)

Misty

Yeti sank into the roll of flesh on my abdomen that she'd been kneading a moment before. As if I needed another reminder that age had taken its toll on my body. It used to be no work at all to stay in decent shape. Those days were far behind me now. Once this horrible situation was over, I'd schedule a brisk daily hike for myself. I wasn't trying to reclaim a beach body I'd never had even on my best days, but it couldn't hurt to be more active.

While Kendall being taken into custody should have freed me from the anxiety I'd felt all day, it had provided little reprieve. There were too many unanswered questions remaining. Why had Cole researched poison on my computer? What had he done with the knowledge he'd gained? Had the allergy medication played a role in Sasha's death and, if so, how had it gotten into her system? Why was Madman giving me dirty looks? Why had Heike reacted so strongly to the news of Sasha's death? Why couldn't I completely shake my suspicions of Brynn?

The only question I had any chance of answering tonight

was the last one. Brynn had mentioned that she was familiar with singing bowls. Might she have wanted the centuries-old bowl to use in her Wiccan practices? To make this determination, I needed to learn more about Wicca.

I spent the next hour reading about Wicca online while Yeti lounged on my belly. I learned that Wicca had its origins in ancient spiritual practices that worshiped nature, and that the practice was often symbolized by a pentagram, or star. Two men, Aleister Crowley and Gerald Gardner, had written guidebooks for practitioners. Gardner's *Book of Shadows* contained spells and rituals. Under Gardner's direction, a woman named Doreen Valiente later revised his spell book. She subsequently split off from Gardner and formed her own coven. Though some Wiccans incorporated witchcraft or magic into their practices, Wicca was now primarily a female and feminist spiritual practice, with a focus on nature and a female deity known as the Goddess. Celtic Wicca incorporated many Celtic myths and traditions. Via various court cases, the practice was recognized as an official religion in the United States. Many practitioners of Wicca were solo practitioners, while others, like Brynn, apparently, belonged to small covens and engaged in rituals together.

I knew already that most religions had some form of the Golden Rule. In Buddhism, practitioners are taught *Treat not others in ways you yourself would find hurtful.* Christianity is a proponent of *Do onto others as you would have them do to you.* Islam preaches *Not one of you truly believes until you wish for others what you wish for yourself.* In Judaism, the thought is expressed as *What is hateful to you, do not do to your neighbor.* I learned that Wicca, too, has its creed, known as the Wiccan Rede, which read *An ye harm none, do what ye will*, with "an" in this context meaning "if." Seems like the basis of all religion was consistent and simple, grounded in treating others with kindness and respect.

My research taught me that Wiccans often used five elements in their rituals—earth, air, fire, water, and spirit—a slight variation on the elements Glenn had mentioned during our meditation earlier. Wiccans incorporated some version of these elements on their altars, such as rocks, small pieces of wood, or leaves. Offering bowls were used to present gifts to the Goddess. Though I didn't find much directly linking singing bowls to Wicca practices, it was clear that practitioners often incorporated elements of other spiritual practices in their worship, based on their individual preferences. It was possible Brynn might have wanted the Tibetan singing bowl to use in her own practices. Still, stealing a bowl seemed to go against Wiccan doctrine—*An ye harm none* . . . Whoever had taken Sasha's bowl had harmed her. Moreover, while many so-called witches had been persecuted over the years, it was clear that practitioners of Wicca were not generally violent in the name of their religion.

When I felt that I had a basic understanding of Wicca, I ran a search for metaphysical stores in the region. To my surprise, there were several. I'd realized the mountains attracted a wide variety of people for a wide variety of reasons, some of them well beyond the mainstream. Survivalists. Loners. Rebels who didn't want to live by the rules of civilized society. But I hadn't known that so many in the area were drawn to the mountains for spiritual purposes. I didn't know why I hadn't realized it. After all, the mountains had appealed to me on a spiritual level.

I closed my laptop and lifted Yeti from my lap, to which she responded with an indignant yowl. "Sorry, girl. I need to get ready for bed and I can't do it with you lying on me."

After changing into my pajamas, washing my face, and brushing my teeth, I aimed for my bed. But first, I pushed a chair up under the doorknob, double-checked that my windows were securely locked, and put both the meat fork and the hiking pole in easy reach. As I turned off the lamp, Yeti settled down on her pillow next to me. "Good night, girl."

She replied with a soft chirrup.

It was no surprise that nightmares bombarded my brain that night, making sleep nearly impossible. When my alarm went off at six o'clock Wednesday morning, I was tempted to stab the clock with the meat fork. I'd set the alarm on my phone for five minutes later as a backup, and I turned that off before it could activate.

My body and mind had felt so light and loose after Heike's massage, the deep stretch class, and the meditation on Monday, but now I felt as heavy as the mountains themselves. After feeding Yeti, taking a shower, and putting on my clothes and makeup, I made my way down to the great room. The tattooed busboy, Brock, was placing trays of food into the warmer. The auburn-haired woman from Patty's waitstaff was with him. They must have used the key I'd given Patty to let themselves in. At least this part of my day was settling into a routine.

Wait . . . Patty's staff had access to a key to the lodge. Could one of them have used it to get inside while the lights were out Monday night? The key wasn't a master key, and couldn't have opened the door to Sasha's room, but it would have opened the front door or the door at the end of either wing. If they'd come in the door at the end of the west wing, the security cameras on the Greasy Griddle wouldn't have picked it up. Her staff might know that door was out of camera range.

I eyed them closely. The woman gave me no cause for concern. Brock, however, caused a jangle in my nerves. The High Life tattoo could be just a humorous play on words, or it could mean he used drugs. And if he used drugs, he'd need money to buy them. A busboy's wages wouldn't be enough to support a drug habit. He might need to find alternate revenue streams. From selling stolen property, maybe?

I also remembered him ogling the backsides of the women raised in the air as they practiced their yoga. Could his staring have been mere surprise? A natural, if tactless, reaction for a young man his age? Or was there more to it? Could he have come into the lodge Monday night with something much more sinister than theft in mind, and taken Sasha's singing bowl and jewelry as a bonus or some kind of sick souvenir?

Brock turned my way and caught me watching him. Alarm flashed in his eyes.

I forced a smile at him. "I appreciate y'all getting up so early to bring the breakfast over here. It's all I can do to get out of bed before nine."

He shrugged. "I like the early shift. Leaves my afternoons free for rock climbing."

Hmm. Was rock climbing what he enjoyed about the "high life?" I wish I knew. I also wondered whether he'd even know that Sasha's singing bowl was valuable. I wouldn't have had a clue if Kendall hadn't mentioned it to me.

I figured I should give Patty an update about Kendall's arrest, but a glance at all of the cars and people across the parking lot told me the Greasy Griddle was busy and it wouldn't be a good time to call her. I stopped Brock before he left. "Ask Patty to give me a jingle when she has time. I've got some news for her."

"Sure."

Attendance at the morning's sun salutations was meager at best. Vera and Vivian. Norma Jean and Chugalug. Joaquín. One of the joggers. My guess was that the rest weren't eager to repeat the particular practice during which their instructor had been found dead. Or maybe, like me, they'd had a difficult time sleeping last night. At least attendance was better at breakfast. Nearly all of the guests came out for Patty's muffins, hash browns, and pancakes. It would take more than a murder to keep them from the hearty buffet.

Rocky caught up with me at the coffee urn, filling a mug with nearly equal parts brew and sugar. He slugged back a gulp of coffee before eyeing me. "You don't look like you slept a wink."

"The dark circles and bags under my eyes gave me away, huh?"

"If I'm being honest? Yeah."

I didn't take offense. I'd seen myself in the mirror this morning, and no amount of concealer could cover things up. "I couldn't settle my mind enough to sleep." *Maybe I should've taken him up on those bedtime stories.*

His brow furrowed. "After the visit from Deputy High-cloud last night, I thought things had been laid to rest."

It was a bad choice of words, but I knew it was unintentional, so I didn't point it out. He followed me over to the breakfast buffet. I grabbed a plate for myself and handed another to him. "There are a lot of loose ends that haven't been tied up. Those loose ends are what kept me up."

Rocky and I were serving ourselves pancakes from the warmer when Patty popped in. "I heard you have news! I figured I'd come over and get the scoop in person."

"Grab some coffee," I suggested. "We can talk on the deck."

A few minutes later, the three of us were seated at a table out back and Patty had been updated: Kendall had left her phone in her room, attempted to abscond down the parkway, and was caught when I noticed her fitness tracker notification and put the clues together.

Patty raised her mug in salute. "Smart thinking, Misty."

I couldn't help but beam, proud of my clever deductive reasoning.

Glenn wandered out onto the deck, a full plate in his hands. I was thankful he wasn't wearing a Third Eye shirt. Many of the others had worn them today, probably in tribute to Sasha, but to me it felt as if her eyes were everywhere, watching us from the afterlife.

Rocky gestured to the empty seat at our table. "Why don't you join us?"

"I'd like that," Glenn said.

Before he sat down, we introduced him to Patty.

He shook her hand and sat. "I've got you to thank for

these delicious banana nut pancakes. I can't get enough of them."

"Happy to hear it," she said.

Patty and I were alike in that regard. Both of us enjoyed being in the hospitality industry and bringing joy and comfort to others, though her comfort came in the form of yummy food and mine came in the form of pillow-top mattress covers.

Patty took a sip of her coffee before asking, "How long have you been at this stuff, Glenn?"

"Yoga and meditation?" Glenn swirled a forkful of pancake in the pool of syrup on his plate. "Since the late sixties. My mother was a devoted yogi. When I was a teenager, we traveled to Rishikesh."

"Wait." Rocky cocked his head. "Isn't that where the Beatles went? Where they met the maharishi?"

"That's the place," Glenn said. "We took classes with masters and swam in the Ganges. Tradition says a dip in the Ganges will wash away your sins. Unfortunately, it's more likely to give you dysentery or cholera these days." He went on to say that the Beatles' embrace of eastern spirituality and transcendental meditation led to acceptance of the practices elsewhere. "The trip was a wonderful experience. The teen years can be hard. We're all trying to figure out who we are, where we fit in. Meditation helped me deal with it. I want to help others experience that same sense of inner peace. That's why I teach. It's only part time, though. I work a day job to pay the bills."

Rocky raised his orange juice in salute. "You're the real deal. A genuine original hippie."

A soft grin tugged at Glenn's lips. "Not many of my kind

left these days. We're a dying breed. I started teaching in my early twenties and been at it ever since."

I dabbed a bit of syrup from my lip with a napkin. "How long have you been with the Third Eye studio?"

"Since long before it was Sasha's." He took a sip of his tea. "I've taught there continuously since some friends and I established it thirty years ago. We called it the Karma Collective, and shared the space and expenses. But when yoga had its recent resurge in popularity, studios popped up all over the place. We lost students to other studios and our landlord kept raising the rent. We found that we couldn't make ends meet anymore. We thought we'd have to shut down, but then Sasha came along two years ago and bought the building and the business."

I wondered where Sasha had obtained the money to buy a commercial property and take over the studio. Had she been in a lucrative career beforehand? Have a trust fund? Married into wealth?

My question must have been written on my face, because Glenn clarified. "I suppose it's more precise to say that Sasha's husband bought the property and business for her. Well, her *ex*-husband, now. Ron Carlisle. You might have heard of him. He comes from a long line of tobacco barons."

Ah. Sasha had married into money. She kept her business and her husband's notable name in the divorce. She must've had a good attorney.

Glenn went on. "Ron is a kindhearted man. He serves on the boards of several nonprofits in Charlotte and has given millions to the children's hospital. He's trying to overcome his sanchita."

I'd never heard the word. Apparently, Patty hadn't either. "What's sanchita?" she asked.

"One of the three types of karma."

"Three?" Rocky held a muffin aloft. "I thought there were only two—good and bad."

"It's a little more complicated than that," Glenn explained. "Karma involves sanchita, or the accumulated sum of karma from past actions. Prarabdha is the term for current actions, what a person is doing now. Agami refers to the future."

Rocky peeled the paper off his muffin and placed it on the table. "Karma sounds kind of like the ghosts of Christmas past, present, and future."

Glenn nodded. "In a sense, yes. The concept transcends culture."

I suspected Sasha had made changes to the studio after she'd bought it, much like I'd made some changes at the lodge. I asked Glenn about it.

"She changed the name to Third Eye, of course. She also added the spa services. I suppose it was a good business decision. It distinguished Third Eye from the smaller studios and expanded the client base. After she earned her certificate, she let most of the instructors go and took over their classes, but she wasn't trained in meditation so she kept me on. I guide meditations most evenings."

Rocky asked, "What's a meditation teacher do for a day job? Manage hedge funds? Run a jack hammer?"

Glenn chuckled. "Neither. I'm an installer for Queen City Sprinkler Systems."

Hmm. You'd think a man who installed lawn sprinklers would be tan, like my ex. Spending time in the southern sun could fry fair skin to a crisp. *Glenn must use lots of sunscreen.* If I hadn't concluded he was innocent before, I certainly would now. With him having a day job and his work for Third Eye being only part time, he could have afforded to quit working for Sasha if he wasn't happy there. As far as I knew, though, Heike worked for Third Eye full time. She'd be much more reliant on the income from her job there. "What's going to happen to the studio?" I asked.

"That's anyone's guess," Glenn said. "For now, I'm just glad the investigation has been resolved, not only for Sasha's sake, but for Heike's, as well."

"Heike?" I poked at my grits. "What do you mean?"

"She lost her husband in a freak accident in April. She's still grieving. I think that's why Sasha's unexpected death hit her so hard."

Rocky and I exchanged curious glances. At the risk of sounding nosy, I asked, "What happened to Heike's husband?"

"She said they'd gone for a bicycle ride in their neighborhood, and when they were done, they rode up their driveway to put the bikes away in the garage. A squirrel ran in front of her husband and he accidentally braked too hard and went over the handlebars. He landed on his back in their garage. The fall broke his neck. Luckily, they were the only two home at the time, so their children didn't see it happen. That would've been so much worse."

Knowing that Heike had so recently suffered a tragic loss made her reaction to Sasha's death understandable. It was no wonder she'd been triggered.

We continued making small talk until we finished our meal, then parted ways. Patty went back to the Greasy

Griddle, and I started my housekeeping rounds. With Brynn having the day off, it would be the first time I'd be responsible for cleaning both wings. *Better move fast.*

After I rounded up my housekeeping cart, I noticed that Madman was on the deck with Joaquín. I figured now would be a good time to clean Madman's room. But when I rolled my cart down the hall, I found the Do Not Disturb sign hanging on the doorknob of his room. Had he put it up earlier and forgotten to take it down when he left?

I walked out to the deck and addressed him. "I'd be happy to clean your room now, but I noticed the Do Not Disturb sign is out."

He skewered me with his gaze and pointed to the table. "Just bring me some fresh towels here."

"Would you like me to take your used towels away?"

"I'll bring them to you later."

Clearly, Madman didn't want me going into his room. Did he have something to hide, and was he afraid I'd find it now that Kendall had been arrested? I wasn't sure, and I certainly couldn't ask him. *Hey, Madman. Did you kill Sasha? Just curious.*

I returned to my cart, rounded up a set of fresh towels, and carried them out the deck. He stared pointedly up at me as I placed them on the table before him.

I forced a smile at him. "Just let me know if you need anything else." I walked back inside to find a deliveryman in uniform looking up and down the hallways. I raised a hand in greeting as I headed toward him. "Hi there!"

He hiked a thumb over his shoulder. "Got a large delivery for you. Where do you want it?"

I saw the large, flat carton on a dolly on the walkway out front. It was my new sign for the parking lot, some assembly required. Of course, I'd turn the job over to my maintenance department, Rocky. "Out front next to the bear would be great," I said. "It'll be out of the way there." I raised a finger to halt him as I scurried around the desk and retrieved a tip for him from the cash drawer. I handed the bill across the counter. "Thanks so much."

He thanked me in return and headed back to his truck.

A glance outside told me Rocky's pickup was gone from the lot. He must be on a handyman call somewhere. I shot him a text to let him know the sign had arrived and asked him to assemble it at his convenience. He responded with a thumbs-up emoji, followed by a red toolbox emoji. I could hardly wait for him to put the sign up. It would mark the final step in making this lodge mine. Despite what had happened here, I felt hopeful. This lodge had been a safe, inviting place for travelers for decades, and it could be again. No, it *would* be again. I'd make sure of it.

CHAPTER 22

Everywhere we look, complex magic of nature blazes before our eyes.

—Vincent van Gogh

Misty

I took my lunch break in my room with Yeti. She stood on the table, daintily nibbling at the shredded salmon in her saucer while I poked at a bowl of salad. I recalled what I'd learned at my previous meal, when Glenn told me and Rocky that Heike's husband had died a sudden and unexpected death. What's more, her husband had died of a broken neck. I couldn't help but wonder if she might have had something to do with it. As a masseuse, she'd have a thorough knowledge of the spine, know precisely where its weak points were located. Could she have killed him with those big, powerful hands of hers? She'd been the only witness to her husband's alleged freak accident. Maybe she'd been the one to snap his neck, and she'd played the grieving widow when the first responders arrived. Maybe those same strong hands had held Sasha's down pillow over her face.

I rounded up my laptop and typed Heike's full name plus the word *obituary* into the browser, hoping to come across her husband's listing. Sure enough, a link popped up to her

husband's obituary, which had been published in the *Charlotte Observer* in late April. The photo that accompanied
the obituary showed a man with a broad smile cradling a
cat in his arms, one of the cats from the photo Heike had
shown me when she checked in. Heike's husband seemed
to share her love of furry, four-footed creatures. Unfortunately, the obituary provided scant information, stating
only that he had passed away suddenly and unexpectedly,
that he had worked as a physical education teacher at a junior high school, and that he left a wife and four children
behind. In lieu of flowers, donations to the local animal shelter were requested.

The gears in my mind began to turn again. I thought
once more of Rocky's quote from Aristotle, the one that
listed the reasons why people acted. Had Heike now made
a habit of killing? Was she controlled by some type of ir-
resistible compulsion to end the lives of those around her?
Did she have a veiled, violent nature? It seemed clear she
wasn't a people person. She didn't eat breakfast with the
others or join in the classes or social activities. She kept to
herself. She seemed to be an introvert, but that certainly
didn't make her a killer. And with four children at home,
things had to be hectic, especially now that she was raising
them on her own. She might simply be taking advantage of
her time at the lodge to decompress and enjoy some peace
and quiet.

My mind went on to appetite, one of the other reasons
Aristotle gave as the basis for action. While some people
had carnal appetites, or appetites for material things such
as designer purses or shoes, the most basic appetite was

actual hunger for food. Though it was clear from Heike's stocky build that she had plenty to eat, she could be struggling to provide for her children now that her husband was gone. I had no idea how much a masseuse earned, so I ran an online search for an answer. According to the internet, a massage therapist earned an average annual income ranging from around $38,000 to $50,000, slightly less than the average of all occupations. Heike would have to support not only herself on that income, but also three cats and four children. I'd heard it cost over $200,000 to raise a child to age eighteen. I ran a search on that question, too. Again, the estimates ranged, but all were well over $200,000, some even closer to $300,000. Four children would cost nearly a million dollars to raise. As a P.E. teacher, her husband couldn't have earned a lot, either. Unless they had some unknown source of other income, or had really good life insurance, she'd be strapped. *Had her husband's death left her in financial trouble? Could she have taken Sasha's jewelry and bowl with the intention of pawning or reselling them for cash?*

I decided it couldn't hurt to see if I could elicit some information from her directly. I finished my salad, gave Yeti a kiss on the head, and headed down the hall to sign up for another massage. I was in luck. Heike was fully booked for today, but she had an opening tomorrow at four thirty. I used the pen hanging from the chain on her clipboard to print my name on the blank line.

By then, Rocky had returned and was putting the sign together out front. I walked out to take a look. It was well built. The wood was solid and stained a nice color. The rustic font had been a perfect choice for spelling out the name of the lodge.

Rocky waved his screwdriver around. "Where do you want it when I'm done? Same place the other sign was before?"

"Put it a few feet closer to the lodge," I suggested. "I think that'll look better."

"I could dig a flower bed around it, too, if you'd like. Make a border of river rock."

Colorful flowers would be pretty and draw attention to the sign, maybe draw in some guests. It was a good idea. What's more, I enjoyed digging in the dirt. "Let's do it."

By midafternoon, I'd finished cleaning the rooms and took advantage of the lull to round up my dirty clothing. After shooing Yeti out of the plastic basket, I carried it to the laundry room and began separating the items, filling one washer with light colors, another with darks. When Rocky wandered in with a drawstring laundry bag, I tossed a blouse over my basket to obscure its contents.

He cocked his head. "Something wrong?"

I'd look ridiculous if I denied it. "Don't want my unmentionables on display."

"Unmentionables?" he said. "You mean your nighties? Panties? Bras?"

I put my hands on my hips. "They're called unmentionables because you're not supposed to mention them!"

His eyes danced with amusement. "I raised three daughters. I've laundered more unmentionables than I can count."

Given that he'd shared the information about his daughters, I took the opening to learn more about them. "*Three* daughters? You've got two more besides the one living at your house?"

He nodded as he loosened the drawstring on his laundry bag and dumped the contents onto the table to sort it. "My middle daughter is a hairdresser in Boone. My youngest is a sophomore at Appalachian State."

I poured the last of my liquid laundry detergent into the machine, shaking it to get the final drops much like Sasha had done with the wine bottle Monday night. "What's your youngest studying?"

"Boys, far as I can tell. That's about all she talks about." Rocky reached over to grab the industrial-sized box of nontoxic granular detergent Brynn had asked me to order for washing the lodge's linens. He poured a scoop of the soap into his machine and dropped a load of whites in after it. "Her official major is industrial design."

"She's in the right place for it." Besides trees, tobacco, and car racing, North Carolina was also known for furniture. An industrial designer would have ample job opportunities with the state's many furniture manufacturers.

He held up the scoop. "Need some detergent?"

"Half a scoop if you don't mind."

"Not at all." He dipped it into the box and handed the half-full scoop to me. As I added the soap to the washer, he said, "I got my start in furniture, too. Building it, not designing it. Spent a year at a factory in Thomasville, then took a few weeks off to come up here and work at the ski resort. They offered season passes as a perk. I figured I'd have to go back down the mountain once winter ended, but I met a homebuilder up here and, when he learned I could handle tools, he offered me a job. Worked for him a while before starting my handyman business."

"And you've stayed in the mountains ever since?"

"Sure have. There's no better place to be."

So, he had three daughters, but no wife, at least not anymore. *Is he divorced? A widower?* As curious as I was, I didn't want to pry. I'd learn more in due time, I supposed.

Leaving my clothes to process, I excused myself and returned to my post at the registration desk.

Brynn showed up around four o'clock, wearing another of her loose, colorful dresses that made her look like an oversized fairy. I gave her an update on the case, including Kendall's arrest.

"Wow," she said. "She tried to flee huh? Like O. J. Simpson in his Bronco. Stupid move. Only guilty people run."

Her comment got me thinking once again about Sammie and Cole. Were they running from something?

Brynn walked out in front of the lodge, clutching colored crystals in her hands and softly reciting words that I suspected were some type of cleansing spell. If I hadn't thought she resembled a fairy before, I certainly would now. She was still out front a quarter hour later when Rocky came up the hall to check on his laundry and stopped at the desk.

I angled my head discreetly to indicate Brynn. "What do you make of my assistant?"

He glanced out the window. "She's a little offbeat, but

she seems like one of those what-you-see-is-what-you-get kind of people. It's the people who try too hard to act normal that you've got to worry about."

Brynn turned and caught us looking at her. A look of concern, maybe even hurt, flittered over her face. I hoped she didn't realize we'd been talking about her, but how could she not? I felt a twinge of shame at the thought that I'd hurt her feelings. She might embrace some unordinary beliefs, but she'd proven herself to be a dependable and productive employee. I was lucky to have her on my staff. I was even growing to better appreciate her unconventionality. It kept things interesting around the lodge, and exposed me to new ideas. Besides, with so few locals on the mountain, I'd hoped the two of us might eventually become not just coworkers, but friends, too.

She turned away before turning back again and coming to the door. She opened it and called, "She's back!"

No sooner had the words left her mouth than Deputy Highcloud's SUV pulled up under the overhang. Kendall sat in the back seat, just like before, but this time her hands were unshackled and her shirt was dry. Both the deputy and Kendall climbed out of the vehicle. Rocky and I walked to the door, meeting them as they stepped inside. Brynn followed them in.

Kendall's pink-rimmed eyes and splotchy, tear-streaked face told me she hadn't slept much last night, either, if at all. After meeting my gaze and giving me a contrite cringe, Kendall looked past me to the great room. "I was wrong," she said to the group. "I didn't kill Sasha, after all."

Vera stood and demanded answers. "How can you be wrong about something like that?"

Deputy Highcloud stepped forward, raising a palm to calm the chatter. "Kendall thought Sasha might have had a reaction to a prescription allergy medication she'd shared with her. Only trace amounts were found in Sasha's system, so Kendall has been cleared of the murder charges."

Vera issued an indignant snort. "I don't see how that information alone clears her."

"There was other definitive evidence," the deputy said. "We were able to determine a time of death by the activity on Sasha's fitness tracker. Kendall's tracker showed her to be in deep sleep at the time."

Vera was relentless. "How do you know Kendall hadn't removed her tracker? Or that someone else wasn't wearing it?"

"If the device wasn't on her wrist, it wouldn't have reported data. And if she'd transferred it to someone else, the system would have reported the temporary break in reporting with an error message. I compared Monday night's data to data from other times. It was clear what happened."

My head spun. *If Kendall is innocent, then who killed Sasha?* We were back to square one. *Or were we?*

"It was those kids, then," Vera said, saying exactly what I'd been thinking. "The hikers."

"We don't know that for certain," the deputy said. "We're still trying to locate them."

My heart fell. With Kendall cleared, it seemed that the odds had increased that Cole, or the couple together, was responsible for Sasha's death. Of course, that theory was dependent on when, exactly, Sasha had been killed.

I asked the next question on my mind. "Can you tell us what time Sasha was killed?"

"Her tracker stopped reporting data at two twenty-nine."

Rocky and I exchanged glances. It was shortly after 2:29 that we'd heard the *bonggg* sound that had drawn the two of us from our rooms. When Glenn had said he'd accidentally bumped into his gong in the night, I'd assumed the sound we'd heard had been his gong. But now I realized the sound must have come from Sasha's room. It would be too much of a coincidence for Glenn to have bumped into his gong in his room down and across the hall at the precise moment Sasha was being attacked in hers. Maybe the noise had been the killer hitting Sasha over the head with the singing bowl. A death from blunt force trauma to the head could explain why there'd been no visible injuries on her body. Maybe she'd been hit on the back of her head, which hadn't been visible since she was lying faceup when she was found.

Kendall looked to Deputy Highcloud, fresh tears welling up in her eyes. "Can I go back to my room now?"

The deputy nodded. Once Kendall had gone, the deputy turned and waved me outside. I followed her around to the far side of her SUV, where prying eyes inside the lodge couldn't see us.

She looked me in the eye. "Sasha had a lot of carbon dioxide in her blood, as we expected. The M.E. has ruled her official cause of death as asphyxiation. He's also ruled her death a homicide, of course."

"She wasn't poisoned? Even a little bit?"

"No."

"That means it's less likely that Cole killed her, then, right?"

"Not necessarily," the deputy said. "He could have changed his mind, decided that smothering her would be easier than poisoning her. Poisons can be tricky to administer, and the results aren't reliable."

Ugh. There's some information I'd never hoped to learn.

"What about other injuries?" I asked. "Had she been hit?"

"There's no evidence of it."

So much for my theory that the nighttime noise had come from Sasha being hit with her singing bowl.

Deputy Highcloud turned to more positive matters, if anything related to this murder case could be deemed positive. "You made a good call with the fitness trackers. Knowing the time of death really narrows things down. We know nobody came out of Sasha's room after she was killed and, if Brynn is correct about the windows and the adjoining door in Sasha's room being locked from the inside, the only logical conclusion is that whoever killed Sasha escaped through Kendall's room and went out Kendall's window. They might have even entered that way, too. Kendall's window was unlocked and open when we searched her room."

"Someone could have snuck in and out of Kendall's room while she was sleeping?" The thought made my skin crawl.

The deputy nodded. "She told me she's an especially heavy sleeper. Her fitness tracker backs that up. She barely moved once she hit the mattress Monday night. She truly slept like a rock."

That might be so, but how would the killer know Kendall was a heavy sleeper? Then again, maybe the killer didn't need to know. Maybe the killer realized that if Kendall woke up and discovered them in her room, they could make a quick escape out her window, or kill her too, so that she couldn't finger them.

The deputy went on to address the issue of the adjoining door. "The scratches on the door frame in Kendall's room could have resulted when the killer used some type of tool to manipulate Sasha's deadbolt and close it from Kendall's side."

"But why would they take the time to do that? Why not just get out of there as soon as possible?"

"That's a really good question," she said. "One I don't have an answer to."

I told her about the key I'd given Patty so that she and her staff could get into the lodge to set up the breakfast buffet each morning. "I caught one of her busboys, a young man named Brock, eyeing the yoga class."

"A horny boy checking out a bunch of women in tight spandex?" She snorted. "That sounds more hormonal than suspicious to me. Besides, the odds of someone from the Greasy Griddle using that key to access your lodge during a short-term blackout and finding the keys to Sasha's room seem very low. That said, I'll swing by the diner and find out who had access to the key. No sense leaving even the smallest stone unturned."

"Could you maybe not mention that I'm the one who

brought it up? I don't want to risk offending Patty. She's the owner of the diner. We're friends." Or we were at least becoming friends. I liked Patty. I didn't want to risk getting at odds with her.

"All right," the deputy agreed. "I'll tell her I'm just looking for information and talking to anyone who's been at the lodge the last few days. That'll give me a reason to ask how she and her staff get inside, and find out where she keeps the key and who has access to it. How's that?"

"Perfect. Thanks." I expected that she'd also ask the staff if they'd noticed anyone suspicious hanging around outside the lodge, maybe a customer of the diner who seemed unusually interested in it. I had another question for her, one that made me feel queasy. "What about Sammie and Cole? Do you think you'll find them?"

"We've put more resources into tracking them down. We've attempted to pinpoint their location by triangulating their phone signals, but it was futile. They're in a large no-service zone that spans miles. It's possible they headed north instead of south to throw us off. They might have even left the trail altogether. Officers have been stationed at crossings both to the north and south, and they'll ask any hikers who happen by to report in as soon as possible if they see the two. I've also notified pawn shops in the region to keep an eye out for the singing bowl and what jewelry the students could remember Sasha wearing. I'll keep an eye for listings online, too, to see if Sasha's things pop up for sale somewhere."

She climbed into her SUV, rolled down the window, and leaned out of it. "Remember when I said '*if* Brynn is correct about the windows and doors being locked?'"

"Yeah?"

"We're also still working that *if.*"

She drove off, heading across the parking lot to the diner, leaving me in a cloud of dust and unanswered questions.

CHAPTER 23

Water is the driver of nature.

—Leonardo da Vinci

Misty

After the deputy drove away, I stood outside and mulled things over for a moment. The possibility remained that Brynn could have been mistaken about Sasha's windows being locked. After all, she wouldn't have known at the time she cleaned the glass that whether the window was locked was going to be an important factor in a murder case. If the window hadn't been locked, the killer could have escaped through it. It was also still possible that Brynn had lied about the window being locked to cover her own hide and direct suspicions away from her and toward the guests in the lodge. Maybe she had slipped in and out through the window and taken the singing bowl and the jewelry herself. I also had to wonder whether Cole could be the culprit, instead. Had he killed Sasha for her valuable bowl and jewelry? Had he turned his and Sammie's hike into a homicidal honeymoon?

But what if Rocky was right, that Brynn was a what-you-see-is-what-you-get kind of person? What I saw was a slightly peculiar but hardworking woman, who was straightforward and direct. What if she was correct about the windows and door? Did that necessarily mean the deputy's theory about someone accessing Sasha's room via Kendall's was correct?

It certainly seemed like a viable theory. The only other options would be that someone rode in on the Tooth Fairy's coattails or came down the chimney like Santa Claus, and the guest rooms didn't have chimneys. That's where the gears in my mind locked up and ground to a halt.

I went back inside. The guests were still moping about the great room and deck. Being cooped up and fretting over Sasha's death was taking its toll on the group. The yoga practices didn't mellow people out for long. I had to find a way to cheer them up, and fast.

I stepped into the great room and addressed the guests gathered there. "What would y'all think about taking a group outing to Lake Coffey?" It would be a two-mile downhill hike to get there, plus another two miles uphill coming back, but we had nothing but time. Besides, a venture through nature might be restorative. What's more, the trailheads for the Upper and Lower Pond Creek Trails were only a short walk from the lake. The lower trail was absolutely gorgeous, running alongside a cascading creek set among a lush backdrop of rhododendrons and other foliage.

Glenn stood, looking relieved. With him being the only remaining instructor, responsibility for the retreat rested on his shoulders now. While he was great at leading classes in *inactivity*, he wasn't much help when it came to planning activities for the students. Understandable, given that he wasn't familiar with the area. I felt a bit like a cruise director on a sinking ship, but he seemed glad to have the suggestion. "A group hike is a wonderful idea, Misty."

He went up and down the hall, knocking on the doors of the few guests who weren't already in the great room or out on the deck. Soon, we had the entire group assembled, all but Heike, that is. While she seemed to like pets, she didn't seem particularly fond of people. That could be why she'd chosen a profession in which she didn't have to talk much and only had to deal with one person at a time. I invited Brynn and Rocky to join us, too. She might as well come along and enjoy the beautiful day. Besides, it would give her a chance to chat with Glenn, compare their spiritual theories and practices.

As we set out down the narrow trail, Rocky said, "Leave the road. Take the trails." Lest he be accused of plagiarism, he added, "Pythagoras gets credit for that one."

I added my own quote. "Nature is cheaper than therapy."

"Who said that?" Rocky asked.

I shrugged. "I have no idea. But I suppose I owe them a dollar for repeating it."

Madman had donned his black wraparound sunglasses, so when he looked my way as we walked along, it was difficult to tell if the looks he cast were dirty or not. I kept a discreet eye on him, trying to determine whether he was simply in a sour mood or whether his ire was for me only. It seemed to be reserved for me. He made small talk with the two joggers as they walked along, and his tone was cordial, not hostile.

Although Kendall had come along with us, she kept

mostly to herself, as if she realized that, even though she was innocent, she'd become a pariah for her attempt to abscond the day before and for putting Sasha's life at risk by sharing her prescription drug. The group didn't seem to entirely trust her. Neither did I. If someone had gained access to Sasha's room via Kendall's, could she have been somehow complicit? Knowingly allowed them inside through her window?

We picked our way down the Overlook Trail before picking up the Upper Pond Creek Trail. As we made our way down to the lake, we spotted a herd of deer munching on grass and a groundhog scuttling about low to the ground, and heard the screech of a hawk overhead. As always, our trek was set against an auditory backdrop of water making its way down the mountain, babbling brooks and trickling rivulets that met up to form creeks, which then emptied into ponds, either here or at the Buckeye Lake reservoir farther down the mountain. Ironically, for as easily as water went down the mountain, it was difficult to bring it back up. Water bills were quite high up here.

Chugalug and Molasses made their way along in the center of the group, the little dog taking five steps for every one of the bigger dog's. Brynn stopped here and there along the way, stooping to gather a fallen leaf, a stone, a twig. I suspected she might be collecting items for her Wicca altar, or to use in a ritual for the upcoming autumn equinox.

Finally, we reached Lake Coffey. The lake was small, only two acres in size. I might be tempted to call it a pond had I not already had this debate with Jack years ago. We'd looked up the distinction between lakes and ponds, and learned that they were distinguished by depth, not surface area. Ponds consisted strictly of photic zones, meaning they were shallow enough that sunlight could reach the bottom and plants could grow across the entire surface. Lakes, on the other hand, had aphotic zones, meaning some parts were too deep for the sunlight to penetrate.

Regardless of the proper nomenclature, the lake was a pretty sight. A boardwalk forming a semicircle on one side and a paved walkway on the other connected to make a complete loop around a quarter mile in length. A man stood on the far bank, a fishing pole in hand. He cast his lure out toward the center, seeking the trout that were stocked in the lake each year.

Glenn stepped over to the edge of the lake and bent down to trail his fingers through the water. Brynn walked over and did the same. Rocky nudged me with his elbow. "I think Brynn's got a crush."

I eyed the two as they knelt by the water. My assistant did indeed look smitten. It would be nice if something positive could come out of this retreat. We had already suffered a death, but maybe this retreat would also mark the birth of a romantic relationship.

Molasses meandered over to lap at the lake water. Chugalug followed. The two seemed to be becoming fast friends.

After walking the loop around the lake, we continued down to the trailhead for the Lower Pond Creek Trail. A short wooden bridge led to steps that took us down to the dirt path. After only a few more steps we reached another wooden bridge. We paused for a moment to admire the tranquil view. A narrow but powerful waterfall poured between boulders above, falling a half dozen feet before forming a pool at its base. Pond Creek continued on from there, carrying the water farther down the mountain over a smooth slide of rock worn flat over the centuries. The rushing, shushing sound of the water was soft and soothing, Mother Nature's own meditation mantra. It was a gorgeous place, a piece of heaven on earth.

Glenn gazed at the waterfall, his faraway expression saying that while his body might be here, his mind was elsewhere. Was he thinking about Sasha? Worried about his future now that the fate of the studio was unknown?

Rocky, who stood next to Glenn, turned his head to speak to the man. "How's our little creek compare to the world-famous Ganges?"

Glenn started, as if Rocky's question had jerked him back to reality. He replied with a laugh. "This water is much cleaner. Less crowded, too. It might be just a little mountain creek, but all water has restorative qualities."

Rocky chuckled. "Good to know we measure up."

We forged ahead. The trail was strenuous in spots, but Norma Jean and Chugalug were determined troopers, only needing a hand or a paw up here and there. My guests oohed and aahed over the verdant scenery. While the rhododendrons weren't blooming this time of year, they remained green and filled the ravine with lush foliage. Boulders provided a visual counterpoint. The creek rushed and tumbled over the gray stone creek bed beside us, softening the sound of our footfalls. The trail and air were damp, and I felt my hair begin to frizz. But that was part of the beauty of the mountains. Up here, you didn't care if your hair wasn't perfect. No one would judge you for it. Life was simply simpler here.

CHAPTER 24

This curious world we inhabit is more wonderful than convenient; more beautiful than it is useful; it is more to be admired and enjoyed than used.
—Henry David Thoreau (1854: *Walden*)

Yeti

While all of the other people were gone, one woman had wandered around the lodge. Yeti was lying on the bed when she'd seen the woman pass by the side window. Curious, she stepped to the edge of the bed and performed the mental calculus necessary to determine just how much force with which to jump and land on the back window ledge without overshooting her mark and smacking into the glass. She crouched and leaped to the still. *Another perfect landing.*

As the woman came around the corner, she spotted Yeti in the window and stepped over to tap on the glass. "Hallo, Kätzchen."

Yeti didn't recognize the words, but she knew the tone. The woman liked her and found her beautiful. *As she should.* Yeti stood and swished her tail to show her appreciation for the woman's good taste.

When the woman walked away, Yeti sat down to watch her. She walked to the deck at the back of the lodge and bent down to look under it. She circled back around the lodge and came at the deck from the other direction. It was the same things Yeti had seen the man and woman in uniform do two days earlier, when there had been all of the uproar and clamor.

The nice woman seemed to be searching for something, or maybe she was exploring, gathering information. Whatever she was looking for, an item or information, Yeti hoped she would find it. Yeti had once misplaced her favorite catnip mouse, and she knew how upsetting it could be when you couldn't find what you were looking for.

CHAPTER 25

Adopt the pace of nature. Her secret is patience.
—Ralph Waldo Emerson

Misty

We stopped at both of the large platforms along the trail to take in the views, then backtracked to the trailhead. When we returned to the lodge, everyone's spirits seemed a bit brighter. Looked like my suggestion for the hike had been a good one. The guests scattered again for dinner, then regrouped at eight o'clock for an evening meditation class. At Glenn's invitation, Brynn stuck around to attend the session.

Afterward, I suggested she remain for a game night, inviting Rocky and Glenn to join us in a game of Scrabble. We set up on a table on the deck. After Brynn had earned a double-word score with SAGE, and I had earned a triple-word score with ZEBRA, Glenn played the word CRICK.

"Crick?" Brynn questioned. "As in 'Let's go skinny dipping down at the crick?'"

"No." Glenn cupped a hand around the back of his neck. "Like a crick in your neck."

Rocky flashed a grin. "I like Brynn's definition better."

"Me too," Brynn said. "It's a lot more fun."

I shook both my head and a finger at my staff. "You two better behave yourselves."

Although we'd been joking around only a moment before, my mind jumped tracks as it considered Glenn's word. A crick in the neck reminded me of Heike's husband, of the neck injury he'd suffered. Again, I wondered if she might have caused it. Had she been unhappy? Had he been bad to her in some way, abusive or unfaithful? I'd see what I could find out during my massage tomorrow.

When we finished the game, we parted ways in the lobby, Brynn leaving the lodge to go home and the rest of us returning to our rooms. As I fell asleep with Yeti curled up behind me, I hoped that tomorrow would bring some solid answers.

On Thursday morning, I joined in the sun salutations. I thought it would give me a chance to assess the group up close, determine whether one of them might have killed Sasha, but I didn't get any vibes. The only thing I learned was that Joaquín had a tattoo of a black flag embellished with a skull and crossbones on his ankle. I hadn't noticed the tattoo before. When I inquired about it, he told me he'd gotten the ink years ago while on spring break with college buddies at the Outer Banks. They'd been sharing stories about Blackbeard, who'd been killed off the North Carolina coast in a sea battle with forces from the British navy. They'd also been sharing a bottle of tequila. Fueled by liquor and lore, they'd made their way to the tattoo parlor for matching pirate flag tattoos.

I was fixing myself a plate at the breakfast buffet after

the class when Deputy Highcloud's SUV pulled up to the lodge. I left my plate at the registration desk and met her at the door.

"Got some news for you," she said.

"Good news or bad news?"

"That's yet to be determined," she said. "We heard from a group of hikers this morning who are heading north on the A.T. They crossed paths with Sammie and Cole yesterday. They said Cole had fallen and busted up his ankle pretty good. He's limping along, but it's slow going."

"That explains why they haven't reached the next crossing yet." It also meant that the newlyweds weren't attempting to flee from law enforcement, didn't it? That was a good sign, right?

"We've sent a team from search and rescue up the trail to find them and bring them in. We should know more soon."

"I really hope those kids had nothing to do with Sasha's murder." Especially now that I knew Sammie was pregnant. I leaned in and asked the deputy the question that had been niggling at me—whether she thought Kendall could have helped someone else access Sasha's room. "Do you think she might be complicit somehow?"

"It's like you've read my mind." The deputy gave me a wry look. "Unfortunately, we can't keep someone in jail based on mere hunches. I don't know who she would've helped, either. From what I could gather, she wasn't close to anyone else in the group."

From what I'd seen, I had to agree. Kendall had glommed onto Sasha, but she didn't seem especially friendly with anyone else from the class.

As the deputy backed away from the counter to leave,

I pointed to the basket of muffins on the breakfast table. "You're welcome to take a muffin with you if you'd like."

"Don't mind if I do." She walked over, reached into the basket, and pulled out a muffin with more blueberries than you could count. She raised a hand goodbye as she headed out the door. "I'll be in touch."

Later that morning, I made my way down the hall, tidying up the rooms. I rolled my cart to the room occupied by Madman Maddox. I'd seen him leave the lodge earlier and hadn't seen him return, but it was possible he'd slipped back inside while I'd been cleaning one of the other rooms. The Do Not Disturb sign had been removed from his doorknob. It appeared that whatever reason he had for not allowing me into his room yesterday was now gone. If he'd been hiding evidence in his room, had he taken it somewhere to hide it?

I knocked on the door as I called out "Housekeeping!" and leaned in to listen for a response. When none came, I used my master key to unlock the door and rolled my cart inside.

I grabbed the duster and headed toward the dresser. To my shock, I heard the bottles of cleaning products jostling on my cart and the *click* of the door closing behind me. I whipped around to see that Madman had, in fact, been in the room while I'd knocked but had failed to respond. He must have stood out of sight while I'd rolled my cart into the room. Now, he'd shut me in with him. My cart blocked the way to the door. *I'm trapped!*

"You liar!" he snarled, stepping toward me. "You told those cops that I slept with Sasha!"

As the NASCAR star came at me, my heart put the pedal

to the metal, racing fast enough to cinch Talladega, my blood roaring in my ears like an engine accelerating out of a curve. Instinctively, I raised the feather duster. It was a useless gesture. The flimsy, soft brush would do little to protect me. The best I could hope for would be to tickle him or make him sneeze. Too bad I'd left the meat fork Patty had given me on the cart, which was now behind Madman. I held the duster out like a sword anyway, stretching my arm out as far as it would go to put as much distance as possible between me and Madman. I got lucky. He stopped an inch or two from it.

I shook my head. "I didn't tell them you slept with Sasha! All I said was that I saw one of her hairs on your pillow when I cleaned your room on Monday."

His jaw dropped. "You're admitting that you lied?"

"It wasn't a lie! I saw a long dark hair on your second pillow." I pointed to the bed. "The far side of the bed was flat, like it hadn't been slept in or had been straightened up. But the hair was there."

He glanced over at his bed, a puzzled expression on his face. His eyes locked on the pillow as he seemed to be trying to suss things out. When he turned back to me, much of the malice was gone. Just as he took corners fast when racing, he'd turned the corner quickly here, too. "Sasha put her head on my shoulder when I was sitting at her table outside. When I came back to my room, I sat on the bed and called my girlfriend. Maybe one of Sasha's hairs had been on my shirt and fell off."

It was certainly possible. No matter how often I ran a lint brush over my clothing, I always seemed to carry some of Yeti's white fur on me.

Knowing he could round another corner and change his mind again, agreeing with him seemed to be the smart move. "That must've been what happened. I saw you and Sasha on the deck. She was all over you." *In for a penny, in for a pound.* "I told the cops about that, too. I said you looked uncomfortable with all of the attention she was giving you."

"I didn't like it one bit," he agreed. "I thought someone might snap a pic and put it on social media and get me in hot water with my girlfriend. Besides, Sasha's not my type. She's too aggressive. A guy like me enjoys a little chase. She was too old for me, too. I'm only twenty-four. She's got to be at least thirty." He made a disgusted face that said thirty sounded ancient to him, but at least he backed away, raising conciliatory palms. "Hey, I'm sorry about all of this. But I've got a lot to lose, you know?"

"I understand." My heart rate slowed like a race car under a caution flag. Still, I didn't completely let down my guard. Madman was a hothead. Something could set him off again.

"I'll get out of your way," he said, and headed to the door.

Once it had swung closed behind him, I exhaled a long breath. Despite the conversation that had just taken place here, I didn't consider him to be fully exonerated. Madman Maddox wasn't someone who was fully in control of his emotions or actions. His temperament could simply be due to immaturity. But it could be indicative of something far more sinister.

At four thirty, I headed to Heike's room for my massage. As before, she'd closed the shutters completely. Today, the room was dimly lit by a trio of candles, and zither music floated on the air. After I'd undressed and climbed up onto her table, she smoothed lavender-scented oil along my back, flattening her hands to distribute it evenly.

As she dug her fingers into my shoulders, I looked down through the face opening in her massage table. All I could see was the hardwood floor, the corner of the white sheet hanging down, and the tennis shoes she wore. Massage sessions were generally a quiet time, but I knew it could be my only chance to confront Heike face-to-face—or, more precisely, her face to the back of my head, but that was close enough. *Time to fish for information.* "It's not fun having to look for a new job," I said. "For your sake and Glenn's, I hope the studio doesn't close."

She bent her arm and put her elbow to the side of my spine, applying a good amount of pressure and moving it in circles. "I have talked to Ron Carlisle. He will make sure we do not lose our jobs."

"Sasha's ex contacted you?"

"No," she said. "I called him."

Hmm. She hadn't wasted any time, had she? "How can he promise you'll keep your jobs? I thought Sasha got the business in their divorce."

"She got the studio and spa business," Heike said, switching elbows, "but he still owns the building. That gives him control over things. If the business was forced to move to a new location, it would be very costly."

In other words, as landlord, he could threaten not to renew the lease if whoever took over Third Eye terminated any of its staff. "You think he'll pay off her estate and run the business himself?"

"He will make sure the business ends up in good hands." She ran her hands over my shoulders.

"*You* have good hands," I said. "Maybe you should buy the business."

I hadn't meant to be serious, so I was surprised when she responded with, "I am considering it."

How can she afford to buy the business? "Glenn said Third Eye was very profitable. Wouldn't it be worth a lot?"

"It is," she said, "but I came into some unexpected money recently."

Before I could stop my mouth from spewing the thought that had popped into my mind, it was too late. The words were out. "Life insurance, you mean?"

Her hands froze around the base of my neck. *Uh-oh. She's not considering choking me to death, is she?*

When she spoke again her voice was low and tight. "Why did you say 'life insurance'?"

There's no backpedaling now. I only hoped she couldn't feel my heart pounding through her fingertips. It was hammering so hard, it threatened to shake the massage table. "Glenn mentioned that your husband passed away unexpectedly." I watched her feet. If she spread them to get leverage to strangle me, I wanted to be prepared. "I'm so sorry, Heike. I can't even imagine how hard that must be. I remembered the photo of your four children that you showed me, and I guess I was hoping that you had some life insurance so you wouldn't have to struggle."

After a few seconds, her hands began to move again, sliding down my back. *Thank goodness.* She must have bought my explanation.

"Ja," she said. "We had good life insurance. My husband

made sure of it." She sniffled, then said, "Excuse me one moment," in a wobbly voice that told me she was crying.

As she walked away to grab a tissue, I turned over on the table and pulled the sheet up to my shoulders to cover myself. "I'm so sorry, Heike. I didn't mean to upset you." My gut shrank into a hard ball and I felt ashamed to have caused her this pain.

She dabbed at her nose before turning to me. "I don't think I can finish."

"I understand," I said. "I'll get dressed. Please forgive me."

She sniffled, nodded, and turned away.

I dressed and left with another apology. She closed her door—*hard*—behind me.

As I sat at the desk later, pondering things, I found myself still wondering about Heike and the call she'd made to Ron Carlisle in an effort to save her job. Would it be normal for an employee to think of such things so soon after their boss passed away? Could Sasha's death be the culmination of an elaborate, long-term plan by Heike to take over Third Eye studio? Had she killed her husband for the life insurance money so she'd have funds to buy the business? Such a scheme would require a lot of planning and a good deal of patience. Many moving parts would have to fall into place. Still, it was possible. But Heike's grief had seemed sincere. And even though Heike wasn't especially warm, could a woman with such an affinity for furry creatures really be so cold-hearted toward humans as to cause their deaths?

I wouldn't be able to sort everything out at the moment, but I could at least sort the mail. I walked out to the mailbox by the road to retrieve it, and carried it back to the desk. I plopped myself down on the stool and began to go through it, dropping the junk mail into the recycle bin below. Advertising circular. *Clunk.* Another advertising circular. *Clunk.* I set the electric bill aside and eyed the return address on the next envelope. It was from the North Carolina Department of Commerce Division of Employment Security. I'd only recently established my account with them, reporting Brynn's earnings for the last week of August and paying the appropriate amount of unemployment insurance tax. *What can this be?*

I opened the envelope to find a letter directing me to garnish Brynn's wages for overpaid unemployment benefits she'd received in the amount of $580. I was baffled. According to the resume Brynn had provided me, she'd been consistently self-employed for years. *What's this all about? Has she lied to me?* I supposed I'd have to ask her when she arrived for work tomorrow.

My cell phone's ringtone drew my attention to the screen. The readout indicated that the call came from the Watauga County Sheriff's Department. I tapped the screen to accept the call.

It was Deputy Highcloud. "We located Sammie and Cole," she said. "Guess what we found in Cole's backpack?"

"Granola bars," I said, willing it to be true.

"The key to Sasha's room. I took an imprint of the one from your drawer before I returned it to you. The key I found on Cole matches it exactly."

My heart sank. *Cole had killed Sasha?* It seemed unfathomable to me. "Did he confess?"

"Of course not."

"Did he have her jewelry and the singing bowl?"

"No," she said, "but he could have sold them already, or hidden them along the trail somewhere so that he could go back and get them later. I'm thinking that might have been how he broke his ankle, wandering off the trail. He said he broke it when he went into the woods to relieve himself and stepped in a hole, but that could be a lie."

"His ankle is broken? Not just sprained?"

"He's got a messy fracture," she said. "We had to take him to an emergency clinic and get a cast put on him before we brought him to the station."

"If he hid Sasha's jewelry and singing bowl," I said, "why not hide her keys, too? Or just ditch them in the woods somewhere?" With so many miles of trail, they'd likely have never been found.

"My guess is he'd forgotten about them. People who commit crimes of opportunity often screw up because they're flying by the seat of their pants. They don't have all the details worked out in advance."

It was little comfort to think that, if Cole was a killer, at least he hadn't planned in advance to kill Sasha. And, while he might not have planned to kill her by smothering her, his online search for poisonous plants said he'd put some thought into ways to end a life. I put a hand to my eyes, as if I could block out this horrible news. "What about Sammie?"

"That's why I'm calling. She's got nowhere to go and very little money. She's wondering if Rocky could come pick her up at the lockup, and if she could stay at your lodge until her parents can come get her. They're driving down from Maine."

"You're releasing her? You don't think she had anything to do with Sasha's murder, then?"

"I don't. She seemed genuinely surprised when we found Sasha's keys in Cole's backpack. Of course, she's standing by her husband. She says there's no way he could've killed Sasha."

Who could blame her? Nobody would want to think that they'd married someone capable of such a violent act.

Though the other guests might not appreciate my allowing Sammie back at the lodge while her husband remained under suspicion for killing their yoga instructor, I figured I could sneak meals to her while she stayed out of sight in her room. She'd probably just as soon avoid the other guests, anyway. They were likely to be hostile toward her. "Tell Sammie she's welcome to stay here. I'll send Rocky to get her."

We ended the call, and I went in search of Rocky. I found him out front with a wheelbarrow full of smooth, colorful river rocks. He was positioning them around a large oval flower bed he'd dug around the Mountaintop Lodge sign. He looked up as I approached.

"Can you do me a favor?" I asked.

"Sure, boss. What is it?"

"Go pick up Sammie at the sheriff's station."

He stood and brushed dirt off his gloves. "They located the kids?"

I bit my lip and nodded.

His face clouded. "What about Cole? He's not coming, too?"

"No. They found Sasha's room key in his backpack."

Rocky spat a curse. "I can't believe it! I just can't. That

boy reminded me so much of myself at that age. Adventur-
ous. Determined. So crazy in love he can't see straight."

*Crazy in love? There's something to ask about at a bet-
ter time.* "I can't believe it, either." But just because we
didn't want to believe it didn't mean it wasn't true. "Bring
Sammie in the side door when you arrive," I said. "I think
it's best we keep her presence here under wraps. She's not
likely to get a welcome reception from the other guests."

"Good call."

When I stepped back inside the lodge, Madman came
barreling up the east wing hallway and skidded to a stop
when he reached the lobby. "Guess what!" he hollered to
those sitting in the great room. He waved his phone around.
"They arrested that hiker for killing Sasha! A report popped
up in my news feed."

Thanks to the internet, news traveled at the speed of light
these days.

While the guests erupted in a fresh round of speculation,
I walked over to Madman and pointed to his phone. "Can
I take a look?"

He handed me his phone and I scanned the article. It said
that Cole was being held as a person of interest, but indicated charges had yet to be filed. I pointed that out to the
group. The reporter had incorrectly referred to my lodge
by its former name, The Ridgeview Inn, rather than the
Mountaintop Lodge. While I'd normally frown on the lack
of attention to detail, it was understandable given that the
name change had taken place so recently. Besides, the reporter's wrongful reference could protect my inn's reputa-
tion. I wasn't about to call them with a correction.

I handed the phone back to Madman and informed the

guests that I'd be stepping out for just a few minutes to grab a to-go dinner from the Greasy Griddle. I didn't tell them that it wouldn't be for me. Sammie would need to keep her strength up, both for herself and the baby growing inside her.

I walked across the parking lot and into the diner. The aroma of fried foods and the tinkling sound of silverware greeted me as I came in the door.

Patty looked up from behind the counter and noted my sagging face. "Oh no. You've got bad news, don't you?"

I gave her the update and finished with, "Sammie's coming back to stay at the lodge until her parents arrive."

"That girl must be heartbroken. You think he really did it?"

"My heart says no, but my mind says maybe." The bad news delivered, I placed a to-go order for Sammie.

After putting in the order with her kitchen staff, Patty turned back to me. "Deputy Highcloud came by the diner earlier to talk to me and my staff. She asked whether any of us had noticed anyone suspicious keeping an eye on your place from the diner." She shuddered involuntarily. "Gives me the creeps to think a killer might have been sitting in one of my booths watching the lodge. Anyway, she asked who all had been involved in setting up the breakfast at your place, whether any of us had noticed anything odd. Nobody had seen anything. Wish we could have been more help."

"Thanks, Patty. It seems like whoever killed Sasha has done a good job of making themselves inconspicuous." Unless it was Cole, of course. His sudden departure was extremely questionable.

"For what it's worth," Patty added, "I told the deputy we

keep the key to your place locked up in our safe. We take it out in the morning when we're getting the start-up cash for the diner. Once we're done setting up at your lodge, it goes right back in. Only my two assistant managers and I know the combination to the safe."

In other words, unless Brock had somehow obtained the combination to the safe, he wouldn't have had access to the lodge key. Good to know. I'd hate for the killer to be one of Patty's staff. It could make things awkward between us, to say the least.

After rounding up Sammie's takeout order from the kitchen service window, Patty reached into the refrigerated dessert case and retrieved the blueberry pie. "I'll add a piece of pie, on the house. That poor girl is going to need some cheering up."

CHAPTER 26

Nature is loved by what is best in us.
—Ralph Waldo Emerson (1836: "Nature")

Misty

At half past seven, Rocky rang my cell phone from the parking lot. "Is the coast clear?"

"Yes," I whispered. "The guests are meditating on the deck." Luckily for us, they all had their eyes closed and were chanting, too.

"All right," Rocky replied. "I'll bring her in."

From my place at the desk, I saw Rocky and Sammie appear at the glass door at the end of the west wing. They scurried inside and he used his master key to let her back into the room she'd shared with her husband earlier in the week. I'd left her meal on the table inside with a supportive note that read "I'm here if you'd like to talk." I wouldn't push her. She might need time to process things.

To my surprise, she sent Rocky up the hall with a message of her own. "She'd like to speak with you. I'll cover the desk."

Rocky took a seat on the stool as I hurried down the hall and rapped lightly on Sammie's door. She opened it and I slipped inside.

Sammie's face was streaked with tears and her eyes were

rimmed in pink. She looked positively defeated. "He didn't do it!" she cried. "There's no way. Cole is the sweetest boy I've ever met in my entire life! That's why I love him. That's why I married him."

Her *entire life* had lasted less than half the length of mine so far, but long enough for her to learn a few things about people. She knew Cole better than anyone. She should know whether he was capable of killing, right? Then again, people often expressed surprise on learning that a loved one had committed a heinous, violent act. They saw only one side of a person, the benign Dr. Jekyll. The perpetrator made sure to keep their Mr. Hyde side hidden.

Fresh tears welled up in her eyes. "I don't know how I can convince Deputy Highcloud that Cole didn't do it, but I have to."

"What evidence does she have against him?" I asked, knowing some of that evidence had been provided by me.

"The keys to Sasha's room," Sammie said. "But he found those in the hallway when he went to get me a snack in the middle of the night. I asked him to get some pretzels from the vending machine. I thought they might settle my stomach. I hadn't been feeling well."

"Pregnancy can take its toll."

She nodded and blinked the tears back. "I was just about to tell you the news. How did you already know?"

"I came across your pregnancy test when I cleaned your room Tuesday."

She swiped an errant tear from her cheek. "I was so excited when I got the results. I'd been feeling sick to my stomach and I thought I might be pregnant, but I didn't want to tell Cole until I knew for sure. He left the room Monday night so I could get some rest. I took the tests while he was out on the deck. I did two, to make sure. They were both positive. When he came back to the room and I told him, he was so happy. We both were. My pregnancy is the big reason we left early. We didn't want to tell anyone then because we know sometimes things go wrong, and we were afraid saying anything too soon might jinx things. Besides, my mother would want to be the first to know. It didn't feel right to share the news with anyone else before her."

I reached out and gave her hand a squeeze. "That's really sweet."

"Before I told him I was pregnant, Cole thought that maybe the reason I was throwing up was because I'd gotten food poisoning from the breakfast buffet or eaten some poison berries on the trail. He didn't want to mention the breakfast and sound ungrateful, especially since you let us stay here for free. But he was so worried. He wanted me to go to the hospital." She barked a joyless laugh. "Guys can be so clueless sometimes."

"They certainly can." It dawned on me then that the reason Cole had been looking up poisonous berries online was because he'd seen his wife feeling sick. Morning sickness, as I'd learned myself when pregnant, could strike at any time of day, despite its name. *His search on poisons had nothing to do with any plans to kill Sasha.* Of course, there was still the matter of her keys. *Why hadn't he turned them in?* I didn't want to pose the question outright and sound accusatory. Instead, I said, "What did Cole say about the keys?"

"He came across them in the hall when the lights went out," she said. "He stepped on them. He said stepping on the pine-cone keychain was like stepping on a Lego. He hopped around in the hall and tried not to yell or curse."

I grimaced. "Ouch."

"He knew he'd wake you up if he called to report that he'd found the keys right then, and he figured since nobody seemed to be missing them they must have had another key to get into their room. He said he decided he'd just turn them in with ours in the morning."

I remembered the deputy saying Sammie had been surprised to learn Cole had Sasha's keys. To see if she might provide me conflicting information, I played dumb and said, "And then the two of you forgot to turn them in?"

"I didn't know about them when we left," she said. "I didn't know until today, when they sent a search and rescue team for us. We thought they'd come to get us because someone had reported seeing Cole hurt. We passed a group of hikers who were going north and they said they'd call for help when they could. It wasn't until we got off the trail and saw the car from the sheriff's department that we realized there was more to it. The deputy searched our packs, and when she found the keys, she asked about them. Cole told her that he'd found them in the lodge when he'd gone to get me the pretzels. By the time he got back to the room, I'd fallen asleep again, so he stuck the keys in his pack. He left the light off so he wouldn't wake me up. He didn't realize he'd put them in a different pocket from our room keys and he forgot all about them by the morning."

Everything she'd told me made perfect sense. What's more, I believed her. Cole was likely too busy thinking about Sammie's pregnancy and getting back to the trail to worry about a spare set of keys someone had dropped, especially keys that surely had duplicates and could be easily replaced.

She ended with, "The deputy told us someone had robbed the woman who was killed, that they'd taken her jewelry. We wouldn't have any interest in her jewelry. I'm not into that kind of thing. My ears aren't even pierced." She pulled back her hair to show me her ears. There were no earrings, nor any piercings. The lobes were intact. She held up her left hand, showing me her wedding band, which was fashioned to look like a leafy vine. "We bought our wedding rings on Etsy for fifty dollars each."

Her innocence showed. She didn't seem to realize that the deputy assumed Cole had stolen the jewelry in order to sell it for cash, not for her to wear. I didn't correct her. Better to let her enjoy what little naivete she had remaining.

She sucked her lips into her mouth for a moment as if to keep them from quivering. When she could speak again, she said, "You've done so much to help us out that I don't feel right asking for more. But if you can do anything to help Cole . . ."

I nodded. The best things I could do to help Cole would be to take care of his wife and figure out who had killed Sasha. "I'll try my best. I want this murder solved too."

With that, I gave Sammie's hand another reassuring squeeze and left her to her dinner and Patty's blueberry pie, though I doubted she could eat much with all the worry and dread sitting in her stomach.

When Brynn arrived for work Friday morning, I followed her to the housekeeping closet. "I need to show you something."

She arched a brow. "Last time I was in a closet and someone said they needed to show me something, I was five years old and it was the neighbor boy wanting to show me how boys and girls were different." When I failed to laugh in response, her face clouded. "What is it?"

I handed her the letter from the Employment Security department.

She read it over, then looked up at me. "I'd forgotten all about this."

"You knew about it?"

"I got a demand letter from the unemployment office years ago," she said. "I didn't pay the benefits back as a matter of principle. Besides, I was broke at the time and couldn't afford it. Losing that job set me back for months afterward."

"You left something off your work history, then? That would be grounds for termination." I wouldn't keep someone on staff who'd lied to me. I had to know I could trust my employees.

"I didn't mislead you, Misty," she insisted. "Your application only asked about my employment for the last seven years. I've owned my cleaning business all that time." She held up the letter and shook it. "This is exactly why. I worked for a hotel in Boone from 2006 to 2009. Never called in sick once, and I was never late, either. They fired me when they noticed I was using my own nontoxic cleaning products rather than the destructive chemicals they supplied. I filed for unemployment and received a couple of weeks of benefits before I decided to stop looking for a job and work for myself. The hotel appealed my benefits claim and said that it was my fault I lost my job. There was some type of hearing on it, but I'd moved up the mountain in the meantime and didn't get the notice. If I had, I would've filed a counterclaim for the unpaid overtime I'd put in for the hotel. I stayed late a half hour or so nearly every shift. By the time I learned about the hearing, it was long since over and too late for me to appeal."

I chewed my lip. She'd been a reliable employee for me so far, and her explanation made sense. Even so, she couldn't have earned a lot with her cleaning business. She might have other financial troubles, too, for all I knew. And those troubles might have given her reason to take Sasha's jewelry and singing bowl.

Brynn sighed and looked me directly in the eye. "Are you going to fire me? I really hope not. Because you're a good boss and I like it here. The lodge feels like a second home to me."

"Trying to butter me up?" I asked.

"No way," she said. "You know how hard it is to clean a butter stain?"

I took the letter back from her. "I'm not going to fire you."

She exhaled in relief. "Thank you, Misty."

I wondered if she'd still be thanking me if she knew that part of the reason I wanted to keep her around was to watch her, see if she might slip up. Someone on this mountain had killed Sasha, and until I figured out who it was, I wouldn't fully trust anyone.

There were no yoga or meditation classes scheduled for Friday evening. With Cole in jail, many of my guests seemed more relaxed and in the mood to celebrate, if respectfully and somewhat somberly. They asked for recommendations for a place to go out for a drink. I happily made suggestions, glad that maybe they might end up with at least one or two fond memories of their time on the mountain.

Rocky and I found ourselves alone on the deck with two bottles of hard cider.

I took a sip. He'd seen the photograph of my sons behind my desk and commented on how much they looked like me, asked what they were doing now. Of course, I'd been happy to talk about them. "You've mentioned your girls," I said, "but I've never seen a picture of them. Got one handy?"

"One? I might have one. Or one hundred." He pulled his phone from the breast pocket of his flannel shirt and tapped the screen. He brought up an image before laying the phone on the table. He motioned with his index finger. "Scroll through if you'd like."

The first pic was of him sitting on the tailgate of his truck with his three daughters surrounding him. One sat to each side with their arms over his shoulders. Those two had his same sandy hair, grayish-blue eyes, and square-shaped face. The youngest was behind him, her arms wrapped loosely around his neck and her chin resting on top of his head. She had dark brown hair and eyes, pale skin, and a heart-shaped face.

"They're all very pretty," I said. I pointed to the one with her chin on his head. "This one must take after her mother."

He huffed a breath. "Not a bit."

"Well, she certainly doesn't look like *you*."

"Yeah, there's a reason for that." His soft voice and the odd tone in his voice told me I might have inadvertently touched on something emotional. I didn't press him further, but he opened up anyway. "I'm not her biological father. But she's as much my daughter as the others."

He went on to tell me about his wife, Monique. They'd married young, or as he put it, "too young." Barely twenty-one. "We went to the courthouse the day after her twenty-first birthday. We'd waited so we'd be able to get champagne at a restaurant afterward." He said Monique had become pregnant almost immediately. "She loved all the attention I gave her. She hadn't gotten enough growing up."

His comment about having once been so in love he couldn't see straight came back to me. Monique must have been the woman he'd been talking about.

He went on to say that the problem was, once the baby came, his attention shifted from his new wife to their little girl. "Monique didn't have a good role model when it came to mothering. Being a mom didn't come naturally to her, either. She seemed almost jealous of the baby. But the less attention she gave our daughter, the more I had to make up for it. I chalked up her behavior to postpartum depression. She'd snap out of it now and then, seem to be adjusting and enjoying our baby, but just as soon as I thought we'd turned a corner, she took off. Said she felt trapped." He shrugged. "She came back a few months later, and we repeated the same mistakes with daughter number two. When Monique left the second time, she was gone for over a year without a word. After that, she'd pop up every now and then, get the girls all excited that we were going to be a family, then she'd disappear on us again."

I couldn't even imagine leaving my children behind. My boys meant the world to me. But I knew not every woman had good maternal instincts. And I'd been lucky enough to have a loving mother and father who showed me what good parenting looked like.

Rocky said, "I filed for divorce in absentia. We had no idea where she'd gone to at the time. Couldn't even serve her the papers. They had to publish the news in the legal notices section of the newspaper." He shook his head. "When she came back the next time, she was pregnant again. She hadn't been home in over nine months at that point, so I knew the baby wasn't mine. The father wasn't stepping up. Monique talked about giving the baby up for adoption, but what kind of man would I be if I let that happen?"

"You'd probably be like most men," I said. "I don't think many would take on a responsibility that wasn't theirs."

He exhaled softly. "She might not have been my baby, but she was still a sister to my girls and, as far as I'm concerned, that meant she was family. My girls were so excited by the thought that they'd have a baby sister. I told Monique I'd raise her as my own. I'd already raised the other two myself, I could do it one more time. Monique had the baby, got her tubes tied, and took off again. She wanted her freedom more than she wanted a family. I only wish both of us had realized that before we'd said 'I do.'" He sighed, but then he smiled. "All this said, I wouldn't change a single thing. My three daughters mean the world to me. Don't know what I'd do or where I'd be without them."

"I feel the same about my situation," I told him. "Even though Jack and I divorced, I'd marry him all over again even if I knew we wouldn't stay together forever."

We sat in companionable silence for a moment before Rocky said, "Funny how life turns out, huh? Here we are, two attractive, unattached people living under the same roof. You're doing your best not to fall for me—"

"Hey!"

He gazed at me intently. "I was hoping it might be true. I get a sense sometimes that you might be interested. Did I misread things?" He cocked his head in question.

I turned to look out in the woods, not quite able to face him. "You didn't misread anything," I said. "But the ink on my divorce papers is barely dry. I need some time to adjust, figure out who I am now, before I start another relationship."

"Understood," he said. "I'm going to have to wear you down slowly, like using fine-grain sandpaper."

My heart, and body, warmed at the thought that he was interested and planned to pursue me, however slowly. "Sandpaper? That has to be the least romantic simile ever spoken."

"I'm rusty." He took a sip of his cider. "Good thing I'll have time to hone my romance skills before you'll be ready to get back in the saddle." He shot me a wink that had me wanting to put my foot in a stirrup right that instant.

Before we took things further, I figured I should know how old Rocky was. He'd mentioned that he and his former wife had their first daughter when they were only twenty-two, and he'd referred to his granddaughter as being five months old. How old was his daughter when she had her? I scrolled through more pics looking for clues. There were several photos of her holding the baby, many of Rocky, too, probably snapped by his daughters. But the photos didn't tell me much. I used what I hoped was a subtle segue. "Sammie and Cole will be young parents, like you were. How old is your daughter? The one who has the baby?"

"She's twenty-five."

I did the math. That made Rocky forty-seven.

His eyes narrowed. "You're trying to figure out how old I am, aren't you?"

This guy had an uncanny knack for reading me. Better even than Jack had ever had. "Busted. If I did my math right, you're forty-seven."

"Yep. What about you?"

No sense in lying. "I turned fifty the day I closed on the lodge."

He hmphed. "You're over the hill then."

"I am not! I'm just cresting the hill. Fifty is the new thirty."

His eyes gleamed with mischief as he raised his palms in mock contrition. "Didn't mean to be rude. My mama always told me I should respect my elders."

I narrowed my eyes at him now. "You're asking for it, buster."

He gave me his roguish grin and I found myself having second thoughts about turning down his offer for a sleepover.

CHAPTER 27

Fresh air is as good for the mind as for the body. Nature always seems trying to talk to us as if she had some great secret to tell. And so, she has.

—John Lubbock

Yeti

When Misty returned to the room, she cracked the windows an inch or two to let the cool evening air inside. Yeti lay on the sill and lowered her nose to sniff the breeze. She could smell the scents of dirt, water, rocks, and trees. It was fresh and wonderful, appealing to her more primal nature. It was much more pleasant than the smells that came through the window at their old place. There, she'd smelled automobile exhaust. Lawn chemicals. Insecticides. The air was much cleaner here.

A light breeze ruffled her fur and carried another scent to her nose, one of a man. She glanced over at the deck. A man sat there on a mat, all alone, the moonlight reflecting off his forehead. He seemed to be taking a nap in a sitting position. She'd seen him and the others do the same thing many times this week. Humans were strange creatures, gathering together as they did and mimicking one another's movements. You'd never catch a cat being such a, well, copycat.

Cats had minds of their own, were independent thinkers. And, right now, Yeti thought she'd climb down and go curl up on her pillow.

CHAPTER 28

A weed is no more than a flower in disguise.
                              —James Russell Lowell

Misty

Saturday morning, Brock and Patty brought the breakfast over to the lodge.

Patty placed a tray filled with pancakes in the warmer before turning to me. "Any updates?"

Brock looked at me, too, as if wondering what I might have heard from the deputy. Was his interest the same general concern shared by everyone on the mountain, or was it more personal? I wish I could read his mind and find out.

I'd already informed Patty about Cole's arrest, and had learned nothing more since. "Nothing new," I said with a sigh.

Her hands now free, she gestured to both hallways at once. "Your guests leave tomorrow, don't they?"

"They do." That meant only one day remained to identify the killer here if he or she was among the guests. Once the group returned to Charlotte, it was unlikely any new evidence would arise. Life would go on, but Sasha's death would never be solved, the case turning cold. I decided to drink a second cup of chai tea this morning, see if the extra caffeine might hone my powers of observation and deduction. *Is there some clue here that I'm missing?*

Patty asked, "How's the news affecting your bookings?"

"I'm not seeing a reduction." Fortunately, because the murder had yet to be associated with the Mountaintop Lodge, it hadn't seemed to affect reservations. They were about the same as they'd been this time last year, according to the records I'd looked at. But I had to wonder and worry whether I was inviting guests into a dangerous situation. If the killer wasn't part of the retreat group, my future guests could be at risk. "Rocky's installed security cameras all around the building," I said, as much to Brock as to Patty. "If anyone tries to harm a guest again on the premises, they'll be caught on camera."

"Good," Patty said. She fanned her Greasy Griddle napkins out on the table and said, "I'll be back in a bit to check on things."

"Thanks."

Just after Patty and Brock left, Glenn came up the hall and dipped his head in acknowledgment. "Good morning, Misty."

"Good morning, Glenn." I handed him a mug. "For your tea."

He smiled. "You're an attentive host."

I returned the smile. "I do my best."

Vera and her daughter came up the hall, their mats tucked under their arms. Vera said, "Please tell me there's a cranberry muffin in the basket."

I pulled back the cloth and peeked inside. "You're in luck. I see two."

She reached in and grabbed one. Her daughter grabbed the other.

Other students wandered in and they moved out to the deck to perform their sun salutations. I watched them on the deck as they shifted positions. Heads raised. Feet raised. Butts raised. I wondered whether one of those spandex-clad butts belonged to a killer.

Could Madman have killed Sasha to prevent another public-relations nightmare, then taken her bowl and jewelry to make it look like a robbery instead? It would be a clever ploy, throw law enforcement off his scent.

Kendall's fitness tracker had cleared her, but I still wondered if she was complicit, whether she'd left her window open for someone else to get inside to enter Sasha's room through the adjoining door. She'd specifically asked for a room next to Sasha, after all. If this was the case, maybe Sasha's killer was someone Kendall and Sasha knew from back in Charlotte. Maybe that's why this case was proving so difficult to solve.

Brynn was still a possibility, though I found it hard to believe that a woman who was so unapologetically and openly herself would kill another person and be able to hide it. Besides, Deputy Highcloud had verified her alibi. Brynn's neighbors said they hadn't seen her car leave the parking lot of her apartment all night. Though it seemed impossible, I had to accept that Rocky remained a viable suspect, too, as did Brock. Just as Deputy Highcloud had made an impression of Sasha's room key, Brock could have done the same with the key to the lodge. A key-maker could have used that impression to make a key. But would a young man know that? And would he have gone to all that trouble and expense on the off chance he'd score some valuables? It didn't seem likely.

But maybe my worries were for naught. Maybe Cole was indeed the one who'd killed Sasha. I'd feel much better if there was more than mere circumstantial evidence to point to him, though. Maybe Deputy Highcloud could wheedle a confession out of him and put this matter to rest.

Thinking of Cole got me thinking of Sammie. She'd probably be hungry for some breakfast. I loaded up a plate with some of everything, and carried it down to her room with a large glass of orange juice. I looked both ways to make sure the hall was empty before rapping lightly on her door. She opened it and gave me a weary smile on seeing the food. She was still in her pajamas and looked positively exhausted. Eyes at half-mast. Cheeks sagging. Hair wild and unkempt.

I raised the glass of juice. "Folic acid is very important when you're pregnant. Orange juice has a lot of it." I gave her my cell phone number and a menu from the Greasy Griddle. "Text me when you're ready for lunch and I'll pick up an order for you."

"Thanks, Misty." She took the plate and glass from me and closed her door to eat alone. Cole might be the murder suspect, but Sammie was serving a sort of solitary confinement here. At least she had a nice view from her cell. I hoped her parents would make good time on their drive down from Maine. She could use support from someone other than an innkeeper she barely knew.

Around nine fifteen, Rocky came up the hall. As was quickly becoming our habit, the two of us had breakfast together.

As I poured syrup over my stack of pancakes, I asked, "What's on your agenda for today?"

"Taking my girls for an afternoon movie then dinner," he said. "It's a tradition we do at least once a month. We take turns picking the movie."

"What are you seeing today?"

"The youngest is forcing me to see a rom-com." He groaned, but the playful look in his eyes said he'd happily watch a thousand rom-coms if it made his daughters happy. "What about you?"

"As soon as I finish cleaning the rooms, I'm going to string up a hammock and start a new book. I've been taking care of guests all week, I thought I'd treat myself to some *me* time."

"Good," he said. "You've earned it."

Brynn arrived at ten o'clock. We figured the guests might sleep in a little later on the weekend, so we'd adjusted her schedule, shifting it back a couple of hours. We were right. The guests who didn't come to sun salutations didn't begin to show their faces until ten or later. Some had stayed out quite late the night before at the local watering holes.

Brynn and I went about our business, cleaning the rooms and answering the occasional phone call or question from a guest. I did some more marketing, targeting groups who might want to come up for a ski trip this winter. I emailed ski clubs at colleges, church youth groups, and ski shops throughout North Carolina, South Carolina, Tennessee, Georgia, and Florida, the entire southeast region.

Around four, I went out front to string a hammock between two of the trees the mountain was named for. I'd wrapped the straps around the beeches and was just about to climb in with my book when Deputy Highcloud's SUV turned into the parking lot. Leaving the hammock behind, I hurried over to the front walkway. Cole sat in the back seat of the vehicle, looking as exhausted as his wife had earlier. He looked even younger than I remembered, too, and scared, vulnerable. He sat slumped, his shoulders up near his ears. He wasn't shackled, but two wooden crutches leaned back against the seat. Even without handcuffs, he wouldn't be able to go anywhere in a hurry.

As he opened the door to get out, the deputy unrolled her window to speak to me. "The boy didn't break. Either he didn't kill Sasha Ducharme-Carlisle, or he's the toughest nut I've ever tried to crack."

While I was thrilled to know Cole had been cleared, I realized this development put the investigation back to square one. The deputy obviously realized it, too. Her face was tight in frustration. "Anybody in the lodge slip up and say something they shouldn't?"

"Wish I could say they had."

She gave me a pointed look. "Keep your ears and eyes open for me. It could make all the difference."

"I will."

I moved to Cole's door and silently held out a hand to help him down. He looked to be on the verge of tears, but I knew from raising two boys that any comfort I might try to give would push him over an emotional edge he'd rather not pass. His right ankle was wrapped in a synthetic cast with an incongruously bright blue outer layer. He held his worn, dusty hiking boot in one hand. I took the boot from him and reached in to assist with the crutches, putting them into position so he could get the padded supports under his arms. Once he cleared the door, I closed it behind him. Deputy Highcloud drove off, leaving the odor of exhaust and a lingering despair behind.

As Cole hobbled along, I walked ahead and opened the front door of the lodge for him. He clumsily *clunk-clunk-clunked* into the lobby on the crutches he hadn't become accustomed to while trapped in his tiny cell at the county jail.

Several people were gathered in the great room. Norma Jean was working a puzzle with Chugalug on her lap, the pug nuzzling the pieces as if thinking about eating one. Vera was knitting, while her daughter watched a video on her tablet, headphones in her ears. The joggers had taken a break from their runs to peruse one of the books on the history of the Blue Ridge Mountains. Madman looked up from a table where he and Joaquín were engaged in a lively game of Battleship they'd apparently turned into a drinking game, judging from the bottle of whiskey sitting on the table between them. He rose from his seat, his face equal parts befuddled and furious. "What the f—"

Before he could finish his thought, I raised a palm to stop him. "Cole was released. He didn't kill Sasha."

"Says who?" Madman demanded.

"Says Cole," I replied, "and Deputy Highcloud. She wouldn't have brought him back here otherwise."

Madman's upper lip quirked in skepticism. Rather than continue to debate the matter with him, I escorted Cole down the hall to his room and knocked on the door so he wouldn't have to take a hand off a crutch and risk losing his balance. In his state, he was likely to fall over and hurt himself again.

A squeal came from behind the door as Sammie evidently peered through the peephole and realized that Cole's presence here meant he'd been cleared—for the time being, at least. She yanked the door open and launched herself at her husband, grabbing him in a bear hug. If not for me providing a steadying hand from behind, she would have inadvertently tackled him to the floor. While he'd kept his emotions in check up until now, they released like a floodgate, a waterfall of feelings flowing freely. Sammie backed off to allow him inside. He *clunk-clunked* into the room and I closed the door behind him.

Rocky was still out at dinner with his daughters at eight o'clock Saturday evening, but Brynn had stuck around to attend Glenn's final meditation class of the retreat. I decided to attend, too. It could be the last chance I'd have to see the group gathered together. The chances of me learning anything new were slim, but it couldn't hurt. Brynn and I took places at the back, sitting on cushions from the patio furniture as I'd done before.

Glenn applied his mallet to the gong to start the class, and the deep tone reverberated across the deck and into the woods. I wondered what the wildlife thought of it. Did they think the sound came from some new species of bird or mammal that had ventured into their territory? Did they find the sound as soothing and hypnotic as humans did? Did they, like me, think how the sound was not at all like the E note that had drawn Rocky and me from our rooms the night Sasha was killed?

I was supposed to have my eyes closed to focus on my

breathing, but instead I opened my eyes and focused on Glenn. He looked every bit the serene master he seemed to be, but could this man have a dark side that had reared its ugly head after we'd all gone to bed Monday night? I hadn't heard him bump into his gong. Rocky hadn't either. Of course, it was entirely possible that Glenn had bumped the gong and that the noise had sounded much louder in his silent room than beyond it. He might have assumed the sound had traveled throughout the lodge, but maybe it hadn't. After all, the walls and doors of the lodge were intentionally thick and heavy to minimize noise. Then again, maybe Glenn had caused a sound with something else, and had hoped to cover it up by telling a white lie. Maybe Glenn had dropped Sasha's singing bowl when he'd gone into her room to take it from her.

His eyes still closed, he said, "Inhale for eight counts. One . . . Two . . . Three . . ."

I took a deep breath as he'd instructed, but continued to ponder this possibility. Glenn clearly had no desire for material things. His jeans and boho bag were faded, evidencing years of use. If he'd been a materialistic person, he would have chosen an entirely different career, one that was more lucrative. He wouldn't have wanted the singing bowl for its value. Then why would he take it? He might consider it to be a wondrous spiritual artifact, but wouldn't it go against his spiritual beliefs to covet it? Wasn't he supposed to be above such things? I was aware that he didn't hold Sasha in high regard, and could have wanted to rid himself of her. But at the same time, his inner peace seemed to allow him to disregard her flaws and failings, to tolerate her condescending treatment. I simply couldn't think of a good reason why he'd take the bowl that wouldn't go against the beliefs he espoused.

What am I missing?

CHAPTER 29

Nothing is softer or more flexible than water, yet nothing can resist it.

—Lao Tzu

Misty

I was sitting at the registration desk at ten o'clock Sunday morning when the chartered minibus rolled to a stop in front of the lodge, its brakes hissing just as they had when the bus had arrived full of guests a week ago. It would be taking one less person home with it. Although the bus had come to transport the guests, it felt as if it would be taking hope with it, too. I could hardly believe the group would be leaving and Sasha's killer had yet to be identified. Deputy Highcloud still hadn't ruled out the possibility that the killer could have been a random person who'd climbed in Sasha's or Kendall's window, but I couldn't shake the sense that her killer was here at the lodge, that there was some clue I hadn't yet found that would point to the killer. But what could it be?

Sasha had been the first to check in last week, and Glenn had been the last. But he was the first to come to the desk to check out today. Unlike Sasha, though, he wasn't forcing his students to wait in line behind him. All of the other guests were still in their rooms and seemed to be waiting until the last minute to leave. I took that as a good sign. I'd always been reluctant to leave when I'd come to the lodge, too, remaining right up to the noon checkout time. My visits to the mountains were always so relaxing and restorative, I didn't want them to end.

Glenn parked his gong by the desk. Once again, it was wrapped in the colorful fringed yoga blanket, held in place by rope for its protection during transport. He placed his keys on the counter. "I appreciate all you've done for our group this week, Misty. It's been hard on everyone, but you did your best to make us feel safe and comfortable. I'm not sure what will happen with the studio, but it was making a good income for Sasha, so my guess is someone will buy it and keep it running. Heike has expressed some interest. We'll do everything in our power to bring a group here for another retreat."

"Thanks, Glenn. I'd love to host your group here again." My words weren't entirely true. While I'd love to see Norma Jean and cute little Chugalug come back, maybe Vera and her daughter, Joaquín, and a few of the others, I hoped I'd never see Kendall again. She'd damaged my inn and lied to law enforcement, caused far too much drama. Madman Maddox could find somewhere else to stay, too. He'd never quite forgiven me for telling Deputy Highcloud about the hair I'd seen on his pillow, even though I'd only told the truth and there'd been no real consequences to him. He'd also been useless as a social media influencer to drive traffic to the lodge. Despite the simplicity of the lodge's name, he had yet to get the name right in any of his posts. In his most recent post, he'd called it the Top of the Mountain

Lodge. *Sigh*. It wasn't that the guy was stupid. It was that he was always in too much of a rush to really stop and listen. He treated everything in his life as a race.

I returned Glenn's keys to the drawer, printed his receipt, and offered it to him with a final smile. "Have a safe trip back home."

He tucked the receipt into his boho bag and carried his vintage green Samsonite suitcase out to the bus. After stashing his luggage in the open bay on the side of the bus, he returned for his gong and rolled it outside, stowing it under the bus, too. Rather than board the stuffy bus while he waited for the others, he took a seat on a bench out front by the bear. But, while his face appeared just as serene as usual, he showed the first sign I'd seen of anxiety. His big toe bounced up and down in his earthy sandal, evidencing a hidden source of nervous energy. *Does Glenn have something to be nervous about?*

Brynn came in from sweeping the deck, and saw Glenn on the bench. "If he's checked out, I'll get started on cleaning his room."

I stood from my stool. "Would you mind covering the desk instead?"

"Whatever you say, boss."

As soon as she'd come around the desk, I rounded up the housekeeping cart from the closet and rolled it across the lobby. Brynn watched with interest as I went by, seeming to realize something was up.

I rolled the cart down to the room Glenn had occupied, parked it against the wall so as not to impede traffic in the hallway, and unlocked his door with my master key. Before

I could step into Glenn's room, Rocky and Molasses came in the door at the end of the hall. Rocky's gaze met mine and narrowed in question. I tipped my head twice to indicate Glenn's room, silently requesting that Rocky join me. He let Molasses into their room and came down the hall, slipping into the room behind me. I shut the door.

"What's up?" he asked.

"Zen Glenn seems nervous." I told him about the bouncing toe. "Something has him agitated."

Rocky cocked his head in thought. "Glenn's emotional dial is always turned down to one. I didn't know the guy could even get agitated."

"Neither did I." I lowered my voice even more, leaning toward Rocky to whisper, "You think he could have killed Sasha, and now he's worked up because he's anxious to get out of here and put all of this behind him?"

Rocky's lip quirked in skepticism. "But we know from Sasha's fitness tracker data that she was killed just before we heard that sound Tuesday morning. The video showed Glenn coming out of his room—*this* room—a few hours later. Sasha's window was locked from the inside, and the footage from the Greasy Griddle showed nobody moving along the front of the lodge, so he couldn't have come in through his window. How could he get from this side of the hall to her side of the hall without getting caught on video? He might be enlightened, but he isn't an apparition that can walk through walls."

"I know that!" My snappishness was unwarranted and undeserved. I hung my head. "Sorry, Rocky."

"No worries. I didn't take it personal." He reached out,

put a finger under my chin, and raised my head, looking into my eyes. "You have every right to be frustrated, Misty. I'm frustrated by this situation, too, but I've been able to take it out on nails with my hammer. It's darn therapeutic."

I looked back down, but this time, rather than hanging my head in shame, I visually examined the wood floor. "Could Glenn have somehow pulled up the flooring and gotten down in the crawl space?"

"Not without making a racket," Rocky said. "When you had me take a look at the rooms, I made sure all the floorboards were securely fastened down." He walked the room anyway, bending down in spots to take a closer look, even reaching out to touch the boards and make sure they weren't loose. "Everything looks the way it should."

I stepped to the door, putting my back to it, and scanned the room, working my way up from floor level, past the window that we'd already ruled out, and up to the coffered ceiling. One dark wood beam ran lengthwise along the wood-paneled ceiling, spanning the twenty-two-foot depth of the room, while three sixteen-foot crossbeams bisected it, dividing the ceiling into eight panels that were eight feet by five-and-a-half feet in size. Protruding from the beam in the center of the room was a metal fire sprinkler head in a sunburst shape. Something niggled at my memory banks.

Sprinkler . . .

Sprinkler . . .

Aha! When Rocky had asked Glenn about his day job, Glenn had said he installed sprinklers for a company called

Queen City Sprinkler Systems. I remembered the name because "Queen City" was a nickname for the city of Charlotte, much like "Cackalacky" was a nickname for the Carolinas. At the time, I'd made the assumption that the business installed lawn sprinklers. I'd wondered why, if Glenn worked outdoors, he hadn't accumulated a tan. I'd attributed his fair skin to high-SPF sunscreen. But what if his light skin was because he didn't install lawn sprinklers at all? What if, instead, he spent his days indoors installing fire sprinkler systems?

I whipped my phone from my pocket and typed the name of the company into my browser as fast as I could. Sure enough, the search returned a site for the company that identified Queen City Sprinkler Systems as Charlotte's #1 Fire Protection Provider. But it still didn't explain how Glenn could travel from his room to Sasha's.

Or did it?

Deputy Highcloud's words came back to me. *Sometimes you find something surprising in the place you least expect it.*

I walked over and climbed up on the unmade bed, reaching for the ceiling. But while I could touch it, I was too short to apply any real pressure. Rocky watched with a puzzled look on his face but said nothing, seeming to realize questions would only slow me down. I hopped down, scurried to the door, and opened it, snatching a broom off the housekeeping cart. Joaquín passed by with his luggage and cast a curious look in my direction before I shut the door.

I hurried over and climbed up onto the bed again. I put the end of the handle against the ceiling panel and pushed upward with all my might. *Whoa!* The panel lifted a few inches before my strength gave out and it flopped back down into place, belching musty attic air into my face. Thank goodness Brynn and I had swept the attic or my nose and eyes would be filled with dust.

Realizing I'd made a critical and shocking discovery, Rocky leaped up onto the bed, grabbed the broom out of my hands, and jammed it upward and forward, the force moving the panel aside and leaving a gap of about eighteen inches. Using the broom as a lever, he forced the panel farther aside and widened the gap. He tried another panel that didn't flank the center beam. It didn't budge. "When this lodge was constructed, the builder must have left the panels that flanked the sprinkler pipes unattached so it would be easier to access them for repairs or replacement." He gaped up at the attic ceiling before turning wide eyes on me. "How did you figure this out?"

Although I'd like to say it was clever sleuthing or deductive reasoning, the truth was I'd solved this crime with wordplay, by interpreting the word *sprinkler* in one of its alternate meanings, much as we had with the word *crick* during our Scrabble game on the deck earlier in the week. I told him so.

As if to test the theory that Glenn could have accessed Sasha's room via the attic, Rocky reached up and put one hand on the beam, the other on the wood panel that formed both the ceiling of the guest room and the floor of the attic. He tried to pull himself up into the attic, but couldn't get enough leverage. "How could Glenn get himself up here? Some kind of bendy yoga trick?"

Though yoga could certainly build muscles and balance,

it seemed that the solution might have been a more practical one. "I bet he used his yoga strap. He could've tied it to the beam for leverage. He probably used it to get in and out of Sasha's room, too." *Now that's* deductive reasoning.

Rocky reached down to his waist and unbuckled his belt. Now it was my turn to gape. "What are you doing?" I hadn't expected an impromptu striptease.

"Testing your theory. My belt is the closest thing I have to a yoga strap." He proceeded to move the other ceiling panel aside just enough that he could fasten his belt around the beam. He made sure to slip it between the beam and the sprinkler pipe so that it wouldn't put pressure on the pipe and risk breaking it. The last thing we needed to do was flood the lodge. He first tried with the belt fastened tightly around the beam, a long part of it hanging straight down, but he couldn't get enough leverage to pull himself up using the belt like a rope.

I rotated a finger in the air. "Put your belt on the loosest setting," I suggested, "so that you've got a loop to work with. Like a stirrup." His recent reference to me getting back in the saddle was proving prophetic and useful now.

He did as I suggested, and the next thing we knew, he'd put a foot in the loop and swung himself up and into the attic. He disappeared into the space and, from down the hall, came Chugalug's *yap-yap-yap.* Though Rocky was doing his best to step lightly, the dog's ears must have picked up his footsteps.

A few seconds later, Rocky's face reappeared as he looked down on me through the hole. "The ceiling panels at the edges of the rooms are nailed in place, but none of the panels next to the sprinkler pipes are fastened down."

I whipped my cell phone from my pocket and dialed the deputy. "Get to the lodge quick! I know who killed Sasha!"

CHAPTER 30

We never know the timber of a man's soul until something cuts into him deeply and brings the grain out strong.

—Gene Stratton-Porter

Misty

Deputy Highcloud was several miles from the lodge. She asked me to hold so she could radio the Beech Mountain Police Department and get law enforcement en route faster. When she returned to the line, she said, "Be careful. If Glenn realizes you're on to him, things could get dangerous."

We ended the call and I turned to Rocky. "I have to protect my guests."

"I'll round up some hammers."

We stepped out into the hallway. Rocky strode quickly down to his room, went inside, and returned with a hammer in each hand and Molasses at his knee. The dog trotted along beside his master, looking up in question. He seemed to sense something was up. He could probably smell our adrenaline.

Rocky handed me a hammer. Armed with the tools, we forced smiles to our faces and walked to the lobby.

Vera and her daughter stood at the desk, checking out.

Brynn glanced over from behind the desk and saw the hammers in our hands. "What's going on?"

My mind went blank, but luckily Rocky had an answer at the ready. "We need to fix the sign. It's wobbly."

I glanced out front. The bench next to the bear was empty now, Glenn no longer sitting there with his bouncing toe. His boho bag lay next to the bench, abandoned. Rocky and I went outside and looked around.

Joaquín was loading his luggage into the compartment underneath the bus. I hurried over to him and, trying to keep my voice calm, asked, "Have you seen Glenn?"

He turned around and gestured to the bench. "He was sitting there just a minute ago. Norma Jean came out and said she'd heard footsteps and voices coming from the attic. She asked if we knew what was going on."

Rocky and I exchanged glances. Was Glenn on the run? Or had he simply gotten up from the bench to stretch his legs before the bus ride?

We hurried together to the east end of the lodge and looked around. *No Glenn.* We went to the west end and did the same. *No Glenn.* We went around to the back of the lodge. *Still no Glenn.*

Rocky glanced over at the Greasy Griddle. "Think he went over to the diner?"

I whipped out my phone again and called Patty. "Is Glenn over there? My tall guest with the bald head?"

There was a pause as she apparently surveyed the place. "No. I don't see him anywhere. Why?"

"If he shows up, call the police."

She gasped. "It was *him*?"

"Yeah," I said. "It was him."

A Beech Mountain Police Department cruiser turned into the parking lot and Officer Hardy pulled to the curb.

Rocky and I hurried over. As soon as Hardy rolled down his window, I said, "Glenn was sitting on the bench in front of my lodge just a few minutes ago, but now he's gone!"

Officer Hardy scanned the surrounding area. "Any idea where he'd go?"

I started to shake my head, but, as I did, it was as if the motion made the puzzle pieces in my head fall into place. "He's headed to the Lower Pond Creek Trail. I'm sure of it."

Hardy reached over and pushed the passenger door open. "Get in. I've got to keep my eyes on the road. You two can watch the woods, see if you spot him."

"I need to warn my staff and guests first."

"Make it quick."

I ran back inside and laid the hammer on the registration desk in case Brynn might need it. "Glenn killed Sasha. He's disappeared. I think he's gone to the Lower Pond Creek Trail. Rocky and I are going with Officer Hardy. If Glenn comes back here, call for help right away."

Brynn gaped. So did Vera, Vera's daughter, the joggers, and Joaquín, who'd followed me inside. The only one who didn't gape was Heike. She pursed her lips and bobbed her head, as if my words affirmed something she had suspected but had been unable to confirm. I realized then that Glenn had likely mentioned the unexpected death of Heike's husband in an attempt to deflect suspicion from himself.

I left the group with their mouths hanging open, sprinted back to the cruiser, and slid inside.

As we careened down the mountain, Officer Hardy radioed Deputy Highcloud to give her an update. Rocky and I kept our eyes peeled, peering through the thick woods. We could get only glimpses of the trail that led down to Lake Coffey and the trailhead for the Lower Pond Creek Trail. There was no sign of Glenn.

Panic gripped me, my heartbeat reverberating through my chest as if someone had banged a gong with all the might they could muster. *What if I'm wrong? What if Glenn went somewhere else?* He could be escaping on some other route while I led law enforcement on a wild-goose chase. But in my heart, I knew I was right.

As Officer Hardy's cruiser came down Lakeledge Road, Deputy Highcloud's SUV approached from the other direction. Officer Hardy turned and braked to a hard stop in the small lot by Lake Coffey. Deputy Highcloud's SUV pulled in right after us. Two men with fishing poles watched as we leaped from the vehicles and scurried down to the trailhead.

When we reached the trail, Deputy Highcloud threw out an arm to hold me and Rocky back, much as mothers do when driving a car and forced to brake suddenly. "Stay behind us." She pulled her gun from her belt to have it at the ready.

She and Officer Hardy crept quietly but quickly along the first wooden bridge and down the steps. Rocky and I followed a few steps behind, also doing our best to be fast but discreet. We made our way along the short stretch of dirt path before reaching the second bridge, the one that overlooked the small pool and waterfall. Sure enough, there stood Glenn, waist deep in the pool beneath the waterfall, his head turned up to the sky, eyes closed, water falling about his face and shoulders. His arms were raised, too, as if in worship or a plea. But while the water might wash away his sins, the North Carolina justice system would feel differently. No doubt he'd be going away for quite some time.

Deputy Highcloud held her gun at the ready by her side. "Come on out of there now, Glenn!"

He didn't respond. It wasn't clear whether he even knew we were here. He might not be able to hear her over the roar of the water in his ears. The deputy and Officer Hardy exchanged glances. They'd evidently never faced a situation quite like this before.

Officer Hardy tried to get Glenn's attention this time. He stuck his gun back in his holster, cupped his hands around his mouth, and hollered, "Hey! Glenn! Hello!" When Glenn still didn't respond, he shook his head. "I'd say 'hands up', but his hands are already up."

The deputy reached down and picked up a stone. "He's left me no other choice." She pulled her hand back and skipped the stone across the pond. It bounced twice before smacking Glenn in the ribs. He raised his head, opened his eyes, and looked our way. On seeing the officers, he lowered his arms, but only to his shoulders. He seemed to realize that keeping them up was the smart thing to do.

Deputy Highcloud motioned him forward. He strode slowly through the water, making his way to the bridge. "Easy now," she said. "No sudden moves."

"I won't hurt anyone," Glenn said, his voice full of sorrow and regret. "Not again."

He put his hands on the railing and pulled himself up and onto the bridge. He stood there, dripping, Sasha's green eye on his Third Eye T-shirt appearing to cry as water ran from it. Like the water spilling over the boulders, Glenn, too, spilled everything.

"I didn't go to her room intending to kill her," he said. "But I didn't like the way she was doing things. Spirituality shouldn't be for sale. She didn't treasure the singing bowl the way she should have, for its spiritual value. It was merely a possession to her, a valuable trinket, not a sacred relic."

He went on to say that he didn't like the way she ran her classes, as if feeling good and experiencing peace was a prize to be awarded in her game show. Sasha had gotten sucked into all the trappings of yoga practice without truly embracing its intent, the mind/body connection, the peace it was intended to provide. She'd only been in it for the income.

He cast a look at me and Rocky. "I snuck into her room through the attic. Misty and Rocky seem to have figured that out. I only meant to take the bowl, to cherish it as it should be. She'd drunk so much wine I didn't expect her to wake up. When she did, she spotted me in her room and I panicked. I grabbed her pillow and put it over her face. I only meant to silence her. I thought if I could render her unconscious, I could leave the bowl behind, sneak back out of her room, and she'd just think she'd had a strange dream. But I guess I held the pillow down too long." He gulped a sob. "When I realized she was gone, I dragged her outside. I thought I could hide her body somewhere. But I couldn't get far in the dark, so I left her under the deck. I climbed back through her window and locked it behind me out of habit. I figured I could make her death look like a botched burglary if I took the bowl and her jewelry."

Deputy Highcloud asked, "Where are those things now?"

"Under the insulation in the attic above her room. I hid them there."

The deputy pulled a pair of handcuffs from her belt. "Turn around please."

Glenn complied, allowing her to pull his wrists together and shackle them.

She put a hand on his shoulder to guide him. "Let's go."

Rocky, Officer Hardy, and I followed along as Deputy Highcloud led Glenn up the trail to her SUV. She placed him in the back and turned to Hardy. "Follow me to the lodge. I need to round up the bowl and jewelry."

Rocky and I climbed back into the cruiser with Officer Hardy. We followed the deputy's SUV as she wound her way back up to the lodge.

We pulled into the parking lot to find all of the guests standing out front, including Sammie and Cole. When the group spotted Glenn in the back of the SUV, they turned to one another and no doubt told how they'd always suspected him, how he'd always seemed *too* serene, how they'd been able to tell he had it in for Sasha.

Madman turned his back to the deputy's SUV and snapped a selfie with his tongue out, his fingers forming his trademark *M*, and Glenn's profile in the background. After taking the photo, he looked my way. "What's the name of this place again?"

Rocky answered for me. "The Tranquility Lodge." He slid me a surreptitious smile before rounding up a ladder from the outdoor storage shed so Deputy Highcloud could search the attic.

She returned a few minutes later with the bowl and jewelry secured in clear plastic evidence bags, and bade the group goodbye. "You folks take care now."

The deputy drove off with Glenn. Officer Hardy drove off, too.

As the last representative of Third Eye Studio & Spa remaining, Heike was now in charge. She pointed her index finger and swung her arm toward the bus. "Everyone aboard. Let's go home."

CHAPTER 31

The earth laughs in flowers.

—Ralph Waldo Emerson

Misty

With Cole exonerated and Glenn incarcerated, the newly-weds could finally put the terrible week behind them. I knew the two were disappointed that they hadn't been able to complete the Appalachian Trail, but what was marriage if not together weathering life's highs and lows, delights and letdowns? They'd learned an important lesson, too. Life will sometimes take you off course, and the best thing you can do is accept it, adjust, and forge a new trail for yourself.

I invited them to stay a couple of nights more so that they could enjoy a proper honeymoon at the lodge, and they happily took me up on the offer. Sammie's parents stayed for two nights, too. For them, what had started as a desperate journey to reach their despondent daughter turned into a celebration of their first, though yet-to-be-born, grandchild. They'd been thrilled to hear the news.

Now that they'd be getting off the trail, Cole and Sammie contacted their employer and arranged to start their jobs in Boston in October rather than January. They planned to stop in Boston to look at apartments on the drive back home with Sammie's parents. As they left, they promised me they'd come back for a stay with their child someday. "Maybe we'll even stay with you before we finish the trail," Cole said as they departed.

Rocky and I stood side by side, waving as they drove off. When they rounded the corner and disappeared from sight, Rocky said, "All good things must zen."

I groaned. "Don't make me toss you off this mountain."

"I'd like to see you try." He raised his hands in a come-and-get-me gesture and wiggled his fingers.

His gesture was a clear invitation to something physical that I wasn't sure I was yet ready for. "Thanks for all of your help this week. I don't know what I would have done without you."

"Me neither," he said with that roguish grin.

"But I do know what I'm going to do without you right now," I said.

"Oh yeah? What?"

"Plant the flowers around the Mountaintop Lodge sign."

I went to my room, changed into gardening clothes, and rounded up a trowel from the storage shed. I knelt down by the sign with the shovel in my hand and Molasses by my side. I leaned over and kissed him on the snout. "Who's a good boy?"

Yeti glared at me from the side window of the lodge as if I'd given the dog affection that should be reserved only for her. *Don't worry, cat. There's plenty to go around.*

I spent the next half hour artfully arranging the flowers in the bed. A buck wandered by and glanced over, as if wondering whether the plants might make a good meal or snack. Rocky and I had specifically chosen ones the deer shouldn't find tasty. The buck seemed to realize this and continued on his way. Molasses didn't even bat an eye. Deer were as common as squirrels up here, and he'd seen so many they held little interest for him. Besides, he was a relatively lazy dog. A chase would seem like too much trouble.

When I finished the flowers, I returned the trowel to the storage shed, changed back into my regular clothes, and took a seat behind the registration desk to check my emails.

On reading the first message in my inbox, I pumped my fist. "Woo-hoo!"

Brynn glanced over from the great room, where she was dusting the mantle. "What's the woo-hoo for?"

"A ladies' motorcycle club from Raleigh wants to rent the entire lodge for the first week of October." Per their email, they called themselves the Dangerous Curves. *Cute name.* They planned to come to the mountains to ride the Blue Ridge Parkway and other scenic routes.

"Biker chicks, huh?" Brynn said. "That should be fun."

I sent back an email telling them the place was all theirs. *I look forward to hosting you at the Mountaintop Lodge!*